Izzy collided into the man, ricocheting off his hard chest.

Her arms flared as she started to fall. Zan's hands shot to her waist so he could steady her. Her own palms slapped those pecs of his—the same glorious ones that she'd been admiring earlier, his skin still slick with sweat.

Once her heart stopped racing, she became aware of their situation. Her towel had fallen off her when they'd collided. She was touching her employer's chest. His warm leg was between her thighs, nestled right against the center of her. His hands continued to clutch her waist. She glanced down for the briefest seconds and saw that her nipples were poking clearly through her bathing suit. Perhaps she should have been embarrassed that he could see her reaction to his closeness, but she was too distracted by him not letting her go.

His hands squeezed where he held her. "Are you okay?"

"Yep," she squeaked before clearing her throat and saying again, "yes."

He let her go then, and perhaps it was wishful thinking on her end, but it felt like his fingertips almost caressed the generous curve of her hips before he released her...

Dear Reader,

How does a family go on when they've lost their anchor? That's the question Zan Chen faces after the loss of his beloved wife, Mary. He decides that what he and his kids need is a fresh start, and what better place to do that than Holiday Bay, Michigan? After all, that's where most of his closest friends now live. More than anything, Zan needs to get his life back on track for both his kids' sake and his own. The last thing he ever expects to find is a light in the harbor, leading him home.

This story is very personal to me, as I based part of it on my own experience of losing someone I loved to leukemia. My mom was our family's anchor, and it was incredibly hard after she passed away. But life keeps moving forward, whether you're ready or not, and somehow, we find the ability to carry on. Writing this book was a way for me to explore that journey of loss and finding one's strength again.

I'm really proud of *The Wedding Promise*, and as my mom was the one who used to buy me Harlequin books when I was a teen, I know she's looking down on me, smiling. I hope you enjoy Zan and Izzy's story.

For more about my books, you can visit my website, kellistorm.com, where you can also subscribe to my newsletter.

Kelli Storm

THE WEDDING PROMISE

KELLI STORM

Recycling programs for this product may not exist in your area.

ISBN-13: 978-1-335-18043-8

The Wedding Promise

For questions and comments about the quality of this book, please contact us at CustomerService@Harlequin.com.

Harlequin Enterprises ULC
22 Adelaide St. West, 41st Floor
Toronto, Ontario M5H 4E3, Canada
www.Harlequin.com

HarperCollins Publishers
Macken House, 39/40 Mayor Street Upper,
Dublin 1, D01 C9W8, Ireland
www.HarperCollins.com

Printed in Lithuania

Kelli Storm graduated with a BA in public relations from Grand Valley State University. Harlequin published three of her books in 2025! Her debut young adult fantasy also came out in October 2025. Kelli resides in the Great Lake State with her three rescue dogs and a fifteen-year-old fish named Henry O'Malley.

Books by Kelli Storm

Harlequin Special Edition

Challenge Accepted

The Wedding Promise
First Comes Marriage
The Fake Dating Dare
His Small-Town Challenge

Visit the Author Profile page at Harlequin.com.

Dedicated to my sister

Chapter One

How old was *too old* to run away from home? Had Izzy Rossi missed out on that window? Probably, considering she was an adult. But what she wouldn't give for a life do-over.

A knot of dread tightened in her gut as she stared at her family's restaurant through her car's windshield.

She did *not* want to work today.

How had her life come to this? It was the same monotonous routine, day in and day out. Get up, spend time on her art, take a shower, go to the restaurant, take her position behind the hostess stand, work until closing, go home, sleep. Repeat everything the next day.

She was twenty-nine and had nothing to show for her life. She had no identity outside of her family's business. Unlike her four brothers, she wasn't married. She hadn't even dated since she'd graduated college.

One problem was that she still lived at home. She couldn't imagine sneaking a guy back to her room with her parents right down the hall. And she certainly couldn't picture spending the night at some man's place, only to do the walk of shame in front of her parents when she got home. The other problem was that she knew practically everyone in Holiday Bay. Most of the men were either already married, easily scared off by her ridiculously overprotective older brothers, or former classmates who used to bully her about her weight.

She'd been working at Florentina's since she was legally allowed to. She practically lived off the rich Italian food that was her family's specialty and, yes, her body carried more than a few extra pounds due to it, but she was perfectly fine with her figure, thank you very much. If the men in this ridiculous town couldn't accept her the way she was, then she didn't want them in the first place.

What Izzy craved more than anything was something *new.* The longer her life went on in the same routine, the more unsettled she felt. She wanted—*needed*—a change.

What she really wanted was to support herself as an artist, and maybe open a gallery in town one day. She already had the building picked out—the old bank off Main Street and Elm. Several years ago, a big corporation had come to town and purchased the property, along with several others. The CEO had planned to tear down the buildings so he could construct an eyesore of a warehouse. But when his plans fell through, he'd left Holiday Bay behind. Izzy still hoped he'd sell the bank property back to someone in town. Someone who would preserve its grand architecture instead of destroying it.

Not that it would be her. She didn't have time to dream about her gallery between her current work schedule and her family's expectations.

Letting out a sigh, Izzy opened her car door. Mustering up the energy to walk into the restaurant, she forced her legs to move toward the entrance. The familiar scents of tomato and garlic filled her nose once she was inside. She made her way to the kitchen, where she could punch in and check on the crew working.

“Hey, Iz,” her third oldest brother, Dante, called out from the kitchen when he saw her. He was busy prepping for the dinner rush along with her fourth brother, Enzo. Both brothers had well-respected reputations as chefs. People came from all around Michigan just to get a taste of their food.

Out of all her brothers, she was probably closest to Dante. He was closer in age to her, unlike her two oldest brothers, who’d already been preteens by the time she came along. They’d been too busy with their own lives to pay much attention to their baby sister. But Dante wasn’t as close in age to her as Enzo, who used to fight with her for their parents’ attention. Not that either of them needed to. Their parents were *more* than involved in each of their children’s lives.

“Hi,” she responded to Dante, then grabbed a bucket of silverware to fold into napkins at the hostess stand in between customers. “Who’s working the floor today?”

“Marcella, Paige, and Luca,” her second oldest brother, Gio, said as he came into the kitchen. Gio was the front-of-house manager, taking care of all server staff.

“Anything I should be aware of?” Izzy asked as she picked up her bucket.

“Yeah,” Gio replied, looking harried. “Two Holiday Boys are coming in with their wives this evening.”

She nodded. The Holiday Boys were one of the biggest boy bands of all time. Three of the five members had grown up in Holiday Bay, while the other two had spent their childhoods in the neighboring town of Clarington. Six years ago, when the town had hit an economic slump, the band graciously reunited after a fifteen-year separation to host a charity concert. The event saved the town. Over the years, several of the members had moved back to the area and inadvertently turned Holiday Bay into a tourist destination.

As she left the kitchen, she went by her oldest brother's office. Antonio had become the GM of Florentina's after her parents retired.

"Hey, Tony," she called out.

Antonio looked up from his paperwork, his face softening when he saw her. "Izzy, hey."

She took in the worry lines deeply etched on his forehead and she frowned. "Everything okay?"

"Yeah, all good. Our food distributor is jacking up their prices again. We might need to make a switch soon."

"Anything I can help with?" Izzy offered, already knowing the answer.

He affirmed it with a shake of his head. "Nothing for you to worry about."

"Right," she replied, trying not to be annoyed by his typical response.

Despite earning a degree in business to satisfy her family, and a minor in art to satisfy her heart, she knew her place in the family business. Behind the hostess stand. And honestly, she should have been okay with that. Izzy didn't want to do this for the rest of her existence. Florentina's was her family's passion, not hers.

Her mother and father met in Florence. Her mom, Tina, had been an art student while her father, Gianni, had studied cuisine. They moved back to her mom's hometown of Holiday Bay and started their restaurant, Florentina's—which her father named in honor of both his wife and the town where they met. His family soon followed from Italy, and before anyone knew it, the Rossi family had businesses all over town. Her cousin Franki's pasty shop was another one of their success stories.

Izzy was happy for their success. But if they expected her to give her life to the restaurant as they had theirs, why couldn't she offer her input and have just one of her brothers listen to her? Maybe if one did, she could somehow change the trajectory of her life, even a little.

Izzy tried not to let her inner frustration ruin her day as she took her place behind the hostess stand. She grabbed the napkins and was about to start wrapping the silverware when their VIP guests walked in. She smiled when she saw her former babysitter, Meg, along with Meg's famous singer/songwriter husband, Tyler Evans. They were accompanied by their friends Kyleigh, who owned an arts-and-crafts store in town, and her husband, Paul Rodriguez. Paul was not only a Holiday Boy and famous reality TV show host, but he'd also become a successful producer, opening up a studio not too far from his wife's shop.

Izzy flashed them a professional smile. "Hello!"

"Hi, Izzy!" Meg said, coming over to hug her.

Her heart warmed as she returned the gesture. Meg practically glowed these days, which hadn't always been the case. She'd gone through a terrible public breakup before Tyler moved back to town. Once the two reunited, he'd quickly swept his former neighbor off her feet, and they'd been happily married ever since, with two kids completing their family.

"Hi!" Kyleigh offered her a bright grin. She and Izzy had grown close over the years since Izzy usually bought her art supplies from Kyleigh's store.

"I'm going to run to the restroom," Tyler said, brushing his lips against Meg's honey-colored hair before leaving them. Paul was off in a corner, texting on his phone, leaving the three women alone.

"So what's new with you?" Meg asked.

"Oh, you know. The same old, same old," Izzy replied, trying not to reveal her underlying bitterness.

Meg seemed to notice it, anyway. "You sure you're okay?"

"Yeah, I'm fine. Just..." Izzy peeked over her shoulder to make sure none of her brothers were around to eavesdrop. "I've been doing a lot of thinking lately. You know, wondering what it might be like to try something new in terms of a career. But it's fine. Everything's good."

"What kind of change?" Kyleigh asked, her head tilted with interest.

Izzy laughed awkwardly, wishing she'd never brought it up. "Oh, it's nothing. Forget I said anything." Kyleigh and Meg exchanged glances, and Izzy rushed to fill the silence just as Tyler rejoined them. "I can show you to your table now."

They nodded and she took them to the best one, overlooking the bay. As soon as her nephew, Luca, came over to take their order, she returned to her stand so that she could finish wrapping the silverware. She was so focused on her task, she didn't realize that Kyleigh had returned.

"Oh..." Izzy said when she noticed the other woman. "Was there something else you needed?"

"No," Kyleigh replied gently. "But I might have something *you* need."

Confusion crinkled Izzy's features. "Sorry?"

The beautiful blonde dug through her purse and pulled out a card. "Paul has a friend who's moving to Holiday Bay. I know the household is looking for a nanny to help with the children."

"I..." Izzy took the black card and glanced down. There was nothing on it. No name or email. Only a phone number written in gold lettering.

"There's no name on this," she said.

"Yeah, sorry about that. You know how eccentric and paranoid some of Paul's friends are," Kyleigh explained. She nodded at the card. "This particular one prefers privacy above all else. The family will be officially moved into their new house next week."

Izzy frowned as she looked at her friend. "Why do you think I'd be a good fit?"

Kyleigh fiddled with her purse strap. "You've always been really great anytime I've needed help with Holly," she responded, mentioning her teenage daughter. Izzy used to watch her whenever Kyleigh and Paul had to leave town for Holiday Boy business. Though now that Holly was sixteen, she didn't really need a babysitter anymore. "And I know you've helped with Meg's kids, too," Kyleigh continued. "You're a natural. And it might be a chance to try your hand at something else. Maybe this is the opportunity that'll help you figure out your own path. Obviously, you don't have to do it, but it's an option for you to consider."

Izzy held the card tightly between her fingers, clutching it like a lifeline.

Putting on a brave face, she said, "I'll think about it."

"Good," Kyleigh replied. She offered Izzy a slight smile before going back to her table.

After she left, Izzy put the card on top of the hostess stand. She ran her fingers over the glossy gold numbers. She wondered who the friend was. Given the circles Kyleigh ran in these days—and the fact that there was no name listed—it had to be someone of importance. Maybe it was some big-time actor or music producer that Paul worked with.

As another group of customers approached, Izzy picked up the card and placed it carefully in her pocket. It sat there like a promise.

Chapter Two

Izzy drove down the hidden driveway, her fingers clutching the steering wheel nervously. She hadn't told anyone—not even Kyleigh or Meg—that she'd called the number on the card. A woman had answered, sounding haughty and annoyed. Izzy had almost hung up. Instead, she'd explained the reason she was calling and in return was given an address and a date to show up. No other information.

She trusted that Kyleigh wouldn't send her off to a serial killer. If Izzy had to make a guess, given the wealthy people she occasionally met through the restaurant, the person she was about to meet was most likely eccentric, not a psychopath. Though given this drive through the thick forest, she started to second-guess herself. It was the perfect setting to get away with murder.

Izzy's brain tried to come up with whom Paul Rodriguez might know that needed this level of privacy. She knew that he and his business partner were getting ready to film a new season of their hit show, *First Comes Marriage*. A lot of residents were excited about that. They hadn't filmed the show in Holiday Bay since the super popular season when Paul married Kyleigh. Due to a contract with the network, Paul had been required to film the next couple of seasons in California. But now that he'd fulfilled those obligations, he'd returned the show to the Bay, much to his and Kyleigh's delight. Even after three years of marriage, they still acted like honeymooners, and the three months Paul had to be gone each season had left them both miserable. Izzy was happy that her friend would have her husband back year-round.

Izzy wondered if another Holiday Boy was up for grabs. There was James Dallas, who'd divorced his husband several years back, but as far as Izzy knew, he'd stepped away from the limelight and only reappeared when the Boys went on tour. Then there was Zan Chen.

Her heart gave a thump when she thought of the handsome widower.

Zan had always been her favorite Holiday Boy. Jake Reynolds and Tyler were considered by many to be the lead singers of the group. Paul had been their resident bad boy. James had been the sweet, shy one. Zan was the boy next door. Smart. Friendly. Creative. And did she mention handsome, with his blue-black hair, eyes the color of dark wood, and cheekbones that could cut metal?

Izzy had had posters of the gorgeous Chinese-American man all over her walls when she was a tween. And the one time she'd gotten to meet him in person, she'd dumped a plate of spaghetti in his lap.

She cringed as she thought back to that horrifying moment. Thankfully, he hadn't even noticed her, since he'd been too consumed by the presence of his gorgeous supermodel wife. People didn't know it at the time, but Mary was sick with leukemia. She'd passed away a couple of years after her diagnosis, and no one had heard from Zan since.

Which was weird, considering that after he left the band, he'd become a bestselling author. There was a lot of anticipation from his fans—herself included—for the next book in his series. But people had started to lose hope that it would ever get published considering the lack of communication from him or his publishers.

Given Zan's circumstances, she doubted he would go on Paul's show. The last anyone knew was that he'd become a recluse in his mansion over in Maine. The whole world knew how much he'd adored his wife. Izzy assumed that Zan would never want to find another love. Not that it was any of her business. She was a grown woman now, not some starry-eyed tween who thought she'd actually have a chance with him.

Glancing at the clock on her car's dashboard, she cursed under her breath. Thanks to the directions she'd received from the snooty woman on the phone, she had gone by the driveway four times before she finally found the hidden entrance. She was now running a few minutes late, which never made for a good impression.

When the thick pines on both sides of the driveway finally parted, Izzy's mouth dropped open as she saw the beautiful mansion in front of her. It was a sprawling three-story home with white siding and enormous windows. The driveway curved into a horseshoe, leading her to a large fountain containing a cupid statue that shot water from its arrow. As Izzy got out of her car, she paused to appreciate the craftsmanship, then walked toward the ten-foot solid oak front door. After smoothing down her beige skirt, Izzy rang the doorbell. She shifted on her feet, trying not to let her nerves get the best of her.

A few minutes went by and no one answered. She glanced down at her watch to make sure she had the correct time. She was five minutes late, but surely she hadn't missed the person? Izzy would have seen a car pass her on the way down the driveway if they'd decided not to wait for her. She rang the doorbell again. Still nothing.

Her shoulders drooped with disappointment and Izzy turned to leave. The door immediately cracked open and she swung back around. A woman who had to be in her late sixties stood in the open doorframe. She wore her silver hair pulled back into a tight bun that only emphasized the severe angles of her cheeks. She was dressed in a rose-colored sweatshirt and black slacks. Her icy blue eyes trailed over Izzy from head to toe, her mouth curling at whatever she found lacking.

"Can I help you?" the woman asked snidely.

Izzy recognized her voice. This was the woman she'd spoken to on the phone. "Yes, I'm Izzy Rossi. I have an interview here today."

"You're late," the woman said. "Is that typical behavior for you? If so, we don't need to continue."

"I apologize. I had trouble finding the driveway," Izzy explained stiffly.

"If Kyleigh Sinclair-Rodriguez hadn't referred you for the job, I would tell you not to bother with your interview," the woman sniped. "But since you have connections..." She looked over Izzy again with that look of distaste. "You might as well come in. Wipe your feet."

It warmed Izzy's heart that Kyleigh recommended her. Izzy should have told her that she'd applied and asked for more information about her potential new employer. She could have pressed her friend for more details on exactly whom she was meeting with. Maybe then Izzy could have been given a head's up about the rude woman who lived in the house.

The hallway was beautiful, with a large crystal chandelier that glinted off the black-and-white checkerboard floor below. The walls were a bright white that seemed to shimmer under the sunlight streaming in through the three large windows next to the front door.

"You'll find that we have very strict rules in this house." The woman continued down the hall. "Aside from being on time, you're to use the servants' entrance whenever you come and go. If you're hired, that is. We have a lot of important guests that visit here. The help is to be seen only when requested."

The woman took her to the back of the house, where there was a large kitchen with gray marble countertops and white cupboards. It was so spacious, Izzy was certain it rivaled the size of Florentina's. Everything in the room looked well organized to the point of being sterile.

Izzy frowned. It was her understanding that she was interviewing for a nanny position. Where were the signs of any children living in the house? There were no smudges on the counter, no artwork on the fridge. She felt like she was in a museum, not a family home.

Izzy was so busy taking in her surroundings that she didn't pay attention to where she was walking. She ran into the back of the older woman, who'd stopped walking and swung around with a glare.

"Sorry," Izzy muttered.

The woman's mouth pursed. "I'll be frank with you. This family has been through a lot recently and they need someone who can take charge and help them. I very much doubt you are that person, but we'll see what my employer has to say about that."

She pressed a cupboard and it swung open, revealing that it wasn't a cupboard at all, but a door that hid a set of stairs behind it.

"Go up the stairs and wait in his office. It's two doors

down on the left. If he's not there, take a seat until he arrives."

Izzy lifted her chin proudly, not willing to let the woman's negativity affect her nerves any more than it already had. "Thank you, Mrs....?"

"Hadley," the dour woman replied before she disappeared down another hall.

Izzy climbed the cream-carpeted steps, taken aback by the eerie silence. Again, where were the children who lived in the house?

Going two doors down, she knocked on the left hallway door. When there was no answer, she followed Mrs. Hadley's instructions and entered the room. The door shut gently behind her.

Izzy paused as she looked around. There was a large maple desk just to the right of the entrance. On top of it was an open laptop, with the screen pointed away from her view. The other side of the room held a gorgeous wood-burning fireplace with antique green tiles surrounding it. On either side of the wood mantel were shelves filled with books from floor to ceiling. The other walls also contained book-filled shelves. Curiosity getting the better of her, Izzy walked over to one shelf and examined the different titles. She frowned as she realized that several of the novels were the same book, but in different editions. She knew the titles well, considering she had the same series at home.

Izzy swung around as some of the comments Kyleigh told her about her potential employer started to filter into her brain. Paul's friend had children. The family preferred privacy.

Her eyes settled on the large portrait behind the desk of a gorgeous woman. Izzy took a step closer to it, her gaze locking on the woman. She wore a flimsy, skin-colored dress that hugged every curve of her lush body. Her long, blond hair had been styled in thick waves, half-covering one eye. Her irises were a hypnotic blue. She had a small, intimate smile on her face that made Izzy feel uncomfortable, as though she was invading a private moment.

She was truly beautiful, but then again, that was why Mary Chen had been one of the highest paid supermodels of her day.

Izzy's stomach twisted as she realized whose home she was in.

The door to the library swung open hard, hitting the wall behind it with a crash. A man entered the room, his handsome face morphed into a thundercloud.

"What the hell are you doing in here?" he demanded.

Izzy froze like a deer in the headlights.

For the second time in her life, she came face-to-face with Zan Chen.

Chapter Three

"I'm… I…" the woman stammered.

Zan took her in while trying to rein in his temper. He'd clearly frightened her. She was vaguely familiar, but for the life of him, he couldn't remember where he'd seen her before. Maybe at a concert or a book signing?

The woman was tiny compared to him. He'd be surprised if she stood at five feet two in her stockinged feet. Hell, his thirteen-year-old son was taller than her. But she had an abundance of curves to make up for it. Her thick black hair was pulled back into a braid and her brown eyes held gold flecks within their depths, reminding him of autumn leaves.

He cursed himself when he realized that she hadn't continued speaking. "You're Kyleigh's friend."

Her chin trembled slightly but she still raised it as she said, "I am."

Zan's mouth almost turned up at that proud, rebellious tilt, but he hadn't smiled in three years. He wasn't about to start now.

He gave a short nod. "You're in the wrong room."

Those interesting eyes darted around the library. "Mrs. Hadley told me to wait for you in the second room on the left."

He stepped back into the hallway and waved for her to

join him. Once she was beside him, he shut the library door firmly. He passed her and opened the door on the opposite side of the hall. He ignored the way her orange-blossom perfume lingered in the air.

"You must have misunderstood. Mrs. Hadley knows that no one goes into the library but me."

He walked into his office and she followed. There was a desk in here that matched the one in the library, but he used this room to handle the business side of his life. Whether it was calls from his literary agent or book publisher, or conference calls with the rest of the Holiday Boys. At least, that was what the office was supposed to be for. He rarely set foot in it, preferring the quiet of the other room.

The library had become his sanctuary. A place where he could hide away from the world and stare at Mary's picture for hours. He'd taken it so long ago. They'd been getting ready to attend an awards ceremony for one of his books. He'd taken one look at her and decided they could be late. It was one of his most cherished moments with her, walking into the show late, holding hands and basking in the joy of being together.

His dead heart tried to thump back to life, but he squashed the urge as he sat down behind the desk. The woman sat down opposite him, rubbing her hands nervously down her skirt.

"So..." he said, looking down at the résumé she'd sent over. "Miss Rossi—"

"Izzy or Isabella is fine."

He nodded. "Isabella, then. Both Meg and Kyleigh told me you're good with children."

"Thank you," she replied, but didn't say anything else. Zan's eyebrows rose. Did this woman actually want the job?

"What's your experience?" he prompted.

"I've watched their kids on occasion." Isabella's face lit up and Zan paused in the middle of picking up her résumé. When she lost some of her reserve, her face changed. Her high cheekbones became more prominent when her full lips tilted upward. "Meg actually used to babysit me when I was a kid," she continued. "It didn't happen a lot, since my brothers usually watched me, but I always enjoyed when Meg could babysit. Now, I feel like I'm returning the favor."

Zan pulled his gaze from her face. "And you work at Florentina's when you're not babysitting?"

She nodded. "My family owns it. I'm the lead hostess."

His eyes narrowed on her at that comment. He'd wondered why she looked so familiar to him, but maybe that was it. Perhaps they'd run into each other at the restaurant. He knew Jake and Tyler liked to eat there. He'd gone with them once when he moved back into town, but the host that night had been a young man, not Isabella.

"How does your family feel about you interviewing for this role?" he asked. "Are they aware that this position requires you to live here? I'm looking for someone who can provide hands-on stability, which includes living under the same roof." When her face morphed into a look of surprise, he added, "Did you know you were interviewing for an in-house role?"

"No," she whispered.

"Will that be an issue for you?"

"No?" she repeated, this time sounding unsure. He lifted an eyebrow.

He put her résumé back on his desk. "Isabella, my children have been through hell and back these past few years. My son has become antisocial, and was on the brink of getting expelled from his former school before we moved him to Holiday Bay. My daughter becomes hysterical at least three times a day. I'm looking for someone who can be a person they can go to with their troubles. Who will be able to step into any situation and calm things down."

Isabella nodded. "I understand. And I feel like that's something I'm really good at. Over the years, my time in the restaurant has taught me to—"

"Ms. Rossi—Isabella—" Zan interrupted when he found himself staring at those voluptuous lips of hers. "I thank you for your time, but I don't feel like this will be a good fit for what this household needs."

Isabella's body drooped, but she didn't argue or try to plead her case. She said, "I appreciate your time. And I'm sorry again for going into the other room."

She jumped to her feet and left, that sweet scent of orange blossoms chasing after her. He did his best to ignore the sad expression that had been on her expressive features.

As Zan got to his feet, he debated what he should do next. The interview went shorter than he planned. Maybe he should try to work on his book. It was going on two years overdue. But the idea of opening his laptop and pulling up that blank document made his stomach wrench.

He heard a scream and went running down the hall. As he reached the stairs, he saw Isabella hurrying down the last few steps so she could get to Alice, who was sitting on the floor in front of the entryway, clutching her favorite book, *Little Women*. Her blond ponytail was askew, her face blotchy, her blue eyes red and puffy. With the exception of those eyes, which were shaped like his, Alice was a miniature of her mom—except when she was screaming and crying, which was all the time these days. He felt at his wits end, unable to give his daughter the assurance she needed to grow into a happy and healthy person.

Zan was failing his kids. And with his former mother-in-law, Astrid, constantly hovering around, waiting for an excuse to file for custody, he knew he needed to figure out how to get his family back on track, and he needed to do so quickly.

"Are you okay?" Isabella said as she crouched down next to his daughter.

"I—I dropped my book and the spine separated f-from the binding."

"Can I see it?" Isabella asked. Alice handed it over to her cautiously. Opening the book carefully, Isabella said, "This looks like a very old copy. Where did you get it?"

"It was—" Alice sniffed "—it was my mom's when she was a kid."

"I see." Isabella looked at it again. "You know, I'm sure Kyleigh's Knits has some type of glue that'll work on this."

Alice wiped her nose with the back of her hand. "It won't be the same."

"But you can fix it and make it better. It'd be a shame if it disintegrated any more and you lose pages. How will you know if Jo ends up with Laurie or not?"

Isabella made a dramatic grimace and Alice giggled, the sound unnatural in the mournful atmosphere of the house. Zan couldn't remember the last time he'd heard his little girl laugh.

Isabella handed the book back to Alice. "I'm sure if you ask your dad, he can take you to the store and you can get the correct glue to fix the issue."

Alice sniffed one more time. "What's your name?"

"Isabella, but my friends call me Izzy, so you can, too. What's your name?"

"Alice," his daughter whispered. "Are you here to interview for the nanny position?"

"I just finished."

Even from the landing at the top of the stairs, he could see the slight slump in Isabella's shoulders.

"It'd be great if you could get the job," Alice replied shyly, giving the other woman a tentative smile. "It'd be nice to have someone around who cares."

She nodded at her damaged book but Zan's heart panged, anyway. She wasn't just talking about the book.

Zan stepped onto the top step. "Alice."

She stood up, clutching the damaged book to her chest. "Hi, Dad."

"Why don't you go put your book in my office? I'll make sure it gets repaired."

She looked at him hopefully, then ran up the stairs. Alice paused when she reached him, giving him a tentative smile. He briefly ran his hand over her silky head before she went by him and headed for his office. He turned back to Isabella, who was staring at him. She jerked a little once their eyes made contact and she pivoted quickly to hurry to the door.

"Isabella," Zan called out, and she froze. "Perhaps I was a little hasty in our interview."

"Oh?" she replied, not looking at him.

Zan walked down the remaining steps. "Alice is ten years old, but emotionally, she's trapped at seven. As I mentioned upstairs, my son barely talks to anyone anymore. I moved my family here for a fresh start, for us to start living again. And for the first time in a long time, I just witnessed Alice not having a complete meltdown like she's prone to do. I…think you might be what this family needs. If you'll still consider the job."

Isabella turned completely around to face him, her eyes wide. "That includes living here?"

"Yes."

Isabella bit her lip. “Can I think it over?”

He tried not to let his disappointment show when she didn’t immediately accept. “Sure, that’s fine.”

She gave him a brief smile before swiftly walking out the door without looking back.

Chapter Four

Izzy walked toward Kyleigh's Knits, her mind in an endless loop of mortification. It had been three days since her disastrous interview with Zan Chen.

Zan *freaking* Chen.

When he'd first entered the library, and caught her gawking at his dead wife's picture like an obsessed fan, she'd sent a prayer into the universe that the floor would open up and swallow her whole. Unfortunately for her, the universe decided to keep her in the land of humiliation. She'd been tongue-tied throughout the rest of the interview, caught between embarrassment and finding herself face-to-face with her longtime crush. Izzy was actually shocked that he'd offered her the job in the end. They both knew she'd bombed the interview.

And that was another thing that had made her toss and turn at night ever since. Would she actually accept the offer? She knew she would have to give her answer at some point, but she didn't know what she was going to do. Because despite whatever silly feelings she'd experienced back when she was a tween with a crush on a megastar, the truth was that the real Zan Chen was kind of a jerk.

Now, she understood the expression *never meet your heroes*.

Sure, she might have misunderstood Mrs. Hadley and gone into the wrong room, but there was no reason for him to act like she'd just tried to break into Fort Knox. Did Izzy really want to work for that man, along with his haughty housekeeper?

But every time she grabbed her phone to tell Zan no, she thought of his daughter. Alice seemed like a sweet girl who carried too much pain and misery in her eyes for someone her age. Even though Izzy's mind told her to tell Zan to shove it, her heart wouldn't allow her to reject the job because maybe she could do some good for his children.

Izzy opened the door and looked around for Kyleigh. She found her friend standing behind the counter, working on her laptop.

"You!" she accused in a sharp tone.

Kyleigh looked up and smiled at her. "Hey, Izzy. What are you—"

"How could you?" she asked as she stomped swiftly to the counter.

Kyleigh's brow furrowed. "Come again?"

"How could you not tell me that I was interviewing with Zan Chen!"

Kyleigh glanced toward the back of the store, then said in a quiet voice, "I promised that I wouldn't tell people he was in town. He's trying to get the kids adjusted without drawing the attention of fans and the paparazzi."

"No excuses. Friends before fiends. Where's the sisterhood?"

Kyleigh glanced again toward the back of the store. She lowered her voice even more, "Iz—"

"He's such a jerk. Clearly the sweet-guy persona he had in Holiday Boys was a lie because he was a complete and utter as—"

"Izzy!"

"Just because he has the face of a god and the talent of a..."

She stopped talking when she noticed Kyleigh staring at something behind her, her eyes horrified.

"The talent of a what?" a deep voice said behind Izzy.

She closed her eyes. No way. No flipping way was this happening to her again. There had to be some universal law that didn't allow someone to humiliate themselves in front of the same person more than once in a week.

"Please lie and tell me Zan Chen is not behind me?" Izzy begged Kyleigh in a whisper.

Amusement crossed her face. "He's not behind you."

Izzy silently cursed. She turned slowly, hoping against hope that it wasn't him, despite Kyleigh's confirmation.

Apparently, the universe really did hate her.

Zan stood behind her, staring at her with that same sexy raised eyebrow he'd given her the other day.

Izzy gaped at him like a fish. "I... Mr...."

"Fiend?" Zan asked helpfully when she didn't continue.

Her mind automatically began listing the Roman gods of her ancestors. Surely, one of them could hand her a favor.

Dear Jupiter, Juno, Neptune...

Oh! Neptune was a good one to plead to. He liked earthquakes, and she could use one to swallow her up.

"Mr. Chen," she finally said. "What are you doing here?"

He raised the bottle of PVA glue he was holding. "You mentioned to Alice that Kyleigh sold glue that could mend her book. She's been upset ever since the cover tore off. I figured I'd get some while I was in town meeting with the guys."

The guys. She assumed he meant the other Holiday Boys who were already living in the area. Which was really weird to think about whenever she gave the matter any thought. That some of the most recognizable people in the world lived within a few miles of her small hometown.

"Mr. Chen," she said, trying again. "What you heard. I'm—"

"Don't worry about it," he said as he walked up to the counter. "And *Zan* is fine."

Kyleigh took the glue and started ringing him up. As she did, he turned toward Izzy, placing an elbow on the counter. He was wearing a white T-shirt and khakis. She didn't know what state of mind the man was in, given his ongoing grief, but he still clearly worked out. His biceps practically busted out of the material.

"Look," Zan said. "I know we didn't start off on the right foot, and I do apologize for that, but I'd really like you to work for my family. I think it'll be good for both of my children."

"I'm still thinking over my options," Izzy admitted.

He nodded shortly before turning to Kyleigh. "Do you have a pen and paper?"

"Sure." She reached under the counter and pulled out what he'd asked for. The pen she handed him had a plastic bee attached to the tip that wiggled with every stroke Zan wrote.

He finished writing and she saw that he had written down a phone number. "This is my personal cell. Once you know your answer, give me a call."

Izzy lifted her chin, trying to salvage a little of her pride. "Who says you can afford me?"

She meant it flippantly. Everyone knew how successful each Holiday Boy was. Aside from his music success, Zan's bestselling books meant he could probably afford three nannies.

His lips twitched upward, revealing that she wasn't too far off with her line of thinking.

"What's your price?" he asked.

She threw out a ridiculously high number and a wicked glint appeared in his eyes.

"I'll triple that."

"Wha…? That's ridiculous. Mr. Chen—"

"Zan," he reminded her. He walked over and handed her the slip of paper. At his nearness, the light cologne he wore enveloped her. He smelled of sandalwood and something else that was all him. She'd caught a hint of it the other day, but without the nervousness of her interview, it registered more fully. She found herself leaning closer to him to get a deeper breath before she realized what she was doing.

"I'll be on the lookout for your call," he said.

This close, she had to tilt her head almost to the ceiling to see him. He was that much taller than her. She never really cared about height before, but there was something about the way Zan Chen carried himself that made her insides scramble.

"I'll let you know soon," she murmured a little breathlessly.

He turned to look at Kyleigh. She'd been watching them, her eyebrows raised practically to her scalp. "Tell Paul I'll call him later, once I have some more information." He turned back to Izzy one more time, giving her a nod goodbye. "Isabella."

"Zan," she replied.

He stilled, his eyes tracing her features. She realized that it was the first time she'd called him anything but Mr. Chen. Without another word, he strode out the door. She watched as he pulled sunglasses out of his pocket, then placed them on his nose before heading down the sidewalk.

Izzy wondered how many people knew he was in town. Surely, fans would start to swarm the area if they did. Then again, with Jake, Tyler and Paul living in the Bay, maybe having another Holiday Boy around wasn't enough to excite people anymore.

Izzy was still staring after Zan when she heard an "ahem" behind her.

Swinging around, she found Kyleigh now leaning with her elbows on the counter, an expectant look on her face. Izzy lifted her head, even while her cheeks burned for some silly reason.

"What?" she asked.

"What was *that*?" Kyleigh asked.

"What was what?" Izzy replied, looking anywhere but at her friend.

Kyleigh snorted. "Forget it." Changing the subject, she asked, "Are you going to accept the job?"

"I'd be an idiot not to," she said. The kind of money Zan was offering would let her pursue her dream. This could give her the foundation she needed to eventually buy the old bank for her art gallery. She could envision it already. She'd change the lower level into a dream studio and gallery, while converting the upstairs into a living space for herself. This money would allow Izzy to finally step out of her family's shadow and live the life she wanted.

She instantly felt guilty about that. Her family was good to her. She was luckier than most. Some people didn't have a family to celebrate life's milestones. She knew she should be grateful. But…

Their dreams aren't yours.

Then again, were her dreams actually based in reality? Few people made it as artists, and galleries closed all the time.

"Why do you look so hesitant?" Kyleigh asked.

"Aside from the fact that I've now embarrassed myself twice in front of one of the most famous people in the world?"

Kyleigh made a huffing nose at that. "Please don't say stuff like that around Paul. His ego is big enough." She smiled, though, her face softening at the mention of her husband. "Zan is just a man. Human. He's not infallible. You could be really good for him."

That got Izzy's attention. "What do you mean?"

Kyleigh lifted a shoulder. "I've known Zan since we were teenagers. He used to be such a happy-go-lucky guy. Ever since his wife passed away, it's like he died, too. I know he tries hard to be there for his kids, but for the past few years, he's been merely existing, not living."

Izzy frowned. "What does that have to do with me?"

"Because, my friend, you made him smile. And that alone makes you a miracle worker."

Chapter Five

Izzy's stomach twisted as she stared at the glass entryway of Florentina's. The slip of paper that Zan had handed to her earlier rested heavily inside her skirt pocket. She reached for it now as she headed inside, the feel of it a balm to the chaos inside her.

Izzy wanted to quit her job at the restaurant. If she had to do the same routine day in and day out until she died, she'd go insane. Zan's offer was a lifeline she didn't know she needed. Kyleigh thought Izzy could be his miracle worker, but the truth was that Zan could very well be hers. With what he said he would pay her, she could eventually follow her heart.

But could she actually do it? Could she quit her family business? She had a duty to them. They had given her everything she had. A roof over her head. Her education.

There also seemed to be an unspoken agreement between her and her brothers. She suspected they wanted her to be the one to take care of their aging parents—living with them, looking after them—when they could no longer care for themselves. Sure, her parents were healthy now, but they weren't getting any younger. And as the only girl in the family, her brothers had dropped enough clues over the years that she'd be the one who took care of their parents.

It was little comments here and there. Like when she'd told her oldest brother, Antonio, that she wanted to get her own apartment.

He'd responded, "It's not a good time. Mom just had her hysterectomy. She'll need help around the house."

If it wasn't something happening to her mom, her dad's vertigo would act up.

"What will happen if Dad falls, Iz? Mom can't lift him by herself," her youngest brother, Enzo, said to her once.

And Izzy was perfectly happy taking care of her family. She loved every single one of them. It was just... Wasn't it okay to want more? Shouldn't she be allowed to follow her own path, one that was of her own free will?

Sighing, she walked into the kitchen to punch in. She could hear Enzo and Dante arguing about some football game in the kitchen as they prepared for the dinner rush. She turned to see Gio walking by with his iPad.

"Hey, Gio, is Tony around?"

Gio glanced up at her briefly before going back to his device. "He's in his office. Mom and Pop are in there as well."

"Thanks," she said, but her brother had already started walking to the front, no doubt to make sure everything was running smoothly with the staff.

Izzy headed to her eldest brother's office and knocked on the door, waiting for his gruff "Come in," before entering. Her parents sat in the two chairs available in front of her brother's desk. Antonio sat behind it, looking at something on his computer with concentration.

"Hey, everyone," she said. She walked over to where her mom was sitting and kissed her cheek. Izzy took after her mom. They were both short with jet-black hair and honey-brown eyes, but her mom was on the slim and petite side, while Izzy definitely wasn't. Her brothers took more after their dad, with their tall frames and thick, dark brown hair. She leaned over to give her dad a side hug.

Her eyed her, a frown appearing on his face. In his light Italian accent, he said, "Antonio, you're working your sister too much. She looks haggard."

Izzy crossed her arms over her chest. "Thanks, Dad."

When her dad noticed her mom glaring at him, he shrugged. "What? She'll never find a husband looking like she does."

Her mom got out of her chair so she could wrap a protective arm around Izzy's shoulder.

"Gianni!" she said sternly to Izzy's father.

He didn't look apologetic in the least. "I'm looking out for what's best for our daughter. She's starting to look forty."

"I'm not even thirty yet," Izzy grumbled.

"She looks perfectly fine," her mom replied.

Izzy briefly closed her eyes. That's exactly what a woman wanted to hear. That she looked *fine.*

Antonio leaned back in his chair, causing it to creak. "I thought you two came in to discuss the restaurant's quarterly statement, not judge whether I'm overworking my sister or not. Which, FYI, I'm not."

Their mom waved her hand at that, dismissing what he said. "We can talk business later. When was the last time Gianni and I had all five of our babies under one roof."

"Mom…" Antonio's voice was amused. "We see each other every Sunday for dinner."

It was true. Her brothers came over to their house once a week, bringing their spouses and hordes of children with them. It was usually mass chaos. Izzy loved it.

"Iz," Antonio said. "Did you stop in to discuss work, or something regarding the family?"

She hadn't really stopped by for any particular reason other than to see if he had an idea of how busy it was going to be that night, but she blurted out, "I was offered another job."

It was as if she'd announced that someone had called in a bomb threat. All three family members turned to look at her with different expressions of disbelief.

"What are you talking about?" her father asked.

"I was offered a job as a nanny."

"When? Who?" her mother said.

"Zan Chen recently moved to the area. He's looking for a live-in nanny for his two kids."

"Zan Chen..." Her father's face looked blank for a minute before he snapped his fingers. "The one you dropped spaghetti all over."

Izzy internally cringed at that memory. "Yeah, that's the one."

"Did you tell him you already have a job?" Antonio said, his attention already starting to return to the computer.

"What's all the commotion about in here?" Enzo showed up at the door, followed by Dante.

"Some guy wants Isabella to move in with him," her father said.

"Over our dead bodies," Enzo said.

Izzy rolled her eyes. "Enz, need I remind you that you're only two years older than me and certainly not one to tell me who I can and cannot live with. Do you remember the Callie Farkle situation from—"

"There's no need to go there," Enzo said, his face hurt.

"What about Callie Farkle?" her mom asked, crossing her arms at the mention of her best friend's daughter.

Izzy tried to steer the conversation back to the topic at hand. "I'm not moving in with a man, like you're implying. I'd be getting my own private room. Besides, he has other staff that also live on the property."

"I bet he does," her dad muttered.

"We should meet the guy before you move in with him," Dante said.

"Oh, for Pete's sake." Izzy threw her hands up. "I'm not moving into a harem."

"The answer is no," her father said. "Your brothers need you here."

Izzy pinched the bridge of her nose. She was starting to feel one of her migraines coming on.

"It wouldn't hurt for Izzy to see a little bit of what the world has to offer," Dante said cautiously after a moment. And this was why he was her favorite.

"Are you serious?" Antonio glared at him.

Dante shrugged. "She's almost thirty. Why do we have her cloistered away like she's some Victorian virgin?"

Her father crossed himself.

"It just seems abrupt," Enzo said.

"Not to mention it's bad timing," Antonio repeated.

"I think it's the perfect time, since we're going into our slow season," Izzy replied. When the weather started getting cooler, they usually had less tourists coming for meals. "Besides, you don't need me. Luca can take over." She mentioned Antonio's son.

"Wait," Enzo said. "If you move out, who's going to take care of Mom and Pop?"

Guilt rippled over her followed by anger. They really only saw her as a means to an end. Someone to greet customers before she rushed off to take care of their parents.

"Who says we need your sister to take care of us?" their mom said, straightening to her full five feet nothing. Her sons might tower over her, but when she got that look in her eye, they usually cowered like babies.

"I didn't mean it like that, Ma," Enzo quickly said.

"You think I can't take care of myself or of your father?" Tina asked sharply. "I raised five children, ran a house, and helped build this business. Despite this offensive conversation, I think all of you turned out okay."

"Nice job," Dante muttered, elbowing his brother.

"But we're not talking about you," Antonio interjected. "We're talking about Izzy."

Izzy went stiff. "What's that supposed to mean?"

Antonio shrugged. "You're not exactly the worldly type, and this guy is."

Izzy went rigid. She certainly didn't need the fact that she was sheltered pointed out. "He's offering me a job looking after his children. He's not inviting me to some orgy."

"Gross," Enzo said, while her father crossed himself again.

"I'm just saying, you won't have one of us there," Antonio replied.

Izzy looked at each of her family members, whose facial expressions ranged from uncomfortable to stubborn to sympathetic.

She swallowed painfully. "Is this how you all see me? Some pathetic loser who can't survive without any of you hovering over my shoulder to make sure I'm breathing okay?"

"No one is saying that," Antonio argued. "But come on, Izzy. Your responsibility is this family. You take care of Mom and Dad, and you help here. We don't need to change those dynamics."

Izzy thought she was going to throw up. "But I do," she whispered.

"What?" her father said, his face darkening. "Are you that unhappy with the life I built for my children?"

"It's not that. It's just… I need to change the dynamics." Taking a deep breath, she announced, "I quit. Effective immediately."

With a nod to her parents, she hurried toward the doorway before her father could say one more thing to her, pushing past Enzo and Dante. She saw Gio at the hostess stand.

He looked up as she approached. "Hey, I put tables three and four together. We have a birthday party coming in—"

"Tell it to Luca," she said. Her nephew was the restaurant's backup host.

"What?" Gio said. His forehead wrinkled as he took in her upset expression. "Izzy, what's going on?"

"I just quit," she said. "I was offered another job."

She gave him a ten-second rundown. Gio looked a little stunned after she was through. "Wow. It sucks to lose you, but you're old enough to know what's best for you."

Izzy sniffed. It was nice to hear one of her brothers outside of Dante recognize that fact.

"Luca will do great," she said.

He gave her a half smile. "So will you."

She nodded her thanks at her brother before glancing around the restaurant one more time. She headed outside and walked to her car. Once she was inside, she pulled Zan's number out of her pocket.

He answered on the second ring. "Hello?"

"Mr. Chen—Zan, this is Izzy. Izzy Rossi."

"Hello, Isabella," he replied in a way that made her shiver.

"If you still want to offer me the job, I'm happy to accept it."

Chapter Six

Izzy looked around her room, making sure she hadn't forgotten anything. There wasn't a lot she wanted to take with her. Most of the items in the house belonged to her parents, anyway. Even the furnishings in her room weren't something she'd bought with her own money. Aside from her canvases and art supplies, she only had a couple of suitcases to show for her life so far.

A knock on the door pulled her from her morose thoughts. "Come in."

Her mom entered, pausing when she saw Izzy's two packed bags on the bed. "So you're really doing this?"

Izzy lifted her head. "I'm too old to still be living at home. It's well past time for me to move out."

Tina tilted her head. "I'm sorry for everyone's reactions earlier. I think it was probably the shock of knowing we won't see you every day."

Izzy's stomach swirled with guilt. "Mom, I need to do this."

Her mom surprised her when she said, "I know." She walked over to Izzy and patted her cheek. "I realize it's been tough for you to grow up with four older brothers who are overbearing on a good day. Tony especially seems to forget that he's your brother and not your father. I've always blamed the age difference on that."

Izzy nodded. Antonio was fourteen years older than her, but sometimes acted like it was forty.

Her mother sighed as she sat down on her bed. "No one should have made you feel like your only job was to take care of your dad and me or to work at the restaurant. And you should especially not have been made to feel like you can't stand on your own two feet just because you're female. Your brothers are hotheads. They always have been. I blame your father for that." She smiled at Izzy, who let out a snicker. "You've always been more like me. We Rossi women are quieter, but we're also what keeps this family going. You're strong, Iz. Don't let anyone make you feel otherwise."

Izzy walked over to the bed and sat down beside her. She laid her head against her mother's shoulder like she used to when she was a kid.

They didn't say anything for several minutes before her mom let out a snort. "It had to be Zan Chen, huh?"

Her mom was well aware of the silly crush she'd had on him when she was a tween.

"Oh… I'm not… He's not…"

Tina wrapped an arm around Izzy's waist and gave her a squeeze.

"He's not married," her mom said.

"He's my employer," she responded firmly. "I'm taking this job because the pay is really good and I'm getting the chance to try something different."

Her mom smiled. "Sure, Iz. Whatever you say."

Izzy pulled her car into the carport near the side entrance of the house, as Zan's instructions had told her to do. She stepped onto the redbrick driveway and opened the trunk to get one of her suitcases. Though she was nervous, she couldn't help but take in the beauty of the grounds. She was able to see more of the backyard from where she stood. The well-manicured lawn wove its way through trees and beds of wildflowers. She could hear the sound of water flowing from somewhere in the distance. Since she knew the property was too far from the bay, she assumed that there had to be some type of creek or river nearby.

Contentedness washed over her. Her fingers itched to set up her canvas so she could try to capture the beauty of her surroundings. Knowing she'd have the opportunity to do that later, she walked to the house and knocked on the large, solid red door. It wasn't ornate like the front doors were, and she remembered that the housekeeper had said this was the servants' entrance.

The relaxed feeling didn't last long when the housekeeper, Mrs. Hadley, opened the door and looked at Izzy like she was dog dung.

"I can't believe you were who he went with." The older woman shook her head, then added, "Well, I don't have all day. Follow me." Izzy wasn't sure, but it sounded like Mrs. Hadley said under her breath, "If you can fit through the door."

Her cheeks burned. It had been a long time—since college, really—since someone had openly fat-shamed her.

They walked through the kitchen and went down a hallway along the back of the house. Sunlight streamed through the home's gigantic windows, reflecting off the natural stone floors. They passed several tables that had vases of fresh flowers on them, no doubt from the gardens out back. They filled the air with a fresh floral scent.

Mrs. Hadley finally stopped at a door and opened it, revealing a steep set of stairs. "This way," she ordered.

The stairway was narrow, making it difficult for Izzy to carry her suitcase. Once they reached the top, they continued up another flight of stairs that led to the attic. By the time they reached the last step, Izzy's cheeks were blotchy red. She put the heavy bag to the side of her as she tried to catch her breath.

Mrs. Hadley looked at her disdainfully. "This will be your room."

She opened a door, revealing a space that was little more than a glorified closest. There was twin-size bed frame with a stained mattress on top of it. The only natural light came from the skylight in the ceiling. The room looked dusty, like it hadn't been used in years.

Izzy tried to think positive. It wasn't exactly what she'd imagined, but it was her own space. And it allowed in enough natural light to be perfect for artwork. "This is great. Thank you." When Mrs. Hadley turned to leave, she asked, "Where's your room?"

Mrs. Hadley sniffed. "I have the housekeeper's suite on the main floor. It overlooks the gardens." Of course, it did. "You already missed breakfast, but lunch will be served shortly. Get settled and your things unpacked. Mr. Chen wants to meet with you before lunch, and then you're to see to the children. They didn't have school today, due to the teachers having a professional-development day."

Izzy's stomach twisted with nervous anticipation at the idea of seeing Zan again. "Got it. Thanks again."

Mrs. Hadley gave her another once-over and shook her head before she left Izzy in peace. Izzy took another look around. She grabbed her suitcase and placed it on the lumpy mattress. The metal bed frame squeaked loudly at the added pressure. Izzy cringed. If it couldn't handle a suitcase without protesting, how would it handle a human being? Turning around, she walked over to the dark wood dresser and ran her finger over it, leaving a trail in the thick layer of dust. She'd have to find some cleaning supplies before this room gave her an asthma attack.

"What are you doing in here?" a voice said behind her, and she swung around to see Alice standing in the doorway.

Izzy tried to put on a polite face. "Oh, I was just about to get settled into my room."

Alice wrinkled her nose. "This isn't your room. We haven't renovated this part of the house yet. It's gross."

The girl walked into the room and hauled Izzy's suitcase off the bed with a grunt. "Come on."

"Oh, but this is where Mrs. Hadley said I should stay," she said. The last thing she wanted to do was to get on the housekeeper's bad side on her first day…at least, any more than she already had.

"I heard Dad talking to Mrs. Hadley this morning. He said to put you in the Rose Room. That's down the hall from our rooms. Mrs. Hadley probably just forgot. She's ancient."

Izzy did her best not to laugh at that. Given the older woman's personality, she most likely wouldn't take kindly to being called "ancient."

"This way," Alice said as she pulled the suitcase toward a set of stairs that Izzy hadn't noticed earlier. Her stomach gave a nervous little flutter. She didn't know what to expect from a room named after a flower, but it sounded ten times more appealing than the one she was currently standing in.

Izzy hurried over to Alice and grabbed the heavy suitcase so that the child didn't attempt to carry it down the stairs. They went down one flight, which opened up to a hallway with warm wooden floors and cream-colored walls.

"Here it is," Alice said, stopping in front of a large white door trimmed in gold paint. She pushed open the door to reveal a corner room painted a soft pink. The bed in here was a queen-size maple-wood canopy with white curtains tied to each post. The comforter on top was a deep violet. Plush, thick carpet in a darker shade of pink cushioned her feet. The room smelled of roses and lemon polish. The perfume of the flowers flowed in from the open windows that overlooked the gardens below.

"This..." Izzy looked around in disbelief. "This can't be my room."

Alice looked at her with those inquisitive eyes of hers. "Why not?"

"Because it's too—" *romantic* "—fancy."

"That's silly," Alice said. "It's not fancy at all. Honestly, Mrs. Hadley snatched up the best room, aside from what the family uses. This one is dated. That's what Dad said, but I think it's a lot better than the rooms upstairs."

"It definitely is," Izzy assured her. "It's perfect the way it is."

"Oh, good, you're getting settled in, then," a deep voice said from the doorway—one that had featured heavily in her dreams as of late.

Izzy swung around to see Zan leaning against the frame. Her pulse leapt at the sight of him. He looked incredible in a dark blue polo and jeans that looked like they were made to fit his body perfectly. Actually...they might have been. After the great spaghetti incident, Zan's bandmate, Tyler, had told her Zan was the fashionista of the group. The man apparently liked his custom clothes.

"I don't know what to say," Izzy finally said, waving her hand around the room. "This is too much. I'm perfectly happy to stay in the room upstairs."

Zan frowned. "In the attic? I wouldn't put my worst enemy up there. That space is for storage. This room is closest to the children, so I'd prefer you use it. Besides, the two bedrooms on the main floor are being used by the other employees. Aside from Mrs. Hadley, we have Simon, who takes care of the grounds. I'm sure you'll meet him at some point today."

"Simon is Grandpa's age," Alice said. "He mostly talks about arthritis and flowers."

Izzy bit back a smile. She could already tell that Alice didn't have much of a filter. Izzy probably shouldn't encourage it by laughing at every naughty thing the kid said.

"Good to know," she told Alice before looking at Zan. "I'm excited to meet him. The landscaping here is beautiful."

He nodded. "Listen, I wanted to meet with you really quick and then introduce you to Xander."

"Sure," she said, her pulse beating loudly in her ears.

Get yourself together. He's still deeply in love with his wife. Everyone knows they had a storybook romance. You don't have a chance. Who cares if he's the most breathtaking man to ever walk the earth?

Zan turned to his daughter. "Mrs. Hadley should have your lunch ready. After you eat, can you give Isabella a house tour?"

Alice stiffened under her father's gaze. Izzy frowned as she watched the earlier light in her eyes instantly dim.

"Sure," Alice replied before looking at Izzy. "See you later?"

She crouched down to be at the little girl's level. "Absolutely. I look forward to it."

Alice gave her a tentative smile before she left the room.

When Izzy turned back to Zan, he was staring after his

daughter with a cross between sadness and frustration on his face. His features went carefully blank when he realized that Izzy was watching him.

"This way," Zan said.

He led her to his office. She noticed that the door to the library across the hall was firmly shut. As they sat in the chairs, he pulled a tablet out of his desk.

As he booted it up, Zan said, "I wanted to go over a few expectations for your employment."

"Of course," she said, trying not to blush like a schoolgirl. *You're not a kid anymore with this man's posters all over your walls.*

He handed her the electronic contract. "This is pretty standard. It's the official copy of the employment agreement I emailed you earlier in the week. But to summarize, it states I will pay you the salary we agreed upon. In addition, you get Sundays off and two weeks' vacation with your first year of employment. If you need more time off, let me know, and we'll make it work. You're welcome to utilize any room that you see fit in the house with the exception of the library, which we've already discussed. The gardens are free for you to use, as are the rooms in the basement."

"What's in the basement?" Izzy asked curiously.

"Oh, you know, normal stuff. The gym is set up down there, in addition to the bowling alley, in-home movie theater, and pool. Any questions?"

A bowling alley and pool were normal? Izzy had grown up knowing her parents were upper middle class, but they certainly were never at this level of wealth.

"Nope, no questions," she replied, her eyes skimming over the document. When she finished signing, she looked up, ready to hand the tablet back to him. She became instantly self-conscious when she realized that he was staring at her. “What?”

“Sorry.” He jerked his eyes away. “I can’t pinpoint why, but I feel like we’ve met before.”

Yeah, when I dumped spaghetti all over your lap and then got on my knees to wipe your crotch with a napkin.

She was *so-o-o* not admitting to that.

Izzy shrugged before changing the subject. “You said something about meeting your son?”

“Right,” Zan replied. As they walked back to the wing of the house where the bedrooms were, he said, “I should probably warn you that Xander isn’t as excited about the idea of a nanny as Alice. As I mentioned before, he’s been—” Zan let out a small sigh “—*angry* since his mom died. He tends to act out by either being closemouthed or downright rude. If it becomes an issue for you, let me know.”

Izzy swallowed, feeling suddenly nervous to meet the teen. “Okay.”

They arrived at another gilded door similar to the one for the bedroom that she had been given. Zan knocked on it and waited a minute. When there was no response, he entered the room. Izzy cautiously followed behind.

She wasn’t sure what to expect. Walls painted black and an emo kid, maybe. Instead, she found a room with painted red walls covered in posters of anime and video-game characters. There was an overflowing hamper outside a large closet, and an unmade queen bed with a rumpled blue comforter on it. In the middle of the room was a teenage boy sitting on a black beanbag chair. He had a large headset on and a game controller in his hands. He had a sour expression on his face as he blasted something on the large TV screen in front of him.

"Xander," Zan said. The teen continued to hit the controller with a level of hostility. Zan tried again. "Alexander."

The boy either didn't hear his dad or didn't care to respond.

Zan breathed impatiently through his nose as he walked over to his son and yanked the headset off his head.

"Hey!" Xander said with a glare at his father. The noise from the headset could be heard across the room.

"You're going to make yourself deaf playing your games that loud," Zan said.

"Like you give a sh—"

"Don't finish that sentence unless you want to lose your Xbox for the next month," he told his son with a sternness that made Izzy want to obey him.

Xander didn't say anything else. He simply gave his father a death glare.

Zan's face was grim as he turned to Izzy. "Xander, this is Isabella. She's going to be helping with you and your sister."

"Izzy's fine," she told the boy gently.

He looked at her like she was a leech there to suck the life out of the room. "I'm too old to have a nanny," he snapped.

Zan folded his muscular arms across his chest. "If that was the case, then I wouldn't have already received a call from your new school that you pulled a fire alarm on Friday. You're lucky they just gave you detention."

"Whatever," Xander grumbled.

Zan's jaw noticeably tightened. "I expect you to treat Isabella with absolute respect. And work on your attitude while you're at it."

Xander gave his dad a mock salute. Zan looked tired as he handed the headset back to his son. Looking at Izzy, he nodded toward the door and they left the room.

Zan shut the door behind them and let out a sigh that came from the depths of his soul. “I’m sorry about that.”

“It’s fine,” Izzy replied, though she was a little unsettled. How was she going to handle a kid who clearly wanted nothing to do with her?

Zan ran a hand over his face. “Let me take you down to the kitchen, and you can have lunch with Alice.”

“Sure, thanks.”

He took her back to the main floor and they entered the expansive kitchen. Mrs. Hadley was standing next to the stove, cutting vegetables on the counter, while a pot of water boiled next to her. Alice sat at the kitchen island, finishing a sandwich.

“Mrs. Hadley,” Zan said, just as his phone vibrated, “can you make sure Isabella also gets something to eat?”

“Of course,” the older woman said, giving Izzy an impatient look.

“Will you stay and eat with us, Dad?” Alice asked hopefully. But Zan missed the look, and was already responding to the text he’d received.

“I have to get back to work,” he replied. “I’ll see you both later.”

And with that, he was gone. Alice started sniffling.

“What would you like to eat?” Mrs. Hadley said, before eyeing Isabella’s figure. “A salad, perhaps?”

Izzy gritted out a smile. “Don’t worry about me. I can make myself a sandwich.”

The witch of a housekeeper pointed at the refrigerator dismissively. Izzy got up and found some jelly. After putting it on the island, she looked around with a frown.

“Could you tell me where the bread and peanut butter are?”

“Oh, for Pete’s sake,” Mrs. Hadley snapped. She walked

over to a nearby cupboard and opened the door, then went over to a drawer and grabbed a knife out of it. She slammed it on the counter before returning to her work.

Izzy quickly put together her meal. The sooner she ate, the sooner she could get out of the old hag's presence.

She sat next to Alice, who'd started to sob quietly.

"Alice, honey, would you please stop that?" Mrs. Hadley said, though her words were much softer than when she spoke to Izzy.

"Sorry," the little girl whispered. She wiped at her face, but the tears didn't stop streaming.

"Hey," Izzy said, nudging her with her elbow. "Your dad said you could take me for a tour after we eat. Does that work for you?"

Alice glanced at her and something inside Izzy ached with sadness. She looked like it was something unusual—an adult actually wanting to spend time with her.

"Okay," Alice replied. The tears stopped rolling down her cheeks as she worked on finishing her meal.

Izzy started to eat her own sandwich, wondering what she'd gotten herself into.

Chapter Seven

At the end of her first day, Izzy was still questioning her decision. She knew that she could return to the family restaurant. Her brothers would welcome her back with open arms…and probably a whole lot of I-told-you-so's.

The idea of going back to that life made Izzy feel physically sick, but she didn't know what to do about her current situation, either.

It was clear to her that Zan Chen's life was a complete and utter mess. Alice had been borderline anxious all day. She was constantly on the verge of tears, the slightest thing setting her off. After the tour, they'd settled in the movie room in the basement and watched *Cinderella*. She'd started crying when Cinderella's dad died, and it took a half hour before she'd stopped. Izzy knew the little girl had connected the loss of the character's parents to her own mother's passing, but Alice refused to talk about it.

Xander was an even bigger concern. She only saw him once during the day and that was at dinner. He'd either treated her with open hostility, or completely ignored her during their meal. But it was the look on his face when he thought no one was paying attention that caused Izzy the greatest concern. There was absolute emptiness, as though he'd suppressed his emotions so deeply, she wondered what it would take for him to ever become a real boy again.

She hadn't seen Zan the rest of the day. He'd locked himself away in his library, not even coming out to have dinner with the kids. She wondered if he'd fire her on her first day if she busted into his sacred space and demanded that he eat with them.

After she tucked Alice into bed later that night, Izzy started to feel a dull pain across her forehead. She hoped with everything in her that she wasn't about to get one of her migraines. She headed for the kitchen to get a glass of something to drink so she could take one of her pills before the pain got any worse. If she took the medication in time, perhaps it would only turn into a dull ache instead of a crippling headache. She paused when she saw Mrs. Hadley sitting at the island, writing on a pad of paper. From what Izzy could tell, it looked like a grocery list. The older woman stiffened when she saw her.

"I just wanted to grab something to drink," Izzy explained quickly. She walked over to the refrigerator and grabbed a can of lemonade.

"I'm making out a list of groceries that we'll need for next week now that we're feeding an extra mouth," Mrs. Hadley said, her tone setting Izzy on edge. "What would you care for? Some fruit?"

She tried not to let her irritation show. "Sure. Except for melons. Honeydew, watermelon… I can't have any of that, or I'll go into anaphylactic shock. I can eat anything but that."

"Clearly," the woman muttered.

Izzy whipped around to face her. It had only been one day and she was already done with the barbs.

"Yes, I get it. I'm overweight," she said angrily. The old

hag merely lifted an eyebrow as though silently agreeing with her. "I don't need you pointing it out every two seconds."

"Salad, it is," Mrs. Hadley said.

Izzy set the can on the counter a little too hard. "What is your problem with me?" she asked.

Mrs. Hadley stood up with a glare. "I've seen your type before. He'll never notice you."

Izzy's face flushed. "I don't have any idea what you're talking about."

"Sure," the older woman said. "Mrs. Chen hired me shortly after my husband died. She gave me a roof over my head and steady employment, despite me being much older than others she interviewed. Aside from being the kindest person I've ever met, she was beautiful. Of course, she was. She was a model. But she was beautiful on the inside as well as out. And I can guarantee that if Mr. Chen ever finds another woman—which I seriously doubt he will, given how in love he was with Mrs. Chen—he'll end up with someone like her. Someone perfect for him in every way. Not someone like *you*."

Izzy paled. She was perfectly aware that she'd never get a man like Zan Chen. But to have it so blatantly laid out for her hurt more than she wanted to let on. A pettiness that she hated to admit took over, and she exited the room, leaving her drink on the counter. The can was probably leaving a condensation ring on Mrs. Hadley's clean countertop.

Good. She hoped it annoyed the hell out of the woman.

Izzy headed back up to her room and paced around, tension thick in her shoulders. She went into her bathroom and grabbed her medication. After swallowing down a migraine pill with some water from the faucet, she thought about the home gym and pool in the basement. Maybe she needed to swim a few laps and get some of her stress out—nothing too strenuous to hurt her head, but something that could help her muscles relax in a gentle way. The idea of soaking her head in some cool water also had a lot of appeal in that moment, though hopefully her medication would kick in soon. After grabbing her swimsuit out of her suitcase, she headed to the basement. She'd finish settling in and unpacking her stuff tomorrow.

Once she reached the home's lowest level, she breathed in the scent of chlorine as she walked down the black tiled floors, keeping her eyes on them instead of the bright white walls. She tilted her head from side to side to relieve some of the pressure in her head.

Izzy paused when she heard the metallic sound of clanking weights. Her pain-inflicted brain tried to think who else could be in the basement at this time of night. She'd met Simon the gardener earlier, and she got the sense that he'd rather be outdoors versus in. Xander most likely went straight to his room after dinner to play video games, which Alice said was "all he did." Mrs. Hadley was probably in her room plotting different ways to make Izzy miserable.

That only left one person who could be in the home gym at eleven o'clock at night. Though her brain shifted between curiosity and slight dread, Izzy carefully peeked into the room.

The gym was truly state-of-the-art. Similar to the hallway, three of the walls were bright white. The other wall was floor-to-ceiling mirrors with black mats sprawled in front of them. Every workout machine imaginable was in the room, from treadmills to a rowing machine. Dumbbells and weights of all sizes rested on sturdy black shelves to the right of the door. This room would have made anyone in the fitness industry jealous.

Zan sat at a weight-stack machine, a large headset over his ears. He didn't see her lingering in the doorway. He had a look of concentration on his face as the heavy stack of weights behind him lifted before falling on top of the other ones when he loosened his pressure on the bar. He repeated the movement over and over, his well-defined arm muscles straining with every motion.

At some point in his workout, Zan must have removed his shirt, or maybe he'd never worn one to begin with. The only thing he had on was a baggy pair of navy workout shorts and running shoes. His six-pack was on display. Hell, six-pack? He easily had a twelve-pack, which was currently glistening with sweat. Izzy's mouth went dry as she watched his pecs flex as he continued working the machine.

He'll never notice you.

Mrs. Hadley's earlier words whispered cruelly in her ear. Izzy needed to stop thirsting after her boss. She went into the ladies' changing room—because, of course, Zan had one, even though people were perfectly capable of changing in their rooms. She stripped off her clothes and changed into her one-piece suit. She stored her clothes in one of the room's lockers, then glanced at herself in the full-length mirror nearby.

The bathing suit did a good job at highlighting the assets of her figure. It was retro style, patterned in blue-and-white gingham. The bottom of the suit was more like shorts. She'd always liked the hourglass shape it gave her. Now, she felt self-conscious as she tried her best to put Mrs. Hadley's poisonous words out of her head. She was no Mary, that was for sure. Not that she wanted to compare herself to Zan's deceased wife. There was no reason to let her mind go in that direction. Zan saw her as an employee. Nothing more. Once he did decide to hop into the dating pool again, she had zero doubt that he would find another model like Mary. Beautiful people always went after other beautiful people.

Izzy grabbed a brush and raked it through her black locks. "Don't you start developing a crush on the man."

Maybe she should put herself out there. It'd be easier to date now that she wasn't living at her parents' house. People seemed to have success on dating apps these days. It'd be a nice way for her to screen men, so that she could avoid the ones she knew in Holiday Bay.

Izzy pulled a folded towel off a nearby shelf and wrapped it around herself, sighing in frustration. She already knew that she'd never join an app. Aside from the fact that the whole idea sounded like a nightmare, there were other things to consider.

Not Zan, though. Zan was her boss.

Gripping the top of the towel so that it wouldn't fall off her, Izzy walked into the hallway. She entered the pool room, relaxing as she examined the aquamarine-tiled pool and deep blue color of the water. After throwing her towel on a nearby bench, she dove in and began her laps. She wasn't sure how many she did until she finally grew tired. She floated on her back for a while, enjoying the serenity of the room. After a half hour, she finally climbed out and dried her hair. Thankfully, her medication had kicked in and her migraine had abated to a dull pain instead of turning into a crippling crescendo.

When Izzy was sure she wasn't dripping water, she headed toward the hallway, adjusting the towel a little tighter around her again as she went. She was so focused on her task that she didn't notice Zan walking down the hall, heading in her direction. Izzy collided with the man, ricocheting off his hard chest and going backward. Her arms flared as she started to fall. Zan's hands shot to her waist so he could steady her. Her own palms slapped those pecs of his—the same glorious ones that she'd been admiring earlier—and his skin was still slick with sweat.

Once her heart stopped racing, she became aware of their situation. Her towel had fallen off her when they'd collided. She was touching her employer's chest. His warm leg was between her thighs, nestled right against the center of her. His hands continued to clutch her waist. She glanced down for the briefest seconds and saw that her nipples were poking clearly through her bathing suit. Perhaps she should have been embarrassed that he could see her reaction to his closeness, but she was too distracted by him not letting her go.

His hands squeezed where he held her. "Are you okay?"

"Yep," she squeaked. She cleared her throat and said again, "Yes."

He let her go and perhaps it had been wishful thinking on her end, but it felt like his fingertips had almost caressed the generous curve of her hip before he released her.

"How'd your first day go?" he asked, going back into employer mode.

Izzy sighed inwardly at the change. "It was good. I didn't see much of Xander, but I plan to slowly win him over."

He smirked and her pulse—which had just settled down—leapt into action.

"I wish you luck with that." He took a few steps back.

"The kids missed you at dinner," she said, and it was like a guard slammed over his face and any previous lightness left his features.

"I was busy."

"Too busy to spend an hour with your kids?"

"What are you getting at, Isabella?"

"Nothing," she said hurriedly. "I just think the kids

would enjoy seeing you. It'd be nice if you could join us tomorrow."

A muscle in Zan's jaw twitched. "I'll see what I can do."

She pasted a happy smile to her lips. "Great, we'll look forward to seeing you then."

His gaze was laser-focused on the upturn of her lips, then he gave a short nod. He moved around her to head to the men's changing room. He seemed to go out of his way to make sure he didn't brush against her as he walked by.

Izzy went into her own changing area, trying to ignore how her skin still tingled from the lingering feel of his touch.

After getting changed into her nightgown, a creamy silk slip that went down her thighs, Izzy threw back her covers and climbed into her bed with a yawn. As she lay in bed staring at the ceiling, her face heated again as she thought back to that moment in the hallway. She silently cursed her body and its reaction to his thigh between her legs. How his large hands felt as they'd held her upright.

Those hands had not only written hits for the Holiday Boys, but also penned some of her favorite books. She wondered what else those talented fingers could do.

As she lay there, letting her mind go wild, she became aware that her leg was itching. She leaned down to scratch it, but that only made the sensation worse. Her other leg soon joined in, her skin becoming almost painful with the need to scratch. Cursing, she turned on the bedside lamp next to her bed and tossed back the sheets. There was a light powdery substance all over the lower half of her mattress.

Thanks to growing up with four brothers, she instantly recognized it for what it was. Itching powder. Letting out a swear so proficient that her mother would have washed her mouth out with soap, despite Izzy being an adult, she went into her en suite bathroom and stripped off the nightgown and her underwear before hopping into the shower to wash the powder off her skin. She scrubbed her legs with soap until they were red.

After changing into a fresh nightgown, she grabbed her silk robe and put it on before going into the hallway to track down some fresh sheets. She stopped when she saw Xander leaning against the wall outside his bedroom door.

"Feeling itchy, are you?" he said.

She stiffened. "You did that? Why?"

He crossed his thin arms over his chest, the pose similar to one she'd seen his father strike earlier. "You're not welcome here."

Without another word, he went back into his room and shut the door behind him.

Chapter Eight

Izzy sat at the dining-room table the next morning, eating oatmeal with Alice. The room was uncomfortably formal, with two large chandeliers dripping from the ceiling, strategically placed over the long table that easily could sit sixteen people. The walls had foiled, flowered wallpaper encasing them, with wall sconces every few feet. The paper was peeling in several areas and was slightly yellowed. Everything screamed 1970s.

Alice noticed Izzy taking everything in and said, "Dad plans on redoing this room. He hasn't had time yet."

That was something Izzy heard a lot on her tour the previous day. Zan had plans for the gorgeous house he bought, but he hadn't seen much of it through yet, other than the basement, his office, and the main rooms the kids used. If it was Izzy's house, she already knew what she would do. The walls deserved to be painted in a classic color, maybe sage—something that would bring out the beautiful woodwork throughout the room.

Izzy ate a clump of oatmeal, swallowing it down without actually tasting it. She'd always hated the texture of wet oats—it felt like mush in her mouth and tasted even worse.

"What do you want to do today?" she asked as she put her spoon down without another bite.

Alice's eyes went wide. "It's Saturday."

Izzy frowned. "Yeah?"

"Don't you have something else to do? I thought Dad gave you weekends off."

"Just Sundays." Izzy waved that off. "But even if I had Saturdays off, I'd still want to spend them with you." She smirked as the little girl preened. "What are your thoughts on painting?"

Alice tapped her chin adorably as she gave the question some serious thought. "I don't know. I haven't really tried it before."

"Well, I happen to love it." Izzy folded her arms on the table and leaned forward. "Why don't you and I paint in the gardens later today?"

"Yeah…okay," Alice said brightly.

"Awesome." Izzy grimaced as she picked up the spoon, contemplating taking another bite.

"It's not very good, is it?" Alice said.

Izzy gave her a puzzled look. "What?"

"The oatmeal." Alice pushed away her half-eaten bowl. "I hate it, but Mrs. Hadley insists that we have it sometimes because it was my mom's favorite, and Mrs. Hadley says it helps keep a part of her with us."

"Have you told her you don't like it?" Izzy asked gently.

"Oh, no! I don't want to hurt her feelings," Alice said. "She means well. I think she only makes oatmeal when she especially misses my mom. Right after Mom died, she made it for two weeks straight. Dad finally told her he didn't want to eat it ever again, but she looked so sad that Dad changed his mind and said she could make it, but only once in a while."

Izzy swirled the spoon in the congealed goop. She

frowned as she looked over at the empty seat next to Alice. "Where's your brother?"

Tears immediately formed in the little girl's eyes. "He never eats with me anymore. All he does is sit in his room and tells me to stay out of it."

"I see…" Izzy put the spoon back down and stood up.

Alice looked up at her. "Where are you going?"

"To speak to your brother."

Alice fumbled her spoon. "Oh, he won't like that."

"I'm counting on it," Izzy muttered under her breath. Her legs still had a bit of a rash from last night. She marched up the stairs that led to the bedrooms and knocked obnoxiously on the door once she reached the teen's room.

She heard a grumble inside.

With a smirk, Izzy knocked even louder. "Are you awake? Because I'm about to come in."

"Go away!" a voice yelled.

"Ready or not," she called out. Izzy opened the door so hard it banged against the wall. Xander shot up in bed, his hair sticking up on one side. His pillow had left creases on the skin of his face.

"Get the hell out of my room!" he snapped.

"Now, now. Language. Also, good morning, sunshine." Izzy walked over to his drawn window shade and lifted it up, causing bright light to filter through the room.

"Get. Out." This time Xander's voice was low and menacing, with the promise of retribution.

Izzy looked around the room. "I've got to give it to you, kid. It's been a few years since I had itching powder used against me, but that was a rookie mistake. First off, I grew up with four older brothers. You think itching powder is going to break me? Second, if growing up with my brothers taught me anything, it's how to fight back."

Her eyes settled on what she'd come for. She walked over to his gaming console and grabbed his controller, as well as the spare next to the TV. She unplugged them and started wrapping the cords around the units before he knew what was happening.

Once Xander realized what she was doing, he growled, "Give those back!"

"Sure," she replied. "You can have them back once you've gotten out of bed, taken a shower, and joined your sister and me outside for a couple hours. We're going to paint."

He folded his arms across his chest. "I won't do it."

She lifted a shoulder dismissively. "I never said you had to paint. I said you have to join us."

Xander glared at her. "Well, that's too bad, because I'm not doing it."

"Fine, then you don't get these back." She waved the controllers.

He eyed it angrily. "Fine," he repeated back. "Then I've got other things I can do."

He started reaching for his phone, but Izzy said firmly, "If you touch that, I'll take your console, too. And if that doesn't give you enough motivation to get out of bed, then how about I go to your father and ask him to turn off the Wi-Fi for the day?"

Xander's expression could have frozen water. "He wouldn't do that."

Izzy lifted one eyebrow. "You want to test that theory?" Giving him an angelic smile, she added, "You've got an hour."

As she left the room, she closed the door firmly behind her. She then leaned against the wall and let out a shaky breath. She truly hoped he'd buy that, because she really didn't want to go to Zan on her first full day and tell him she had just blackmailed his son.

* * *

One hour and three minutes later, Xander showed up looking like he'd just swallowed poison. He was wearing black sweats, a matching T-shirt, and sunglasses so dark she couldn't see his angry eyes. But she certainly felt them.

"Xander!" Alice called happily. She ran over to her brother and gave him a hug. Izzy half expected him to pull away from her, but he didn't. Instead, he gave his little sister a one-arm embrace before moving to sit in the lounge chair behind where Alice and Izzy were set up to paint. He sprawled on it and opened a book that he'd brought with him.

He didn't say anything to Izzy, but even with shades on, she could feel his icy eyes on her. She ignored him as she started explaining the basics of using acrylic paint to Alice.

As they began to work on their individual canvases, Izzy gave the little girl a rundown of her methods for creating art.

"Everything you're looking at has shapes that you can paint. The planter box in front of us, for example. What do you see?" Izzy asked Alice.

Alice scrunched up her face before answering. "I don't know. I see a box of flowers."

"You're not wrong there," Izzy replied. "But what I see are lines. Straight lines that form the box." She ran a thinly edged brush across the canvas, creating the front of the box. "I see the curves of the daffodils' petals, the circle at its center. Can you see it?"

Alice nodded hard, and Izzy had a feeling that even Xander was listening.

"I can see it," Alice said excitedly as she got to work on her own canvas.

They worked for hours with only the sounds of nature and Xander turning pages in his book to fill the silence in the air. But it was peaceful and Izzy felt more relaxed than she had in a very long time.

By the time Mrs. Hadley came out to tell them that lunch was ready, Alice had created a painting that was a very impressive first attempt, given her age and experience.

"Can we do this again sometime?" she asked, trying not to look too wistful.

"We can. Absolutely," Izzy assured her as she started to pack things up. Alice threw her arms around Izzy, giving her an unexpected hug. Izzy melted at the feel of those reedy arms squeezing her—as if Alice hadn't experienced affection in years, despite the moment of closeness Izzy had seen her share with Xander earlier.

"You better go wash up," she told Alice, who nodded and left.

When Izzy grabbed the canvases to take them inside, she was startled to see that Xander was still there. He got up from the lounger and walked slowly over to her.

"Can I have my controllers now?" he asked, though his voice wasn't filled with hate like it had been earlier.

Izzy nodded. She reached inside the bag she'd brought outside and pulled out the devices. He took them from her and left without another word.

Izzy let out a slight sigh as she continued to clean up. She couldn't help but feel like someone was watching her. She glanced over her shoulder to see if Mrs. Hadley was standing nearby throwing hexes her way. But the feeling wasn't coming from the kitchen area. Looking up, she saw Zan staring down at her. She wondered how long he'd been watching them. She gave him a little wave before picking up Alice's canvas off its easel.

When she glanced back up at the window, Zan was gone.

Chapter Nine

Zan paced around his library. His laptop sat open on his desk, the blank Word document taunting him from across the room.

He couldn't write anymore.

Words used to come so easily to him. Now, every time he sat down to try, his mind went blank. Maybe if he was lucky, he'd get a few paragraphs down, but they were usually such complete and utter garbage that he deleted them.

He moved over to his window and stared down at the garden below. His mind flashed to earlier in the day, when he saw Isabella outside with the kids. He'd been so stunned at the sight, he'd only been able to stare, like an outsider looking in. Alice had been *happy*, her smile so bright he could see it even from a distance. More surprising, Isabella had gotten Xander out of his room and away from his gaming. Sure, given the way his gaze had been locked on her, Zan assumed he'd been silently cursing her out, but she had actually gotten his son outside, breathing fresh air. It was a damn miracle.

Against Zan's will, he thought back to the night before, when he'd run into her in the basement.

He'd been shocked by his reaction. For just a second, as he'd kept her from falling, he'd become enraptured by the smooth warmth of her skin. More surprising had been the yearning that had hit him to explore those generous curves of hers. He remembered in vivid detail the way his thigh had fallen between hers, pressed against the very center of her. He wondered what she would have done if he'd pressed his leg against her harder, to see how'd she'd react to that delicious friction. Probably sue him for sexual harassment.

But that hadn't stopped him from dreaming of that moment in vivid detail for most of the night, only to wake up with his body hard and aching. He'd solved that issue by taking an ice-cold shower. Despite his body suddenly remembering that it had needs, he certainly wasn't going to give in to temptation.

Because, again, Isabella Rossi was his employee, and he damn well needed to remember that.

Maybe what he really needed was a night on the town, to find a woman to spend the evening with. He could almost guarantee that if he picked up the phone and called his best friend, Paul would be able to provide him with a long list of willing companions who'd give him their company.

He couldn't remember the last time he'd indulged in that pleasure. Probably shortly after Mary died. He'd gone on a book tour and slept with some random woman he'd met at a book festival. He didn't even remember what she looked like. The sex had been unremarkable. The only thing that particular exercise in carnal pleasure had left him with was a sickening sense of guilt. As though he'd cheated on Mary. He hadn't bothered since.

He turned to look at the picture of his wife hanging on the wall behind his desk, and his heart broke all over again. God, he missed her. It wasn't even about them making love, which had always been amazing. He missed *her*. He missed parenting with her during the day and spending their nights in each other's arms. He missed her companionship as much as he missed the sex.

He tried to stay focused on Mary, but Isabella slipped back into his brain. He didn't want to admit it, but she fascinated him. Perhaps it was the way she carried herself—her posture was perfect, even when she painted in the garden. Or maybe it was the way she walked, with those ridiculously tempting curves emphasized with each step she took. Not only did she have a body that any man would long to caress—even though the thought of any other man touching her irritated him, for some reason—but she also had a face that Michelangelo would have begged to sculpt. What made her even more attractive was that she seemed completely unaware of how beautiful she was.

Mary always knew she was good-looking, going out of her way to look perfect before they'd go out in public. They'd been late to more than one function because of that. To be honest, it used to get on his nerves.

Zan scowled at that wayward thought. Mary was the love of his life. He didn't want to think about any faults she had. They were minor compared to the incredible woman she was.

Rubbing his face, he went back to his desk. He frowned when he realized he didn't have the journal where he kept his notes. He had just opened the library door to go across the hall so he could retrieve it from his office when his phone rang. He went back to answer it.

Dread filled his stomach when he saw the caller.

Taking a deep breath, he hit Accept.

Izzy couldn't sleep. She'd tried, after carefully inspecting the sheets first to make sure Xander hadn't tried to mess with her bedding again, but her mind kept whirling.

She felt like her first full day on the job had been somewhat successful. Sure, after she'd given Xander back his controllers, she hadn't seen him for the rest of the day but… baby steps.

She and Alice had spent a fun afternoon swimming in the basement pool, followed by a walk around the property. It was truly beautiful, though she missed the view of the bay she used to get at her parents' house. But Alice had shown her the creek she'd heard the other day. It had a gorgeous little waterfall and large rocks that broke up the flow of water. Izzy had ached to paint it, and she knew she'd be back to that spot someday. She could appreciate why Zan had chosen this house. Aside from how peaceful it was, it was also completely isolated from other people, allowing nature to reclaim the land.

After continuing to lie in bed for another half hour, she finally gave up and tossed back the sheets. Glancing at the clock next to her bed, Izzy saw that it was almost midnight. Everyone was probably in bed. She poked her head out into the hallway to double-check that fact, then headed toward the kids' study, which was next to Zan's library.

Though she respected Zan's request that no one go into that particular room but him, she ached to explore it and discover what books were inside. Zan hadn't been completely ungenerous when it came to novels, though, and he'd made sure there were still plenty available in the children's study. They might be out of her age range, but she wasn't opposed to reading a middle-grade or young-adult book if it helped her sleep.

But as she got closer to the room, she realized that Zan was, in fact, not only awake, but also on the phone in his library. She became very much aware that she'd forgotten to grab her robe and that her silk tank top and matching boxers showed more of her body then she wanted to display in front of her boss. She was about to turn around and hightail it back to her room when the tone of his voice caught her ears.

Zan was upset at whomever he was speaking with. No, he wasn't just mad, he was downright pissed.

"You don't want to take me to court. I can promise you that," Zan said, his voice filled with cold rage.

Izzy really needed to get out of there—this conversation was none of her business—but she was frozen to the spot.

"You'll take the kids over my dead body," Zan snapped. There was a hard sound of plastic hitting wood, as though he'd slammed his phone on his desk.

Before Izzy could react, he came storming out of the office, his face menacing. He came to an abrupt halt when he saw her standing there.

"Isabella," he said, his voice tight. His eyes trailed over her and she mentally kicked herself for not remembering to grab her robe. "What are you doing out here?"

"I…" Her cheeks flushed as his eyes seemed to linger on her hips before slowing moving up her chest to her face. She felt as though she was standing in front of him naked. "I couldn't sleep. I was going to grab a book out of the study."

He nodded, his shoulders loosening slightly, then said, "What kind of books do you like to read?"

She crossed her arms over her chest, aware that her nipples were probably poking out from the thin material of her camisole.

"Oh, um, mainly romance, but I do like mysteries as well."

He nodded before he said, "Come on."

Zan turned and went back into his library. Her mouth dropped. She didn't think he allowed anyone inside his precious sanctuary. She followed before he could change his mind.

He went over to a shelf and pulled out a book. "I don't read romance, but I do have quite a few mysteries. You're welcome to borrow them if you want."

"Thank you," she said as he handed her the book.

Zan didn't immediately release it. "Did you overhear my conversation?"

Izzy's eyes widened. They were barely a foot apart and she had to look up to meet his eyes.

"I…not really. Only that you said you'd fight someone on custody."

A muscle in his jaw twitched. He released the book and went over to his desk to stare at the painting of his wife.

"My former in-laws have been making threats since Mary died. They want to take the children away from me."

"On what grounds?" Izzy asked in disbelief.

He snorted, but there was no amusement to the sound. He turned and sat on the desk, his hands gripping the edge until his knuckles were white.

"They think I'm a terrible father, and that they could do a better job raising the kids."

"That's ridiculous."

"Is it?" Zan said so softly that she barely heard him.

"Of course, it is. I've only been here a day and can tell that the kids love you."

That might have been a stretch, but she had to believe it. It was in the way Alice looked for her father whenever they entered a room. She still had to figure out Xander, but she guessed that he loved his father every bit as much as Alice did.

"Thanks," he said. "I'd appreciate if you didn't bring this up in front of the kids."

"I won't. I promise."

Awkward silence fell between them before he nodded at the book. "I hope that helps you sleep."

Taking that as her cue that he wanted her to leave, she murmured her own thanks and started to head toward the door.

"I saw you earlier," Zan said once she was almost to the hallway. When she glanced over her shoulder questioningly, he added, "In the garden."

"Oh…yeah. I thought the kids could use some fresh air. Is that okay?"

"Of course." Zan's face lost some of his tension. "How'd you manage to get Xander to leave his room?"

Izzy's cheeks turned red. "Um, blackmail."

Zan's eyebrows snapped down. "Come again?"

Izzy eyed the ceiling, hoping that he didn't fire her. "Blackmail. I took his game controllers away and told him he could get them back once he came outside for a little bit."

"And it worked? Just like that?"

"Well, no. I also told him that if he pushed it, I'd have you turn off the Wi-Fi."

She expected Zan to end her employment on the spot for threatening his son. Instead, he threw back his head and laughed.

"If you ever need me to actually do that, let me know," Zan told her.

Feeling much lighter, she said, "Will do."

"Good night, Isabella."

The way he said her name. It did something to her that she would *not* analyze.

Pulling herself together, she murmured, "Good night," and left him to his evening.

Chapter Ten

A few weeks into the job and Izzy found herself back in the garden painting. She had to pick up the kids from school in a few hours, but until then, she was pretty much free to do what she wanted. In all honesty, she felt a little sick charging Zan so much for her services. The kids were gone most of the day. She had to be the most overpaid nanny in the country.

The sound of her phone ringing broke the focus she had on her canvas. She answered it and was surprised to hear the school principal on the phone.

"Hello, Izzy," Anita Spencer said.

"Hello, Mrs. Spencer," she replied. Even though Izzy was a grown woman, Mrs. Spencer had been her principal, too. Calling her by any other name made her feel like she was being disrespectful.

"Mr. Chen listed you as an emergency contact for his children. I understand that he's recently employed you as their nanny."

"Yes, that's correct."

"We're having a bit of an issue with Alice today," Principal Spencer went on and Izzy went on instant alert.

"Is she okay?"

"Unfortunately, she can't seem to stop crying. It's become disruptive and we simply can't keep her in class. Are you able to stop by and pick her up?"

"Yes, of course," Izzy responded. "I'll be there shortly."

"Perfect, and while you're here, there are a couple other things I'd like to go over with you."

Izzy's stomach twisted at the seriousness of the principal's tone, but she agreed to meet with her.

Once she parked outside the school, she entered the familiar halls of Holiday Bay's school. The town was small enough that they only had one—a brick two-story building that had been around for decades. The lower floor housed pre-K thorough sixth grade. The upper floor was for the junior-high and high-school kids. Izzy could still remember the thrill of walking up the stairs leading up to the second floor. She thought she'd made it, big-time. She hadn't come to realize yet that teenagers made even worse bullies than elementary-school kids did.

As soon as she entered the principal's office, she could hear Alice hysterically crying. She quickened her pace and found the little girl sitting outside the office, rocking back and forth.

"Alice?" Izzy said, hurrying to her.

"I lost it," Alice responded, hurtling herself into Izzy's arms.

"What?"

"Mom's book. I can't find it a-anywhere." Alice buried her face against Izzy and started sobbing harder.

"Shh," Izzy said. She pulled back a little so she could see the girl's blotchy, tearstained cheeks. "You didn't lose it. You left it at home."

"No." Alice shook her head, "I always have it in my bag and it's not there."

"Sweets, I promise you. It's in your room. I saw *Little*

Women on your bedside table when I was gathering your dirty clothes."

Alice's chin wobbled as she stared at Izzy. "Do you promise the book's there?"

"Yes, I promise."

Alice seemed to collapse in on herself as she slumped back in her chair, clearly exhausted.

"Izzy," a voice said to her left and she looked over to see the principal watching them. "Can I have a moment of your time?"

"Of course." She cupped Alice's chin gently. "I'll be right back."

The little girl sniffed in response.

She entered the principal's office. She'd been here a few times when she was a student. Not because she'd gotten into trouble, but because of how badly her bullies had treated her sometimes.

Not much had changed since she'd graduated. Mrs. Spencer had her degrees on her wall. Beneath her honors was a bookshelf filled with books that she probably kept more for the aesthetic than because she actually read them. Behind the desk was a large window that had lavender and lemongrass plants on the sill.

"Close the door behind you, will you?" the principal said as she walked across the vinyl beige flooring to sit behind her desk.

Izzy did as instructed and took the seat opposite, sitting in one of the same yellow hardback chairs that Mrs. Spencer had for years. And, yep, as Izzy shifted in the seat, she silently confirmed that they were still as uncomfortable as they'd been when she was a student.

"I tried calling Mr. Chen earlier, but wasn't able to get

ahold of him," Mrs. Spencer explained, her mouth pursing in disapproval.

"He had a meeting," Izzy explained. At least, that's where she assumed he was. He'd muttered something about needing to see Paul when she'd passed him in the hall that morning, their arms brushing. He'd left the house without another word.

"The children have been enrolled here for almost six weeks now," Mrs. Spencer said. "I'm going to be blunt. Neither of them are adjusting well. Xander was caught trying to skip school yesterday."

Izzy's stomach dropped. "He did what?"

"Our first-grade teacher saw him trying to leave the property and ordered him back to class. He called her something that I won't repeat in this office. We called Mr. Chen's house to let him know. The housekeeper who answered said she'd pass on the message. I assumed either Mr. Chen or you would be told." She gave Izzy a disappointed look, as though it was Izzy's fault for not responding before today. "I emailed him asking for a more direct way to contact him, and that's when he gave me your number, as well as his cell."

Anger simmered inside her. Freaking Mrs. Hadley. Why hadn't she passed on the message that Xander was acting up?

"Feel free to reach out to me moving forward," Izzy said. "I'll make sure to take the call."

Mrs. Spencer nodded. "Xander will be serving detention today for his behavior yesterday, but we can't let this develop into a pattern."

"I understand," Izzy replied. She hadn't been able to make any further breakthroughs with Xander, but they would talk later today. He couldn't leave school whenever he wanted, just because he didn't feel like attending.

"And then there's Alice," Mrs. Spencer continued. "To be honest, I'm deeply concerned about her. Aside from how she reacted today—which completely disrupted her class—well, there's this."

She pulled out some papers and handed them to Izzy, who glanced down. Her face furrowed into a frown. Alice had always insisted that she didn't need Izzy's help when it came to her homework, so she never looked it over. She thought she was doing her job by ensuring Alice completed it.

Clearly, she hadn't done her job well. The homework in front of her didn't look like it was done by a ten-year-old. If it was Alice's writing, she had the skills of a seven-year-old instead of someone her age. Several of the letters were backward, and many of the sentences didn't make sense.

"You're saying that Alice wrote these?" she asked, looking through the rest of the papers.

"Yes, which you can see is a concern. I'm not sure how the school system functioned where the Chens originally moved from, but I think it might be best if Alice is held back a year. I wouldn't be surprised if she dropped out of school by the time she's sixteen."

Izzy's head shot up at that comment. She didn't like the direction this conversation was going. "Alice is a brilliant girl. She's simply gone through a lot." When the principal opened her mouth to say something else, Izzy interrupted. "Thank you for making me aware of this situation. I'll take care of it from here."

"I hope so, because if things don't change, then I'm going to be forced to make some difficult decisions. In the meantime, you're welcome to take Alice when you leave.

She's already upset most of the students in her class with her tantrum."

"Tantrum?" Izzy seethed. "That little girl has been through hell and back. Do you think you'd be okay if your mom died and you were Alice's age?" The principal opened her mouth again, perhaps to argue with her, but Izzy had had enough. "I appreciate your time, Mrs. Spencer."

She stepped out of the office, and walked over to where Alice was still slumped, staring miserably at her shoes.

"Let's get out of here," Izzy said gently.

"Am I in trouble?" Alice asked, her chin starting to wobble.

"No." Izzy offered the girl her hand and pulled her out of the chair.

As they walked to Izzy's car, she kept thinking about what the principal had shown her. Alice wasn't just having random outbursts, she was also developmentally behind her classmates.

"Hey," Izzy said. "When we get home, why don't we grab your book and you can read it to me."

Alice's hand instantly tightened around hers. "Oh. Why don't you read it to me instead?"

"Because I'm always the one reading to you," Izzy said. It had become their habit at night. Alice loved having stories read to her. But she never offered to read them herself. Izzy wondered how she'd missed that fact.

Xander was another issue. She'd have to speak with him soon. In the meantime, it looked like she'd have to confiscate his gaming console. Not just the controller this time, but the whole system. She wasn't looking forward to that argument.

No. What she needed to do was talk to Zan. He should be aware of what was going on with his kids. She was just their nanny. He was their parent. She didn't understand why he hadn't answered the phone when the school called. What if one of the kids had been injured? It was unacceptable.

"Listen," Izzy said, moving the car toward the center of town. "I want to pick up some art supplies at Kyleigh's Knits. Maybe there will be something there that catches your eye, too."

"What would I need?" Alice asked. Her eyes were so puffy that Izzy's heart ached.

"Oh, I don't know," she replied. "Have you ever thought about what you want to be when you grow up?"

Alice's face dimmed a little. "I—I want to be a writer, like Dad."

"That's great!" Izzy enthused. "Have you told him that?"

"No," Alice whispered. "He wouldn't care."

"Of course, he would. He might be able to give you pointers."

"I…don't think my dad likes me very much." She said it so quietly that Izzy had to strain to hear what she said.

Once the words registered, she frowned at the little girl. "Why on earth would you think that?"

"Because I look like my mom and I think it's too painful for him to look at me."

It was true that, aside from her eye shape, she was the spitting image of her mom. It broke Izzy's heart that Alice seemed to think that made her father not love her. He deeply loved his wife. There was no way on this planet that he wouldn't love the very extension of her. She thought back to the angry conversation she'd overheard weeks ago, when he'd told Mary's parents that he'd never give up custody of his children.

Nodding at that memory, Izzy said, "He loves you. Very much. I just think he might be sad."

"Because Mom died?" Alice asked.

"Yeah."

The little girl nodded solemnly. "I'm sad, too."

It was another thing that Izzy would bring up to the man the next time she saw him.

After pulling into a spot in front of the store, they got out and entered the building.

Kyleigh greeted them from behind her counter. "Well, hello!"

"Hi, Kyleigh," Alice said, going over to hug her.

"Hello, my sweet girl." She frowned when she saw Alice's puffy eyes. "Everything okay?"

"Yes," Izzy answered. "Alice, why don't you see if you can find a writing journal? I think they're along the wall."

Alice nodded and disappeared down the aisle.

Kyleigh asked in a low voice, "You want to tell me what's up?"

Izzy bit her lip. "She freaked out at school because she thought she lost her mom's book. It was so bad that they had to pull her out of class. The principal also showed me some of her recent homework. Her writing is really underdeveloped."

"Was Zan at the meeting?" Kyleigh asked.

Izzy frowned. "No, he said he had to meet Paul today."

"Oh, that's right. I think Paul's interested in turning one of Zan's books into a TV series."

Izzy was half-tempted to ask which one, since she loved Zan's novels, but she had bigger concerns. "Xander also tried to skip school, apparently. When he got caught, he swore at the teacher." She rubbed at the space between her eyebrows. "These kids are so lost. I'm not sure I can help them as much as they need."

Kyleigh gave her an encouraging smile. "The fact that

you're seeking out answers to help them shows me that they're in good hands."

"I guess," she said just as Alice walked around the corner with a small journal in her hand. It was pink and had a unicorn on it.

"Can I get this one?" she asked hopefully.

"Sure," Izzy replied. "Let me get what I need and then we can head home."

As they made the drive back to the house, Izzy said, "You know what I'd love to see you do this afternoon?"

"What?" Alice said.

"I want you to write five of your favorite story ideas and then bring them to me. Maybe it can be a side project we work on together. Like your art."

"Okay." Alice beamed. As soon as they pulled into the driveway, Izzy noticed Zan's car in the garage, meaning he was back from wherever he'd gone that morning.

Alice disappeared into her room to work on her project. While she was doing that, Izzy went in search of Mrs. Hadley.

The woman was dusting one of the tables in the hallway on the main floor.

"Can I speak to you for a minute?" Izzy asked.

"About?" the older woman said, her tone cool.

"Why you didn't tell me that Xander tried to skip school yesterday?"

"It was nothing," the housekeeper said.

Izzy went ramrod-straight. "He got detention."

Mrs. Hadley's eyes simmered. "He's a thirteen-year-old boy who's lost his mother. Perhaps as their nanny, you could have a little empathy."

"I understand that he lost his mom, but that doesn't mean he can act however he wants."

The woman scoffed. "I've watched over Xander since he was a toddler. Who are you to say how he should and shouldn't act!"

"Because Zan put me in charge of their welfare. Not you!"

Mrs. Hadley's lips pursed. She turned away from her and continued dusting as if Izzy wasn't standing there.

Izzy tried her best not to say or do anything that would get her fired. Instead, she stormed away and headed to Xander's room to get the gaming console. She didn't usually go into his room, leaving that to Mrs. Hadley. Other than that one time, she tried to respect his space, but he'd gone too far by swearing at a teacher and trying to skip school.

She grabbed the console, and headed to the kids' study next to the library. Rifling through the desk Alice tended to use, she found several papers that the girl had written on. She shifted the console in her arms, so she could pick up Alice's work.

Izzy returned to the hallway, went to the library, and knocked on the door. A few moments later, Zan answered, a scowl on his face. It softened a little when he saw it was her.

"Hey," he said. He glanced down at her occupied arms, taking in the gaming system and paperwork. His face shifted into concern. "Xander in trouble again?"

"He tried to skip school yesterday and then swore at the teacher who caught him."

Zan's eyes flashed. "He did *what*?"

Izzy looked down the hall to make sure no one was eavesdropping. "Look, do you have a second to talk?"

"Sure, come in." He closed the door to the library but invited her into his office across the hall.

She placed the console on his desk. "I'm confiscating

that from his room for a week. Or should I say, you're confiscating it."

Zan nodded. "That's fine."

"Can I speak freely?" Izzy asked.

Zan's eyes narrowed for a second but he said, "Go ahead."

"Your children need help. More than I can give them. Xander is antisocial and doesn't seem to care about anything but gaming, and Alice had to be picked up from school today because she had a complete meltdown."

"Why didn't the school contact me about this?" Zan asked.

"Apparently the school did attempt to contact you about Xander trying to skip yesterday, but I'm assuming Mrs. Hadley didn't give you the message."

He stiffened at her tone. "Of course, I didn't get it."

"I just asked her about it. She basically said that because Xander lost his mom, he should get a free pass."

A muscle flinched in Zan's jaw. "She has a tendency to spoil the kids. I'll talk to her."

Izzy doubted very much that it would make a difference. "They said they tried to call you today, too."

Zan frowned before pulling his phone out of his pants. He thumbed through several texts and missed calls before he finally settled on the one call he should have answered. "Oh."

"Yeah," Izzy said. "And that's not my only concern." She placed Alice's papers on his desk. "Look at how she writes. Her letters are mixed up and the writing is childish. Has she always been like this?"

"Her other school never told me about it, though Mary usually attended the parent/teacher conferences."

"Of course, she did," Izzy muttered.

Zan's head snapped up at that. "What's that supposed to mean?"

"Alice needs to be in therapy. Maybe Xander as well. They both experienced something traumatic at a young age, and they are not doing well. And their father doesn't seem to care one way or the other."

Zan rose slowly, placing both palms on his desk. "Say that again."

Izzy lifted her chin. "When was the last time you sat down with your children for a meal? Because it sure as hell hasn't happened since I've been here. Those children need you. Xander acts like he can get away with anything because he doesn't think you care either way. And as for Alice…did you know she wants to be a writer? Just like her dad. But she can barely string together a sentence. Don't you understand that these children need more than just material things from you? You didn't die when your wife did and it's damn well time you remember—"

"Enough," he said quietly, but his voice was like ice. "I suggest that if you want to keep being employed here, you leave this office immediately."

Izzy was very tempted to tell him to shove the job, but she thought of Alice's face earlier. She couldn't—wouldn't—abandon that little girl. Or Xander, for that matter.

Without another word, she left the room. She swiped angrily at the tear that escaped her eye as she went.

Later that evening, Alice and Izzy sat in the dining room eating their dinner, talking over a few story ideas Alice had come up with. There was another place setting for Xander, but he'd only just returned from school after his detention.

A few minutes later, he came storming into the room. "Where's my Xbox?"

"I took it," another voice said. The other three occupants turned to see Zan walking into the room carrying a plate. Izzy tensed, remembering their earlier conversation.

Xander glowered at his dad. "Why?"

"Because you tried to skip school yesterday and then swore at a teacher. Your actions have consequences. You've lost gaming privileges for the next two weeks."

"This is such crap!" Xander yelled, heading for the exit.

"If you leave this room, you'll lose privileges for a month," Zan threatened. "We're going to have dinner together for once."

Alice's jaw dropped and even Xander lost his rage to stare at his dad in disbelief.

"Sit down," Zan told his son before turning to Alice and Izzy. "So what are you two talking about?"

As he reached for the bowl of stew, he gave Alice a soft smile.

She flourished before Izzy's eyes. "I-I'm working on a writing project. I had some ideas for a story about a witch."

"Hmm," Zan replied before grabbing a dinner roll. "Tell me more about it."

As Alice launched into the premise of her story, Zan glanced at Izzy, giving her a slight nod, and some of her tension left her. She had gone too far speaking to him like she had, but he was here now, and he hadn't shown up with her pink slip, telling her to vacate the premises.

Xander slowly walked back to the table and sat down. He didn't say anything even as he grabbed his own bowl of stew.

And for the first time since Izzy started working there, Zan ate a meal with his children.

Chapter Eleven

Later that evening, Izzy hummed as she headed to her room. She passed Xander's and heard music blasting behind the closed door, but no accompanying sounds indicating he was gaming. He could very well be playing something on his tablet or phone, or one of the million other devices kids had these days, but by taking away his favorite option, hopefully he'd learn some sort of lesson.

Farther down the hall, she saw light seeping around the frame of Zan's bedroom door, suggesting that there was someone inside. Was he in there? Maybe he'd just wrapped up his evening workout. She hadn't gone down to the gym after their first run-in, but she knew that he liked to spend his evenings working out.

Izzy entered her room but didn't settle on her bed. It was still relatively early, just after ten. She was used to working late hours at the restaurant, and her body hadn't adjusted to a different schedule yet. She eyed the book on her bed, the one that Zan had let her borrow. She'd only gotten a couple of chapters in, but she could already tell that she was going to love it. It was funny how he'd picked the perfect choice for her. Izzy was simply waiting for the right time to devour it. Since she wasn't sleepy yet, she decided to change into her pajamas and then read for an hour or two. More likely two.

Her phone beeped and she went to see who'd texted her. It was a message from Dante.

Hey, call me.

She frowned. It was a bit late for a conversation. Aside from check-ins from Dante and her mom, she hadn't heard from anyone else in her immediate family since she'd quit her job. Honestly, she wouldn't have expected anything less from Gio and Enzo. They were usually wrapped up in their own lives. But it did hurt that she hadn't heard from her father or Antonio. Maybe that was why her brother wanted her to call. Something had happened to a family member.

With anxiety now pummeling her, she picked up her phone and called her brother.

"Hey," Dante said after the first ring.

"Hi, is everything okay?" she asked.

"Yeah, everything's good," he said. She could hear the noise of the restaurant kitchen in the background.

"You're at work?" Why would he text her during the evening? They'd be serving late customers at this point and wrapping up the late shift.

"It's a little slow right now and I wanted to tell you my news. Mallory's pregnant," he said, mentioning his wife.

Mallory and Dante had been together since they were teenagers, and they'd been married for over ten years, trying without success to get pregnant. Tears of happiness welled up in Izzy's eyes.

"Oh, Dante. I'm so freaking happy for you."

"Thanks. We told everyone during Sunday dinner, but I know you weren't able to make it."

Izzy swallowed over the sudden lump in her throat. She'd been avoiding her family like they apparently were avoiding her. She'd skipped out on the past few dinners. A part of her was a little hurt that Dante hadn't called her until days later, but she was at least happy that he had.

"That's amazing. Congrats again. You'll have to let me know when the baby shower is."

"We will, or I can tell you in person once we know. You know, like during a family dinner or something?"

Izzy sat on her bed with a plop. "Maybe."

"You ever going to talk to Dad or Tony again, Iz?"

"They don't want to talk to me," she argued. "Why should I make an effort to speak with them?"

"You people are the most stubborn to ever walk the earth, you know that, right? Eat your pride and come to dinner, Iz." Dante huffed loud enough that she heard it through the phone. In the background, she heard Enzo call his name. "Listen, I need to get back to work. Please come soon, okay?"

"I'll think about it," she told him and they disconnected their call.

Trying not to feel morose at being excluded from the happy family tidings, she went to use her en suite bathroom and change into her pajamas. After brushing her teeth, she bent over the sink to wash her face. Just as she got a good lather going, she felt something slither over her feet. She jumped back and tried to wipe the soap away from her eyes to see what it was.

A snake hissed back at her.

Izzy let out a terrified scream and booked it out of the room. The remaining soap dribbled into her eyes, causing them to sting, and she stumbled over the edge of the bed frame, adding a bruise to her terror.

She ran into the hallway and slammed into a warm, bare chest.

"What the hell?" Zan said.

"Th-there's a s-s-snake in my bathroom."

"What?" Zan said it like she was hallucinating. Maybe she was.

She tried to wipe the soap out of her eyes, but it only made them sting harder. She took a shuddering breath but said in a short and clear voice. "There. Is. A. Freaking. Snake. In. My. Bathroom."

"Okay," Zan said. She was positive that he was humoring her. "Let me see if I can find it."

He disappeared into her room. She wanted to throw up. What if he didn't find it? She'd have to move out. No. She'd have to move to Pluto if it meant getting as far away from that thing as possible. She'd been terrified of snakes ever since Enzo put a snake in her sleeping bag when the family had gone camping when she was nine. Gio and Dante had chased him down and made him pay for it, but she'd had to sleep in the car for the rest of the trip, refusing to get back in the tent.

Loud swearing shot through the air, confirming that she was right. A few moments later, Zan came out with an amused expression and a snake in his hand. It slithered and twisted in the air. Izzy wanted to throw up.

"It's just a garter snake. It won't hurt you."

"Please get it away from me," Izzy said, her face turned away from them.

Zan snorted. "Yes, ma'am." He started to turn away, but he said, "I triple-checked your bathroom. I didn't see anything else in there if you want to finish what you were doing. But don't go to sleep just yet. I want to talk. I'm going to let this little guy out of the house first."

She nodded shakily. There was zero chance that she'd be able to sleep after that, anyway.

She tiptoed back into her room after he was gone, and looked carefully around as best as she could, considering her eyes burned as if they were on fire. She forced herself to enter the bathroom. After grabbing a washcloth out of the cupboard, she dampened it and wiped the remaining soap off with the cloth instead of washing her face from the faucet. She'd rather keep one eye on the scene of the crime then close both lids and risk something else happening.

A short time later, she walked into the bedroom to find Zan already there, leaning against her closed door. She almost jumped out of her skin, not expecting him back already.

"Cheese and rice!" Izzy placed a hand over her chest. If she had one more scare, she worried that she'd have a heart attack.

"I wanted to make sure you were okay," Zan said. His eyes ran over her, causing her to remember that she was in a short silk nightgown that barely went past her thighs. He was in low-hanging jeans and was still shirtless.

"You're staring," he said lightly, but there was something curious in his voice.

"Why aren't you wearing a shirt?" she asked, pulling her eyes away.

"I was in the process of changing into my gym clothes when I heard you scream. I came to check on you, and you know the rest."

"What'd you do with the snake?"

"I put it in the backyard, what else?"

"Where?" she asked because that was one section of the yard she wouldn't go in ever again. And then she realized it didn't matter because the thing would be long gone by the time she ever ventured outdoors, *if* she ever went outside again. She got back to the matter at hand. "How'd a snake get in my room?"

Zan's face lost some of its amusement. "I don't know, but I have a feeling that Xander might have a clue."

Izzy nodded. "Because of today."

"That and who knows what else." Zan folded his arms over his chest. The pose only emphasized those chest muscles. "How would you like me to handle it?"

Izzy's eyes narrowed as she thought of an idea. "Give him back the gaming system."

"What?" Zan said in disbelief.

"Tomorrow morning. We'll give it back to him together, okay?"

"O-o-okay?" Zan said.

An evil smile formed on Izzy's lips. "Trust me."

Early the next morning, Zan and Izzy stood outside Xander's room. Zan held the console in his hand.

"You sure about this?" Zan asked.

"Absolutely," Izzy replied brightly.

Zan shook his head but knocked on his son's bedroom door.

"Go away!" Xander yelled out.

"Alexander, open the door," Zan demanded.

A short time later, the teen answered with a scowl on his face.

"Yeah?" His expression darkened when he noticed Izzy standing next to his dad. "What is *she* doing here?"

"She has a name, and you'll use it respectfully," Zan replied.

"I actually asked your dad to give you your gaming

console back," Izzy explained sweetly. "I'm here to make sure it's delivered."

Xander's eyes narrowed. "What's the catch?"

"No catch," Izzy said. "It's my way of saying thank you for the gift you left in my room last night."

The teenager's face switched to one of pure innocence. "I don't know what you're talking about."

"No?" Izzy placed her hands on her hips. "You must be pretty good at video games, given how much time you spend on them."

Xander lifted his chin. "Yeah, I am."

"Okay, how about a deal then?" she said. "We play a game. Right here and now. If you win, I quit my job."

"Wait, wha—" Zan began, but Izzy raised her hand.

"However, if I win, no more pranks. Not on me, not on classmates—nothing. And no more trying to skip school."

Xander's face turned cocky. "Fine." As they sat down in front of the screen, he murmured so his dad wouldn't hear, "You should just start packing now and save yourself the humiliation."

Izzy simply gave him a look, silently telling him to get on with it.

Xander shook his head. "It's your funeral."

He reconnected the system and handed her a controller while he took the other. He pulled up some racing game. "Best of five wins, deal?"

Izzy smirked. "Deal."

One hour later, the cocky confidence had completely left Xander. There was a little bead of sweat forming at his temple, and he kept swearing under his breath as he jammed the buttons on his controller. As Izzy's character crossed the finish line a second before Xander's did, he threw the device on the ground in disgust.

Izzy stood up and wiped invisible dirt off her leg. "It was a pleasure doing business with you."

"You cheated. You didn't tell me you knew how to play this game," Xander whined, but dare she say it? There was also a tiny spark of respect in his eyes.

"You never asked," she replied. "This is my nephew's favorite game. We usually play a couple of rounds whenever I see him. And like I told you, I grew up with four older brothers. You think I wasn't their stand-in when they couldn't find someone else to game with?"

She winked at him before turning to leave the room. She was surprised to see Zan still there, leaning against the doorjamb. She would have thought he'd left a half hour ago. She couldn't describe his expression. There was amusement on his features, but there was something else. Something much softer as those deep brown eyes locked on hers.

As she started to walk toward him, Xander spoke up. "Do you think we can play again sometime?"

Izzy turned to look at the boy. "Yeah, we can do that."

He nodded and gave her the slightest of smiles. When she turned back around, Zan was gone.

Chapter Twelve

When Izzy pulled up to the house, she was in a foul mood. It was her day off, and she'd finally caved and gone to a Sunday dinner after missing so many. Antonio had acted like she'd turned her back on her legacy by not returning to the restaurant by now. Her father straight-up ignored her, spending most of the day in his office. Even working at her cousin Franki's pasty shop would have been better than leaving the family business entirely, apparently.

The only one who'd seemed to act like everything was normal was Dante. He'd stuck by her side when he could, asking her about her job and telling her about the milestones of his wife's pregnancy. No matter how old they got, Izzy didn't think he'd ever let go of his need to protect his baby sister, even if it was from their own family.

When her mom had asked her if she'd had any chance to work on her art, Antonio had scathingly asked, "Are you still doing that?"

Like it was just some silly, girlish dream. It made her feel small, like all she had in value was working for her family, and to hell with everything else.

Dante had replied to Antonio with anger. "What are you good at, besides being *un pene*?"

It got him in trouble with their mother, who'd snapped, "Language, Dante."

But knowing that her family still couldn't get past her leaving Florentina's only solidified Izzy's decision not to return for Sunday dinners anytime soon.

Things were at least improving in her job, and she was glad to finally be home. Because that's what Zan's house had become to her. Home.

Alice was blossoming. Zan had taken her to see a specialist in Traverse City, and she'd officially been diagnosed with dyslexia. She'd also been diagnosed with PTSD relating to the loss of her mother. Zan found a great therapist in the neighboring town of Clarington who was helping Alice channel her emotions in a healthier way. The school's guidance counselor also set her up with an amazing tutor, who showed her how to learn in a way that worked with her disability instead of against it. Alice still had a long way to go, but she wasn't having as many emotional breakdowns as she'd had before.

The best development, though, was that she was thriving under her dad's watchful eye. Ever since Izzy had told him off for ignoring his children, he'd made sure to make it to every breakfast and dinner. He sat and spoke with his daughter about their mutual love of writing.

Even Xander didn't seem as angry with the world as he had been, though he still preferred to be by himself than with others. Izzy had her moments of tension with him, but things between them had slowly gotten better—especially since he discovered there was someone else in the house who knew how to game.

After Izzy parked her car, she took a walk out back so that she could enjoy the garden. The gardener was busy replanting some flowers in the light of the setting sun.

"Good evening, Simon," she said.

"Evening, Izzy," he replied somewhat gruffly.

She hadn't gotten a chance to really get to know the man well since she moved in, but she knew he was normally a cheerful guy. Today, his face was grim.

"Everything okay?" she asked.

He looked over his shoulder before he leaned toward her and said in a low voice, "The mood in there is as somber as a graveyard. I'd avoid Mrs. Hadley if I were you."

Izzy looked at the house in concern. She didn't give a crap what kind of mood Mrs. Hadley was in—the woman still treated Izzy like she was fungus—but she was concerned for the kids.

"Did something happen while I was out?"

"Not sure. All I know is that the little one won't stop crying, and the boy has locked himself in his room. Mrs. Hadley told him she wouldn't feed him his dinner unless he came out to eat with his sister, and he said something I won't repeat in polite company. Mrs. Hadley looked fit to explode. Then she yelled at *me*. Told me to take myself and my filthy shoes outside immediately. I didn't argue with her."

Izzy's didn't try to hide her surprise. While Mrs. Hadley couldn't stand her, the woman was always polite to the gardener.

"Thanks for the heads-up," she said. "I think I'll go check on Alice."

He nodded and went back to what he was doing.

When she entered the house, she could hear Mrs. Hadley slamming things around in the kitchen. Avoiding that area, she headed to the bedrooms. There was a heaviness in the air that Izzy couldn't explain. She passed Xander's room and could hear the sounds of explosions screaming loudly from whatever game he was playing. She'd try to get him to eat some dinner later. She continued on to Alice's room. She could hear the little girl crying.

She knocked gently on the door. "Alice, it's me. Can I come in?"

Izzy only heard a sob in response so she let herself in. Alice was lying on top of her bed, her face buried in her pillow. She was sobbing so hard, Izzy worried she'd make herself sick.

She sat on the mattress beside the girl and gently rubbed her back. "You want to tell me what's upset you so much?"

Because once Izzy found out who'd made her cry like this, she would track them down and make them weep just as bad. Alice had made such progress, and in an instant, she'd gone back to crying hysterically.

Alice mumbled something into the pillow.

"What?" Izzy asked.

She flipped over on her back and stared at Izzy with swollen red eyes. "My m-mom died three y-years ago today."

"Oh." Izzy ached inside for the pain she saw on the girl's face. "I'm so sorry."

Alice stared at the ceiling, wiping her nose with her hand. "It's not fair. Why did she have to die?"

"I don't know, sweets. But I do know that she loved you so much. I remember seeing pictures of her and your dad in magazines when you were born, and she absolutely adored you."

They'd been publicity shots taken for some big-name celebrity magazine. The media apparently paid them a million dollars for the pictures, but the Chens had donated the money to charity.

Izzy looked around the room helplessly. "Where's your father?"

Tears sprung up in Alice's eyes again. "In his library. He asked Mrs. Hadley to make sure we ate something at breakfast this morning. I haven't seen him since."

"Did you eat dinner already?" Izzy asked. Alice nodded. "What about your brother? Did he get his dinner?"

"I don't think so."

"Come on," she encouraged. The two went down to the kitchen. It looked like Mrs. Hadley had finally retired for the evening, which Izzy was grateful for. She grabbed some food out of the refrigerator and made up a plate for Xander. They took it back to his room and Izzy knocked on the door.

"Xander, I have food for you." He didn't answer and she sighed. "I'm going to leave it outside your door."

She doubted he heard her through the noise still coming out of his room. Izzy turned to Alice. "You want to go watch a movie? I'll let you pick out what we watch."

Which was how she soon found herself watching one of the freakiest movie's she'd ever seen in her life.

"How on earth did you ever find this movie?" Izzy asked, looking at the screen in horror.

"*Return to Oz* is my Aunt Mei's favorite movie."

Izzy stared at the screen, where a little Dorothy was walking through a room full of heads in cabinets. She didn't know much about Zan's sister, other than she was a doctor. She made a mental note to never use the surgeon.

After the movie was over, Alice started to yawn. Izzy said, "Come on. Time for bed."

They made their way back to the hallway. She was pleased to see the plate that she'd made up for Xander was missing. Hopefully, the teen had eaten something.

After she got Alice settled in for the night, she made her way to Zan's library. She was trying not to let her frustration get to her. Didn't Zan realize how much his kids were hurting today? She understood that he had to be hurting as well, but he should have been there for them. He was the only parent they had left.

She reached the library just as she heard a crash inside the closed room. She pushed the door open without thinking. At first, she didn't see Zan. He wasn't sitting behind his desk. A fire roared in the fireplace on the other side of the room, catching her attention, and that was when she noticed the figure lying on the floor. She hurried over to see what happened. She came to an abrupt halt when she noticed the shattered bottle all over the floor in front of the fire.

"What are you doing in here?"

Izzy pulled her gaze away from the glass reflecting in the firelight to look at Zan. She drew in a sharp breath at the sight of him. In all the time that Izzy had worked for him, Zan always looked put together, but in his current state, he was a hot mess. His hair was disheveled, like he'd run his fingers through it nonstop all day. The shirt he had on was wrinkled, and there was a stain on the leg of his gray jogging pants.

Which was another thing.

She'd never seen him in jogging pants before. She tried not to thirst over the sight of the pants hanging low on his hips, providing a glimpse of the skin underneath. They did little to hide what was beneath the material and she swallowed hard.

Now was not the time to ogle her boss.

His bare feet pointed toward the fireplace as he was lying on the floor with only his head propped on the chair behind him. In the light of the fire, Izzy could see that his eyes were bloodshot and she didn't miss the smell of alcohol wafting off him.

"I heard something crash," she said. She nodded toward the broken glass. "I guess I know what it was."

He reached around and grabbed another bottle of bourbon that was beside the chair. "And let me guess. You're here to judge me. You're very good at that."

"I don't judge," she said, trying not to be offended, given that his words were slurred. "I just call it like I see it."

"Sure." He gave her a little finger-gun salute before taking another swig from the bottle. "I know what you think of me. I'm a crap dad who continuously lets my kids down."

"You're not a crap dad," she argued. Lost, sure. Locked in his own pain? Absolutely. But he loved his children. She knew that without a doubt.

"But I do let my kids down," he told her. "We both know it. I shut myself away after Mary died, and now I don't know how to reach them."

"They're right here, and they love you." Izzy wasn't about to lecture him in the state he was in. She'd talk to him about this another time.

"Humph," Zan stared at her like she was an apparition before he patted the spot next to him. "Well, don't just stand there."

She stood rooted in place. On one hand, he was clearly drunk and she didn't know if she wanted to be around him like this. On the other hand, she didn't want to leave him alone like this. Making up her mind, she sat stiffly on the floor beside him.

He rolled his eyes when he saw her posture. "Relax. I'm not going to push myself on you."

She looked at him in surprise. "That was the last thing I thought you'd do."

He looked at her, a frown forming on his lips. "Why?"

"What do you mean, why?" She waved her hand between them.

"Is it because you spilled spaghetti on my lap once?" he asked before taking another swig.

She was unable to breathe as mortification danced through her system. She finally blurted, "You remember that?"

"Took me a minute, but when we ate spaghetti the other week, things clicked into place. I knew you were familiar the day of your interview, but I couldn't figure out why until then."

"I'm sorry," she whispered.

"Why is that, Isabella?" He gave her a sexy smile. "Because you tried to rub me off with a napkin?"

"I—I didn't. I—" she sputtered.

"I'm kidding." He waved off the conversation like it was nothing, while she wanted to die on the spot. "That happened years ago. I'm more interested in why you think I wouldn't push myself on you now."

"First off, you're a gentleman," Izzy said.

He smirked. "Is that what you think?"

The way he said it made something sizzle down Izzy's spine.

She cleared her throat. "And second," she continued, "I'm not your type."

"Is that what you think?' he repeated, this time in more of a rough-edged whisper.

Izzy's pulse sped up. "You're drunk."

He laughed, but the sound was cold. "That I am. Mary died three years ago today. I'm acknowledging the day like I always do."

"Alice told me. I'm sorry."

Zan didn't say anything for a minute as he stared into the

fire before he finally spoke. "Do you know what it's like living with someone who has terminal cancer?"

She shook her head. "No."

"It's like you're living with a person who has a bomb inside them. You don't know when it's going to go off, only that it will. And once it does…" He took another drink, deeper this time. "Once it does, the person is gone, and you're left with scars from standing too close to the explosion. No one else can see them, but they're there. And because no one else can see them, you're expected to just continue on with your life, as though you don't have shrapnel embedded in your heart, slowly killing you, too."

Tears formed in her eyes. "Zan…"

"Hmm?"

She cleared her throat. "I think you should try to get some sleep."

"You going to tuck me in, Nanny Izzy?"

It was the first time he'd ever called her Izzy. It felt foreign to her ears, and she almost missed the deep timbre of him calling her *Isabella.*

"Yes, I am," she said firmly. She stood up and held out her hand. He looked at it for a minute before letting out a breath. He grabbed for her palm and got to his feet. He swayed for a second and she wrapped her arm around his waist to steady him.

"Let's go," she said.

He slung his arm around her shoulder, and they carefully went around the broken glass. Once they got in the hallway, they headed to the bedrooms, with zero space between their bodies as they walked. She'd deal with the glass after she knew he was safe and nowhere near a liquor bottle.

They made it to his room and he opened the door with his free hand, the other arm still holding her shoulder in a hot grip. But he let her go once they were in his room. It gave her a second to look around.

She'd never been in here. On one side of the room were two open doors. One led to a bathroom, while the other revealed a walk-in closet. The room had dark green walls and thick white carpet. In the center of the room was a king-size, four-poster bed. Next to the bed was a lit lamp and pictures of the kids. She looked at the bed again, only for her eyes to drift up to the painting above it. This one was of Mary and Zan looking at each other so intimately, Izzy felt wrong for even laying eyes on it.

She quickly looked away to see Zan face-plant on his mattress. His pose was so similar to Alice's, Izzy almost smiled.

"Hey," she said, going around the bed until she was standing almost above him. "Lift up for a second so I can grab your sheets."

He got up on all fours and she pulled the comforter back. Once he lied back down, face up this time, she drew the blanket up to his chest.

"You're probably going to feel like crap tomorrow," she said.

"What's new?" he grumbled. She pursed her lips and he smiled. His hand shot up and traced the corner of her mouth. "You know when you do that, you get these adorable lines. Right here."

His index finger touched the side of her mouth.

Izzy's heart jumped several beats. "Pull the other one."

He moved his hand so that the back of his fingers brushed her cheekbone. "You know what I think?"

"What's that?" she asked, barely getting out the words.

"I think you don't know how beautiful you are. It's nice. I think you also smell really good. Like orange blossoms."

"I use body soap with that scent," she whispered.

"I like it a lot. Probably too much." With that, he dropped his hand and promptly passed out.

She stared at him, wondering if she'd heard him correctly. Forcing herself to move away from him, she went into his bathroom and looked around. Feeling like a snoop, she opened a couple of cabinets until she found a bottle of painkillers. She grabbed a cup that was next to the sink and filled it with water. She carried both back to his bed and placed them on the table for when he woke up.

A lock of Zan's black hair had fallen on his forehead and she brushed it softly back.

"I don't think you know this," she whispered. "But I think you're beautiful, too."

Chapter Thirteen

Zan woke up the next day feeling like tiny sledgehammers were going off in his head. He tried getting his bearings as his mind went to the night before. He remembered consuming a crap ton of alcohol as he did his best to drink the loss of Mary out of his brain. Once he'd finished a bottle, he'd thrown it into the fireplace. Or at least, he'd tried. He'd missed his target and the glass had shattered all over his rug—something he was going to need to deal with today. He then remembered the scent of orange blossoms surrounding him and resisting the urge to bury his face against the source. He was pretty sure he'd touched someone's face, the skin like silk under his fingertips. He'd wondered what that tempting flesh would feel like against his lips, underneath his body.

Zan shot up in bed, causing his head to spin. With a groan, he covered his face with his hands. When the pounding lessened a little, he looked around and noticed a glass of water and painkillers next to his bed. He had no idea how they got there, but he gratefully took a couple of pills and swallowed them down before getting out of bed. He glanced toward the bathroom and let out another groan. What he needed was coffee, but he probably smelled like a brewery, so he stepped in the shower and washed the previous night down the drain.

After he finished, he stared at himself in the mirror. He looked like hell. There were dark circles under his eyes and he looked pale. He honestly wasn't sure if all the alcohol was out of his system yet, given the way his head felt a little fuzzy. He rubbed at his face. He needed to find a healthier way to deal with his grief. He was getting too old for this.

Going down the stairs, the hairs on the back of his neck stood up as he heard unexpected voices conversing with Mrs. Hadley. Following the sound, he entered the kitchen but came to an abrupt stop when he came face-to-face with his former in-laws, Astrid and Arthur Westwood. They were sitting at the kitchen island drinking coffee.

Had Mary lived, she would have grown to look like her mother, though she would have lacked the poisonous expression Astrid always wore. Mary's father was a tall man, with grayish-blond hair and a year-round tan that only emphasized that he preferred spending more time at the golf course than with his wife. Astrid glanced over at Zan as he entered the room, her eyes cool as she looked him up and down.

"Well, so nice of you to join us," she said with fake cheerfulness. "We were afraid you were going to sleep the day away. And on a school day, too."

Zan's jaw tightened. "It's seven a.m. School doesn't start until eight."

Astrid looked at her nails, inspecting her manicure. "The children need structure and a good, hearty breakfast before they leave for that backwater place you enrolled them in."

"Their school is one of the highest rated in the state, but okay," Zan replied. He looked at Mrs. Hadley, who was standing by the stove, drinking from her own mug of coffee. "What's on the menu for breakfast this morning?"

"Oh..." the woman said, her face filled with a remorse he didn't trust. "I'm so sorry, Mr. Chen. I didn't have time to cook anything this morning, what with the arrival of the Westwoods. There is cereal available."

"Cereal?" Astrid said, as though Mrs. Hadley had suggested the kids eat slugs.

Zan's jaw clenched as he turned back to his in-laws. "What are you doing here, Astrid?"

Arthur shifted over to his wife, putting a hand on her shoulder as if to restrain her. Out of the two of them, Arthur had always tolerated Zan more. The man was simply indifferent to Zan, always had been. And because he truly cared less about him, he often acted as the peacekeeper between his wife and son-in-law. Probably for his own mental well-being. The man drove around with a bumper sticker on his Beemer that read I'd Rather Be Golfing.

"We were in the area and thought we'd visit our grandchildren," Arthur explained.

"Have you been drinking again?" Astrid asked, ruining whatever congenial atmosphere her husband had tried to create.

Drinking again? Like it was an everyday occurrence. Sure, after Mary died, he'd been a mess, drinking almost every day, while Paul and Kyleigh had stood helplessly by, not trying to stop him, but not letting him drink himself to death, either, like he'd been tempted to do. During one of those occasions, Astrid had stopped by the house. It was the first time she'd threatened to take the kids away from him, and it certainly hadn't been the last. She'd seen him at his absolute worse and she'd never let him forget it, either.

"What I do in my free time is none of your damn concern," he stated.

"Excuse me," Mrs. Hadley said, clearly not wanting to stick around for what was most likely going to be an intense argument.

"It is my business when my grandchildren are affected by their drunken lout of a father!" Astrid snapped as the other woman scrambled out of the room.

Zan's teeth gritted. "Having a couple of drinks on the anniversary of my wife's death doesn't make me a drunk. Or did you forget that Mary died three years ago yesterday?"

"How dare you!" Astrid replied, seething. "Of course, I remembered."

And how convenient that you show up at my house the very next day—knowing how hard that date is for my family.

"We truly just came to see the children," Arthur interjected. "We've missed them since you moved to Michigan."

Zan gave them an insincere smile. "Why don't you check into Holiday Bay's hotel and we'll catch up with you at a different time."

"No need," Astrid replied with the tone of a viper. "Mrs. Hadley knows Mary would never want us to sleep in a hotel and miss out on spending time with the children, so she got us set up in one of your guest rooms."

At that revelation, Zan froze. The sickly headache he'd had from his hangover turned his stomach to acid. And just like that, he was done playing these ridiculous games.

"What are you really doing here?" he asked.

Astrid stopped playing as well. "We're here to speak with the children about returning to Maine with us."

Zan's hands clenched at his sides. "You're not taking my kids away from me. You have no legal right to."

"According to Charles Cavendish, we have a very good shot."

Zan froze. Charles worked at the law firm the Westwoods had used for years. He'd been in the news more than once, building a reputation for winning impossible custody battles for the extremely wealthy, and that's exactly what the Westwoods were. While Zan had more money than he could ever spend in three lifetimes, his in-laws were old money, with high connections to judges, senators… hell, Arthur even played golf with the president a couple of times a year.

"You'll never win," he whispered.

Astrid waved her hand at him. "Look at you. You're a complete mess. From what I hear, you barely see the children, even while they're living under the same roof as you. Xander got expelled from his last school and Alice cries at everything."

"They're doing much bett—" He tried to defend himself, but Astrid overrode what he was going to say.

"The children need two parents to see to them. We can give them the life they need, not the life you're giving them."

Isabella breezed into the room, wearing a thick beige sweater over leggings. Her hair was piled into a messy bun and she hadn't bothered with makeup. She looked fresh and adorable.

"Good morn—" Izzy began, but came to a halt, her expression turning to surprise as she stared at the unexpected guests. "Oh! I'm sorry. I didn't realize you had company."

She turned to leave, but he grabbed her arm and pulled her against him. His hand went to her waist in a way that said they were more familiar with each other than they actually were. Out of the corner of his eye, he saw her jaw drop.

"Who is this?" Astrid growled.

"You were so busy lecturing me, I didn't get a chance to tell you my good news," Zan replied.

Astrid's eyes narrowed with suspicion as her gaze went from him to Isabella.

He smiled broadly, his mood improving with each second. "Arthur. Astrid. Let me introduce you to Isabella Rossi. My fiancée."

Chapter Fourteen

Izzy tensed next to Zan, not able to comprehend what the man had just said. It was bad enough that she'd woken up with the start of another migraine. She'd already taken her medication, but this announcement made her temples ache.

The woman stared at her like she'd grown a second head. Her eyes ran over Izzy from her head to her toes and her lip curled in disgust.

"You're kidding," she said. Izzy stiffened, feeling offended despite her confusion. "Isn't she your nanny?"

"The heart wants what it wants. This is still very new," Zan replied, squeezing Izzy's shoulder in warning. "We just talked about it last night, in fact."

"You talked about it last night, of all nights?" The woman sounded like she was ready to throw hands.

"Sweetheart," Zan said and Izzy's nerves jumped at the word. "I'd like you to meet Astrid and Arthur Westwood. They're my former in-laws. They're in town and decided to stop by unexpectedly to say hello to the children."

He squeezed her arm again and something clicked inside Izzy's addled brain. Mainly, the conversation she'd overheard a a while back, when Zan had mentioned that his in-laws were trying to get custody of the kids.

She looked into his brown eyes with a promise that they

would talk later before she plastered on a fake smile and said, “It’s nice to finally meet you. I’m sure this comes as a surprise.”

“To say the least,” Arthur replied.

Izzy put her hand on Zan’s chest, trying to ignore how good it felt under her touch.

Astrid, of course, missed nothing. “No ring, I see.”

“Like I said, we just got engaged. The ring is being custom-made, but I’m afraid I couldn’t wait any longer to make Izzy mine.”

Izzy tried her best to remain composed. “Honey,” she said in a threatening tone, “we should get going. We still need to drop the kids off, and then you promised to take me out to brunch.”

“That I did.” Zan leaned down and brushed his lips against her temple. She sucked in a breath at the light pressure, that incredible cedarwood scent of his filling her nose. He stepped back as the sound of two pairs of feet shuffling down the stairs.

“Stay calm,” Zan whispered before Xander and Alice entered the room with their schoolbags.

“Grandma! Grandpa!” Alice said, hurrying over to the older couple.

The cold look on the woman’s face instantly warmed as she embraced her granddaughter. “Hello, darling.”

“Xander, how are you, my lad?” Arthur asked as he stood up to greet his grandson.

Xander moved closer to his father. “I’m fine. I didn’t realize you were coming to town.”

“Oh, your grandma wanted to surprise you,” Arthur said.

I bet she did, Izzy thought.

“How’s school going, dear?” Astrid asked Xander.

"It's going fine," he replied, giving his dad another look. His eyes narrowed at how close Zan was standing next to Izzy.

"And you must be so excited about your dad's engagement to Isabella," Astrid said.

Both kids froze before Alice looked at Izzy, her eyes as wide as an owl's. "For real?"

Zan tilted his head, staring at his daughter with soft curiosity. "Would that be okay?"

"Yes!" she shrieked. "I love Izzy."

She raced over and hurtled herself at Izzy, who was starting to feel sick. How were they going to explain this to the kids? Alice had been doing so well in her therapy, and Xander had stopped causing issues at school. What would this do to them when they learned the truth?

As if reading her mind, Xander said, "We should get going."

He grabbed a banana off the counter and stomped out the door.

Alice turned to her grandparents. Arthur looked bemused. Astrid looked like she'd sucked a lemon.

"You'll be here when we get back?" Alice asked.

"Of course, we will. We're not going anywhere," her grandma said, brushing back a bit of Alice's hair. Zan's jaw clenched at that. He grabbed the keys from the closet closest to the door.

"You'll have to excuse us," he said to his in-laws as Alice grabbed a granola bar for her breakfast and raced out the door after her brother. "If you get hungry, ask Mrs. Hadley for something to eat."

He waited for Izzy to join him before he grabbed her hand to haul her outside.

As soon as the door shut behind them, Izzy hissed, "What in the ever-loving hell was that about?"

"Let's drop the kids off and then you can ream me." He handed her the keys. "I don't think I can drive."

"No kidding," she muttered.

They drove in strained silence for most of the way to the school. Alice was the only one who seemed unbothered by the morning events.

"Can I be your flower girl?" she asked Izzy.

"Well, you see—" Izzy began.

"Of course, you can," Zan interrupted.

"I can't wait to tell my teacher and everyone in class," Alice chirped.

"Would you shut up already?" Xander snapped.

Tears immediately started to form in Alice's eyes and she sniffed.

Zan breathed loudly through his nose. "Don't talk to your sister like that." To Alice, he said, "Do me a favor? Keep this a secret for now. You know how I like my privacy."

Alice's shoulders drooped. She wiped a couple of tears away as she said blandly, "And this will get reporters at our door if it gets out."

"That's right," he said. Izzy wondered how many times he had to remind the kids that he was actually an extremely famous guy.

Izzy parked the car at the curb outside the school. Alice got out of the car, waving to someone that she knew before taking off. Xander stayed in the car.

"What's on your mind?" Zan asked his son.

Xander slouched. "You're not really getting married, are you?"

Izzy's heart sank at the look he was giving them. Sure, she wasn't actually going to marry Zan Chen, but did Xander have to look so disapproving? They'd been getting along so well lately.

Zan frowned at his son's response. "Would it be so bad?'

Xander picked at his leather seat. "It's because Grandma wants custody of us, right?"

Zan paled. "What?"

"Before we moved to Holiday Bay, Grandma kept asking me how I'd like to live with them. And you always get super on-edge when they're around. I put two and two together." He nodded at Izzy. "Is that why you're suddenly engaged?"

"Xander…" Zan began, but the sound of the school bell going off stopped him from speaking any further.

"I have to get to class," Xander said, reaching for the car handle. He looked at it with a frown, then added, "For what it's worth, I don't want to leave. So I'll go along with this if it gets them off your back. But it's not fair to Alice to get her hopes up when you know this is fake."

He shut the door behind him, leaving them in stunned silence. Zan rubbed at his face. Izzy glared at him and he grimaced.

"I know," he grumbled. "We need to talk."

There were several women outside of the car, whispering and pointing excitedly at Zan. He never usually took the kids to school, leaving that to Izzy. The women clearly recognized that there was a Holiday Boy in their midst.

Zan swore when he noticed their attention as well. "We should talk somewhere else."

Izzy pinched the bridge of her nose as her head gave a slight throb. Thankfully, the headache seemed to be dulling instead of getting worse. She really couldn't handle a migraine on top of everything else.

"Let's go to Franki's," she suggested. "He just introduced a new breakfast pasty."

Once they pulled up in front of Holiday Bay's famous pasty shop, Izzy got out of the car and slammed the door behind her.

Zan got out and muttered, "I'm too hungover for this."

She swung around to face him. "Oh, I'm sorry. Are we feeling a bit under-the-weather? Perhaps that should have been your first clue not to tell people *we're getting married*."

As Izzy turned to open the door of the shop, she practically ran into her two friends, Meg and Julie as they stepped out.

"Hey!" Meg said, embracing Izzy before giving Zan a hug, too. She turned back to Izzy. "How's the job coming along?"

"It's something, that's for sure," Izzy said with false cheer.

"It's a bit weird not seeing you at Florentina's anymore," Julie added. "You know Jake and I love to go there for date nights."

"And we appreciate the business," Izzy replied genuinely. The Reynoldses had always been some of her favorite customers.

Meg held up a bag of pasties she was holding. "Are you here to try Franki's new breakfast pasties?"

"That we are," Zan said.

"I'm glad he made a vegetarian option along with the other breakfast meals."

Izzy grinned despite her mood. "Considering how much publicity it is having anyone associated with the Holiday Boys eating here, I'm sure Franki's more than happy to come up with recipes to accommodate you both."

"That's sweet of him," Julie said.

"Hey, I need to get to the campground, but I'll drop you

off at the store on my way," Meg offered to Julie, mentioning the two businesses in town that they were in charge of.

Julie nodded before she turned to Izzy. "Jake and Tyler are going to watch the kids for us next Saturday so we can have a girls' day out. Kyleigh's coming, too. Would you like to join us?"

"Oh, I..." Izzy said. She looked at Zan. She technically was working that day.

"It's fine with me," Zan replied. "I'll take care of the kids."

Izzy smiled at the other two women. "That'd be great. Thanks for the invite. Where were you thinking about going?"

Meg smirked somewhat evilly. "Kyleigh and I want to officially introduce Julie to Wine & Stuff. She's never been there, if you can believe it. What about you? Have you ever gone?"

"Not on purpose," Izzy muttered. Wine & Stuff had a reputation for serving the worst wine in all of Michigan. It had somehow become a tourist attraction because of how awful it was, but the owners, bless their hearts, didn't seem to realize that fact.

"We'll text you later with the details," Meg said before she and Julie left.

Zan opened the door for Izzy and waved her in. "After you."

As soon as Izzy smelled the familiar scents of dough and spices, she relaxed a little.

Franki poked his head out from the back and broke into a grin when he saw who was standing there.

"Iz!" He hurried over to her and wrapped her in a bear hug. "How've you been, cuz?"

Some of her earlier anger with Zan dissipated as she

returned her cousin's embrace. It was familiar and safe. Maybe Antonio was right and she should stick with being employed by the family, instead of whack jobs who randomly announced to people that they were marrying their nannies without asking the person first.

Speaking of…

She pulled away from Franki and turned back to Zan. "Franki, have you met Zan Chen?"

"Not formally, no," her cousin said. "Though your bandmates are in here so much I feel like I know you by extension."

A corner of Zan's mouth ticked up. "They've been telling me to come here since I moved back to the area."

Franki grinned before looking back at Izzy. "I heard some interesting news today. Did you hear Farmington is going to sell the bank?"

Izzy's mouth dropped. "No, really?"

Franki nodded. "Yeah, Meg just told me. I guess Farmington was going to raze it as sweet revenge for the town not letting him build that warehouse he wanted for his business. However, Lucas Beaumont, the mayor's son," he said in way of explanation to Zan, "stepped in and used his new position to list the bank as a historical site. Sounds like it was the final straw for Farmington, and he put the few remaining properties he owned in town up for sale."

"Huh…" Izzy fought the sudden urge to cry. She wanted that building so much, but there was no way she could afford it at this time.

She could feel Zan's eyes on her as she said to her cousin, "Thanks for letting me know."

"Yeah, of course," Franki replied before going back behind the counter. "So what can I get you today?"

They placed their orders before sitting down at one of

the few tables there were in the restaurant, as it was designed as a grab-and-go type of establishment. Izzy ran her fingers over the cool, white metal tabletop, feeling despondent. Zan scraped his chair across the bright red tile floor, getting comfortable.

"What's the significance of the bank?" he asked as they waited for their meal.

A sigh escaped her lips. "Just a silly pipe dream."

"Tell me about it."

She folded her arms on the table. "How about you tell me why you told your in-laws we're getting married?"

"You know why," Zan said, his voice low and urgent. "They didn't pop up randomly, today of all days. They know how hard the anniversary of Mary's death is for me. They came to show what an awful father I am so they can take my children from me."

Izzy rubbed at her temple. "Okay, but surely there's a better way to stop them than throwing me under the bus."

Zan leaned back in his chair, no expression on his face. "Tell me about this dream of yours."

She glared at the change of topic, but said, "I want to buy the bank and convert it into an art gallery. But I'm not in the position where I can afford it right now. So can we get back to the topic at hand?"

"I see." Zan didn't say anything further as Franki came over to drop off their food and drinks, then patted Izzy on the back before heading back to the kitchen to prep for lunch.

Zan cut into the pasty and took a bite, then said, "I didn't realize you were that serious about art."

Izzy lifted her chin in defense. "Why? Because you don't think I have any talent?"

"I never said that," Zan replied. "I think it's great that

you want to open a gallery. But why Holiday Bay? You would have better luck in Detroit or New York."

She shrugged. "Holiday Bay is home."

"So that's what you want to do with your life? Open up a gallery?"

"No, that's not all I want." She cursed herself as soon as she said it. She cut into her own food with a vicious swipe of her knife. She had zero desire to confess anything to Zan, given the state of things between them.

Zan took a sip of his orange juice. "What else do you want, then?" he persisted.

"Freedom," she muttered. She thought back to her last meeting with her family, and the pressure her dad and brothers had put on her to return to the restaurant. She shoved a piece of pasty in her mouth and chewed it aggressively.

Zan tilted his head, reminding her of a confused puppy. "What do you mean?"

She closed her eyes briefly, before thinking *screw it*. "My family wants me to return to Florentina's. They mean well, but I'm not only the youngest child, but also the only girl. They tend to be overprotective of me. It can get a little smothering. My brothers act like I can't survive without them hovering over me, making sure that I don't screw up my life. But I never wanted to work at the restaurant until the day I die. I've always wanted to be my own business owner, sharing art with the world. I have a knack for painting murals, and I'd love to do that while I build my gallery and reputation. Art's the only thing I've ever wanted to do."

"Oh..." Zan's expression was thoughtful. "And...marriage?"

"What about it?" she asked.

"Have you ever thought about it?"

Izzy frowned. “Not really. I know most of the men in this town already, and there’s no one I could see myself settling down with.”

Except for the one sitting across from her, but he was so far out of her league, she mentally squashed that notion. The only reason the word *marriage* was brought up in the first place was because he’d lied to his in-laws to get out of a sticky situation. Not because of love.

And didn’t that cheery thought leave her feeling crushed.

“Great,” Zan replied brightly and her discontent deepened.

“Great?” she repeated.

“Then you shouldn’t have any objections to marrying me.”

Izzy gaped at him. “You can’t be serious.”

“But I am.”

“I… Why?”

He gave her a no-nonsense look. “The same reason I mentioned before. My in-laws are making my life hell. If I get married, they won’t have any further arguments as to my ability to provide a stable home for the kids.”

“But why me?” Izzy clarified. Because there was no way Zan Chen didn’t have a million other women around the world who would give their left arm to marry him.

Zan gave her a half smile that did something to her insides that she quickly squashed. Now was not the time to have hot thoughts about one’s boss.

“I think you and I could have a mutually beneficial relationship,” Zan replied. “The kids love you—”

“I think Xander would disagree with that.”

“He likes you,” Zan insisted. “If he didn’t, he wouldn’t ask you to play video games with him.” When she still looked hesitant, he said, “Look, I don’t mean to toot my own horn here, but I'm a very wealthy man. You want the bank? I'll buy it for you, and you can start your gallery. Not only that, but I'll give you the financial freedom to do whatever else you desire. In exchange for that, you marry me, and help me get my in-laws off my back."

"I—I can't let you do that. It wouldn't be right for you to buy the bank for me." There was something so dirty about the suggestion. She might as well go walk Main St. like some prostitute while she was at it.

"Don't look at it that way," Zan said, as though reading her thoughts. "Consider it a loan, if you don't want to take the money outright. You can pay me back as you see fit. Or… I could be a backer and get a small percentage of your profits in exchange for the loan. Businesses get investors all the time. In exchange for that, you get the building of your dreams, and I give my kids some permanency."

"This is a crazy idea," she whispered. But…there was something very tempting about it as well.

"It might be crazy, but will you think it over, anyway?"

Izzy frowned. "When you say you want to marry me, exactly what kind of marriage are you talking about?" Her face heated as her eyes glanced over his toned body.

"What kind of marriage do you want?" he asked, his voice half-amused, as if he'd guessed where her mind was going, and half something else. That something else made a shiver slither down her spine.

"I—I asked you first," she insisted.

Zan lifted a shoulder. "I'll let you define what you want this marriage to be. If you want it to be normal, I'll give you that."

"And by normal you mean…"

"You. In my bed."

She sucked in a breath at his bluntness. Her cheeks

bloomed red and a million different fantasies tried to push through to the front of her mind.

"But…" Zan went on. "If you prefer separate bedrooms, we can do that, too. It's up to you."

"You'd be okay with us having a normal marriage?" she asked, her voice barely above a whisper.

He pushed aside his food. "I won't lie and say that I don't find you attractive. The fact is, I find you very attractive. Trust me when I say it'd be no hardship to take you to bed."

"I—I…" Izzy tried to speak, but her brain had stalled somewhere between Zan admitting he found her attractive and that he'd be open to sleeping with her.

"But to be clear, I'm not talking love here," he continued. "I…can't love anyone else. Not after Mary. I'll treat you right. I'll give you my money, freedom, and sex, if that's what you want. I just can't give you my love. Everything else is yours."

Izzy swallowed, not sure where the painful lump in her throat came from. Could she marry a man that would never love her? She could see herself falling in love with Zan, and to know those feelings would never be returned devastated her—which she should probably take as a warning that she was already in too deep.

Forcing the words out, she said, "And if I go through with this, what if I decide I want out?"

"Then we end it…" Zan said with a shrug of his shoulders. "After a certain waiting period, though. I need my in-laws to believe our marriage is real."

Izzy shook her head in disbelief. "All I have to do is marry you, and you'll help me get my business off the ground?"

"Yes."

He was handing her everything she ever wanted. Her

business and her freedom. And in return, she'd give the kids that she was already growing to love the stability they needed. Not to mention she'd get Zan…in every way but the one that mattered to her most. Could she live with that?

Looking into his handsome face, she read the certainty of his decision there. God, how was she going to not fall in love with him? She was already halfway there.

"If I decide this isn't working out," she said and he tensed, "do you promise that you'll let me go if that's what I want?" She lifted her pinkie to him.

He looked at it and smirked as though already sensing his victory. He wrapped his pinkie around hers and shook it.

"Yes. Consider it my wedding promise to you. So what do you say? Will you marry me?"

Before she could stop herself, Izzy found herself nodding. "Okay."

Chapter Fifteen

Izzy put the finishing touches on her makeup as she got ready for her Saturday night. It felt weird going out, but she was looking forward to spending the evening with Julie, Meg, and Kyleigh. It had been a tense week, with Mary's parents staying in the house and Astrid watching Zan and her with eagle eyes, waiting for one of them to slip. Izzy was ready to get out of the suffocating atmosphere. But first things first—she needed to go to her parents' house and break the news that she was engaged. Who knew how her family would react to that.

Alice sighed dramatically from where she was sitting on the side of the bathtub watching Izzy get ready. "You're so pretty, Izzy."

She smiled at the little girl. "Thank you, my favorite girl."

Izzy turned back to the mirror and eyed herself critically. She had on a jean dress with white tennis shoes for comfort. The dress flowed to her knees and flattered her curves instead of showcasing her weight. She'd piled her black hair into a bun on top of her head and applied minimal makeup. She was no beauty queen by any means, but she felt good.

"Don't you think she's pretty, Dad?" Alice said.

Izzy dropped the lip gloss she was applying. She swung around to face her fiancé. Zan leaned against the doorjamb, a playful smirk on his lips.

"Sorry, I did knock," he told her, his face one of complete innocence. "I heard you and Alice speaking, so I figured you weren't running around the room naked or anything."

A blush formed on her face while Alice giggled.

"And to answer your question, Alice, yes, I think Isabella looks absolutely beautiful."

"Thank you," Izzy breathed. She didn't miss the way Zan's eyes roamed over her body before returning to her face. Did he also think the dress flattered her, or did he realize that she was no Mary in any way, shape, or form?

"Alice, can you give us a second?" he asked. The little girl nodded.

She ran over to Izzy and gave her a brief hug. "I'm so glad you're marrying my dad."

"Me, too," she choked out, still trying to get used to the idea.

After she left, an awkward silence fell between them.

Izzy grabbed her earrings and put them on. "Did you need to speak with me about something?"

"Hmm?" He was distracted, his eyes looking over her again before his gaze snapped back to hers. "Oh…yeah." He reached inside his pants pocket and pulled out a small jewelry box. "I figured the sooner people learn about the engagement, the better."

He handed her a red velvet ring box. Izzy gave him a tentative smile before opening it. She gasped at the stunning ring inside. A huge, black oval-cut diamond on a white gold band nestled in the center of the cushion. Smaller white diamonds surrounded the larger jewel, sparkling brightly under the bathroom light.

"I wasn't sure about the color of the diamond," he said. "So if you don't like it, we can exchange it." He gave her a sheepish smile. "It reminded me of your gorgeous black hair."

Her eyes shot to his.

"You think my hair is gorgeous?" Izzy whispered.

He reached up with his free hand and twirled a loose strand of her hair between his fingers before tucking it behind her ear. "It's incredible. Like night spun silk."

"Oh…" She didn't know what to say to that. Thanks to Astrid's presence, Zan had gone out of his way over the past week to act like they were a loving couple. He'd found a million different ways to touch her, and Izzy's body had responded accordingly. As much as she tried to remind herself that this was all part of their agreement to act like a loving couple, she was becoming addicted to his touch. Just the graze of his fingers against her skin had her fighting the need to kiss him, to finally release the desire that was building inside her. Zan said he'd be open to them have a physical relationship. Izzy was beginning to wonder not *if* they were headed down that path, but *when*. Because, God, did she want this man.

"So…do you like the ring?" he asked.

"It's the most stunning ring I've ever seen."

He smiled at her and her heart flipped. Zan took the ring out of the box and slid it on her finger. The weight of it was like a promise. He lifted her hand and kissed the knuckle right beneath the band.

"Have fun tonight," he said. His eyes roamed over her again, as if he couldn't stop himself, and his mouth turned down slightly. "And if any man hits on you, don't forget to flash your ring at him."

Izzy let out a light laugh. "No one is going to hit on me."

He didn't return her smile. "Call me if you need anything."

And then he was gone, leaving nothing but the lingering scent of cedarwood in the air.

Izzy walked up the driveway to her family house. She could tell that her parents were home, given that almost every light in the house was on. As she entered through the front door, she heard their voices, along with those of Antonio and his wife, Tonya. Before Antonio met Tonya, he would have been at Florentina's on a Saturday night. Now, he gave that responsibility to Gio one Saturday a month, so he and his wife could have a weekend date.

Swallowing down her nerves, she entered the kitchen to find them playing euchre around the table.

Her mom spotted her first. "Izzy! What a surprise. We were hoping you would swing by tomorrow."

Izzy's stomach panged with guilt as her mom's gentle reminder that she had skipped the last two family meals.

"I'm sorry, I didn't mean to interrupt your night," she replied, ignoring how her father placed his cards on the table. He looked like he was about to stand up and walk out of the room, but Tonya grabbed his arm, restraining him.

"Nonsense," her mom said, getting up from the table to give her a hug. "What brings you by? I thought you had to work."

"Why are you so dressed up?" Antonio asked and his wife elbowed him.

"You look lovely," Tonya said.

"Thanks," Izzy replied.

"Did you finally decide to come back to my restaurant?" her father asked. And, of course, that was the only thing on his mind. Not, *hello, daughter that I'm no longer speaking to.* It was only and always about the restaurant.

"Actually..." Izzy lifted her chin before flashing her hand and the five-carat diamond on her ring finger.

"What is that?" Antonio asked sharply as Tonya squealed and raced over to her to examine it.

"What do you think it is?" Tonya said with a roll of her eyes, then she muttered to Izzy, "Men. This is the most gorgeous ring I've ever seen."

"Thank you," she told her sister-in-law.

"I'd love to know what's going on here," her mom said, hurt and concern written all over her face.

"Well, the thing is..." Izzy began. Swallowing down her nerves, she blurted, "I'm engaged to Zan Chen."

"Your boss," Antonio said through narrowed eyes. "Did he compromise you?"

"Please tell me he compromised you, and often," Tonya said so low that only Izzy could hear. She would have laughed if she didn't feel like throwing up.

Izzy glared at her brother. "Who even uses that word anymore?"

"No," her father said, the sharp word filled with emotion. "You're not getting married."

"I am," Izzy retorted.

Her father glared daggers. "A man who doesn't respect a father enough to ask for their daughter's hand in marriage will not respect his wife once they're married. And where is he as you tell us this news, huh?"

"He didn't know I was going to tell you tonight, or he would have been here." Of that, Izzy had no doubt. Despite the circumstances that led to their engagement, she knew that Zan would be here supporting her if she'd asked him to. But this was something she needed to do alone.

Her father folded his arms across his chest, giving her a stern look. "The answer is no."

Izzy tried hard to hold on to her temper.

"Dad, I love you." She looked around the room at her family. "I love all of you. But I'm a grown woman. I don't need to ask for anyone's permission here."

"So that's it,' Antonio said, adopting a pose similar to their dad's.

"Yes." Izzy raised her chin. "I'd love your support, but if you can't offer it, then I'll just have to live with that. I'll let you know when the wedding is taking place. I'd love for you to be there."

She left, blinking back tears as she hurried to the front door. She refused to cry right before she met up with her friends. She made it to the front door when a hand landed on her arm, stopping her. Izzy turned to see her mom beside her.

"Do you love him?" she asked.

Izzy opened her mouth then closed it. She couldn't lie to her mom. But would it be a lie? She'd thought she was in love with Zan Chen when she was a teenager, but that had been the celebrity, not the real man she'd gotten to know. The same guy who would set the world on fire for his children. Who made her feel like he'd give her the universe if only she'd ask for it. Zan set her blood sizzling just by looking at her. Not even an hour ago, her heart had been on a speeding train when he'd said her engagement ring reminded him of her hair, his gaze all over her.

"Yes," she answered her mom and she knew it was true. "I love him."

Her mom cupped her cheek. "Then be happy and don't let the overprotective men in this family ruin it for you."

Tears formed in Izzy's eyes. "Thanks, Mom."

She hugged her tightly before leaving for a night out with the girls.

Izzy took a sip of her wine, trying not to wince. The drink, named Beautiful Bounty to go along with Wine & Stuff's pirate theme, was anything but. Kyleigh and Meg had wisely chosen beverages other than wine. Izzy and Julie were the only ones gullible enough to try the winery's specialty. It felt like a rite of passage at this point. Every legally aged adult in Holiday Bay had to try Wine & Stuff's house wines at least once in their lives. It was Julie and Izzy's turn tonight.

"Here's to Zan and Izzy," Julie said, her voice slurring as she took another sip of her wine.

"To Zan and Izzy," Meg and Kyleigh repeated.

The girls had been stunned but supportive when Izzy had shown up wearing her engagement ring.

"Do you know where you're going to get married yet?" Meg asked.

"No, everything is still so new that we haven't gotten that far into the details." Izzy was still reeling from the realization that she'd fallen in love with Zan. And he had already warned her that he would never return her feelings.

Meg's face turned diabolical. "We should plan a bachelorette party."

Julie groaned. "I'm still recovering from the last one you threw."

Meg lifted a shoulder. "It's not my fault that you can't hold your liquor."

Izzy lifted her glass to her mouth as her friends squabbled, but the putrid smell of the wine made her nauseous.

She placed it back down on the table just as Julie jumped up with her hand covering her mouth.

"I'm going to—" She didn't finish her sentence as she hurried to the bathroom.

"I should go check on her," Meg said, her tone amused.

After she left, Kyleigh said, "I can't believe you and Zan are engaged. I never thought I'd see the day. He must really love you."

"I…" Izzy replied. Tears spilled unexpectedly from her eyes, but she dashed them away. Before she knew it, she was telling everything to Kyleigh, including the real reason they were getting married.

"So it's not going to be a real marriage. I'm helping him out," she explained just as Julie and Meg made it back to the table. "And he's going to help me start my career as an artist."

"Who has a career as an artist?" Julie asked, looking like she regretted everything in her life.

"Me, hopefully," Izzy said. "Zan's going to help me open an art gallery. I'm hoping we can purchase the old bank on Main Street."

"Oh! I'll talk to Lucas and see if I can pull some strings," Meg said, mentioning her former fiancé.

"I… That would be amazing," Izzy replied, so thankful for this squad of women in her life. "I'm hoping to start off small. Maybe get work as a muralist while we get the art gallery up and running. I was thinking it'd help bring some credibility to my name."

"You do murals?" Julie asked. When Izzy nodded shyly, she said, "I've been thinking that the wall behind my sales counter could use a little pizazz. Something that captures Holiday Bay. Would you be interested?"

“Are you serious?” Izzy said, trying to clear her head of the sudden lightness caused by the wine.

“Absolutely,” Julie said, before she moaned, clutching her stomach. “Let’s talk some more later, when my insides don’t feel like they’re being karate-chopped.”

Sarah, one of the winery owners, came over to their table with a wine bottle. There were daffodils woven in the threads of her dark hair, which was styled in a braid around the crown of her head.

“Can I top you off?” she asked.

“No!” all four of them said at the same time.

Chapter Sixteen

Zan read on his tablet at the kitchen island while he waited for Isabella to wake up. She'd come home pretty late and he was letting her sleep. But he wanted to talk to her. He wasn't sure about what—only that he did.

Mrs. Hadley was cooking food at the stove, her movements abrupt. Zan pinched the bridge of his nose. The old housekeeper had been with the family for years. Mary had hired her shortly after the woman had lost her husband. Mrs. Hadley, in return, became a second mother to Mary, making sure she lacked for nothing, especially when Mary got diagnosed with leukemia and the disease grew worse. After she died, Mrs. Hadley made sure that the kids ate three meals a day and wore clean clothes, instead of wearing the same dirty outfit for a week straight, like Zan had done. When he'd decided he and the kids needed a fresh start, Mrs. Hadley had moved with the family to Michigan.

He'd promised Mary that he'd look out for the older woman, and Mrs. Hadley had continued to be something comforting and familiar to the kids. But Zan had to admit, he was getting a little tired of the attitude she seemed to have all the time lately. He'd had to remember his promise to Mary more than once, otherwise he probably would have fired the housekeeper by now.

Putting down the tablet, he said, "What's on your mind, Mrs. Hadley?"

The housekeeper faced him, placing a hand on her hip. "It's none of my business, Mr. Chen, but I think you're making a mistake marrying that woman."

"Oh?" he said, trying to hold back his anger.

"Well, she's certainly not Mrs. Chen, is she?"

"She's not Mary..." When Mrs. Hadley's face started to relax, he said, "But she will be Mrs. Isabella Chen soon enough, and I expect everyone to treat her with the respect she deserves. Including you. However, if you don't think this situation is working out for you anymore..."

He didn't finish his sentence, but Mrs. Hadley heard the threat to her job loud and clear. Her lips pursed. "No, everything is perfectly fine."

She turned back to her cooking and flipped the pancakes with a little more aggression than was needed. Zan reminded himself again to honor Mary's wishes and not fire the woman on the spot. But who the hell did she think she was, insulting Isabella?

"And when *is* the happy occasion?" Astrid said from behind him as she entered the kitchen. Mary's parents had been staying with them for almost a week now, and Zan was ready to boot them out. Aside from the constant snips at Isabella, they also couldn't stop getting their barbs in him. He would have already, if the kids—mainly Alice—weren't so excited to have them around.

"We haven't set a date yet," he muttered, "but you'll be the first to know."

Arthur came into the room and grabbed some coffee before sitting down at the kitchen table. He carried a newspaper—where he got one from, Zan had no idea—and started reading it as he took sips from his mug, ignoring everyone else in the kitchen.

"Well, I hope the nuptials are soon. We can't stay here forever," Astrid said.

Zan stiffened at that. "What are you talking about?"

"Of course, we're staying for your wedding. You're family, after all," Astrid said, a gleam in her eye that Zan didn't trust. She'd probably guessed that her appearance was the reason behind his sudden engagement.

Isabella stumbled into the kitchen at that moment, and Zan's stomach did a funny little lurch at the sight of her. She hadn't bothered to get dressed yet, so she approached them in nothing but her silk robe and slippers, her shapely legs on full display. Her hair was sticking up in the back and she had dark circles under her eyes.

Paul had come over to work out with Zan the previous night while the ladies had gone out. He couldn't stop laughing when he'd told Zan how awful Wine & Stuff's house wines truly were. Apparently, he and Kyleigh had gone there once on a date that ended with her getting physically sick in the parking lot.

It was a miracle that Isabella was up so early. Zan watched her bumble her way to where the mugs were. She poured herself a coffee and took a sip of it with a happy little murmur. His face softened as he took her in. Despite the hangover she most likely had, she looked gorgeous, as usual.

"Zan…" Astrid said. "Zan!"

"Hmm?" Zan said, pulling her eyes away from his fiancée.

Astrid looked like she was ready to spit venom. "I said when are you planning on getting married?"

"Next weekend," he replied out of nowhere.

Isabella dropped her mug on the kitchen island, spilling coffee everywhere.

"Next weekend?" she squeaked.

He didn't miss the narrow-eyed gaze Astrid was giving them.

"Yes, love. I was able to get everything arranged." He hadn't, but it was a good thing he knew a guy who had a whole reality TV show based on marrying strangers quickly. Paul surely had some connections that Zan could use to pull this off. He wanted Astrid and Arthur gone. He looked at Isabella again, and something shifted and settled. The quicker they got married, the better he'd feel about everything.

"I..." Isabella said.

"In fact, I thought I'd go with you today to personally invite your family." Zan knew that she'd mentioned Sunday dinners with her family at one point since she'd started working for him, though he couldn't remember the last time she'd actually gone to one. He turned to Astrid. "You don't mind watching the kids today, do you? After all, you'll be gone soon."

Zan needed to remind her that her stay under his roof was coming to an end. He wondered if Astrid would say no just to thwart him, but she had to know that once he was married, her chances of fighting for custody were gone. She might as well get her time in with her grandkids now.

"We'd love to," Arthur said, folding his newspaper to take in the scene. He looked pointedly at his wife.

"Yes, of course, we'd be happy to watch the children," Astrid added through clenched teeth.

Looking over at Isabella, he found that she was staring at him with wide, shocked eyes. He wondered if she knew her hair was still sticking up from her bedhead. It was adorable. *She* was adorable.

Zan smiled—a true, real smile. It was the kind that warmed your insides. It felt like the first one in forever.

Zan watched Isabella's knee bounce up and down as he drove them into town.

"I have to get my car at some point," she said, staring out the window. "Meg drove me home last night."

"Sure, no worries," he said. "We can get it after dinner."

"I told my parents and Antonio about us last night before I met up with the girls."

That caught his attention. "How'd that go?"

Isabella leaned her head back against her seat. "Not well. I'll be honest, you probably won't get the best reception today. My dad is really old school and is mad that you didn't ask his permission first."

"Would he have given it?" he asked curiously.

"No, probably not."

"You're a strong, independent, beautiful woman. No offense, but the only person's consent I need is yours."

She stared at him with wide brown eyes. "You think I'm beautiful?"

"Of course, you are."

Isabella's leg continued to bounce.

"So why are you so nervous?" he asked. "Nothing is going to stop me from marrying you."

Aside from a major earthquake or some other natural disaster, he had every intention of marrying Isabella on Saturday. Luckily for him, the Great Lakes had a tendency to protect Michigan from most bad weather.

"Talk to me," he urged.

Isabella let out a soft sigh. "Other than the fact that my

family will most likely try to kill you as soon as you step foot in my parents' house, how are we supposed to get married next weekend? Are we going to the courthouse or something?"

"Would you be okay with that?" he asked curiously.

She turned her head away from him and her leg stopped bouncing. "That'd make the most sense. You've been married before, after all."

He could hear the disappointment in her voice, though. She wanted the full wedding experience—a wedding dress, flowers…the works. He could tell by her body language, the weary acceptance in the slump of her shoulders. He refused to give her anything but the best. If Isabella wanted a full wedding, she'd get it.

"Well, we're not doing a courthouse wedding," he told her.

Isabella looked back at him. "We're not?"

"No. I haven't had the experience of a full wedding, either. Mary and I eloped."

Isabella stared at him in surprise. "You did? I mean, I remember when it was announced in the magazines that you'd gotten married, but I didn't read the details. I assumed you had the big affair that others did, but you'd kept it hidden."

Zan snorted. "You've met Astrid and Arthur. You think they wanted their princess to marry some guy who made a living from being in a boy band and writing books? They wanted her to marry some hedge-fund billionaire they knew. Mary told them to forget it, and we ran off to Vegas."

He smiled at the memory, the normal crushing depression he felt whenever he thought of Mary not there. He felt sadness, sure, but it wasn't accompanied with the desperate need to get plastered just so he could forget the pain.

Huh. How about that?

Zan realized Isabella was staring at him and glanced her way. She immediately turned her head, but he could see the tension in her profile.

He was about to ask about it when she muttered, "We can't plan a wedding in a week."

"I know." He grinned, though she didn't see it. "That's why I called Paul while you were getting dressed. He's using every connection he has from his show to arrange everything, but I thought we could get married in the gardens in our backyard since you like them so much. Paul said he could get that arranged. I'm going to owe him a bottle of his choice, and that knob-head's taste isn't cheap."

Isabella wore a stunned expression, and he had the sudden crazy notion to pull the car over so he could kiss that look right off her face. He forced his eyes back on the road.

"So..." he began and had to clear his throat. "Why, um, why do you think your family is going to kill me?"

"Aside from the fact that my Italian father is very old school and is ticked you didn't ask him for my hand in marriage? He's taking it as a personal insult, which has most likely trickled down to the rest of the family."

"Good thing hostile in-laws are my forte," Zan half joked. "Maybe we should have brought the kids to soften the blow. They can't hurt me in front of my own children, right?"

She snorted. "Coward."

They pulled up to a large house in the middle of town. Cars filled the driveway and part of the street as well.

Isabella sighed. "Great. Looks like the whole family is here."

She got out of the car and he followed, hurrying to meet her so that he could grab her hand. He squeezed it in reassurance, but he also just wanted an excuse to touch her.

She glanced down at their joined hands, and he realized how little affection he'd shown her when others weren't around. For all intents and purposes, this was going to be a real marriage to the world. Whether they had sex or not was up to Isabella, but this wasn't some fake marriage for a TV show. This was real.

Zan looked down at the navy dress she wore, which hugged the lush curves of her body, and felt a pang of desire. He wouldn't mind at all if she said yes to sex. In fact, he was starting to look forward to the possibility. At the back of his mind, there was something that tried to stir up the normal guilt he felt whenever he looked at someone that wasn't Mary, but it never surfaced. He pulled Isabella a little closer to him as they headed up the walkway leading to the front of the house.

"Ready?" she said as her free hand grabbed the door.

He couldn't resist anymore. He leaned down and brushed a kiss to the top of her head, the sweet scent of orange blossoms filling his nose before he pulled back.

Her wide eyes were like pools of melted chocolate. She opened her hypnotic mouth to say something just as the door opened. A woman stood before them. She looked like an older version of Isabella. The woman had to be her mother.

"Izzy, I was worried you wouldn't come after yesterday. Come on in," the woman said, stepping back.

Zan let go of Isabella's hand so she could go in first, but he put his hand on her back, unwilling to break contact.

"Mom," she said, "this is Zan Chen."

"Mrs. Rossi," he said, offering his hand and shaking hers. "Thank you for letting me join you today."

"He's charming," she said to her daughter. "I can see why you had his posters on your wall." Zan watched in fascination as a bright blush hit Isabella's cheeks. Her mother turned back to him. "And call me Tina."

He nodded his thanks as they headed to the back of the house.

"You had my pictures on your wall, huh?" he teased quietly enough that only she could hear.

"Every girl in Holiday Bay had the Holiday Boys on their wall. Don't let it go to your head."

He snorted as they entered the kitchen. He could see a large, screened-in porch with a gigantic table set up through a large archway. There were people everywhere—adults, children, and even a few babies. He recognized Isabella's cousin Franki speaking with someone who had to be a brother or cousin of hers.

"Look who's here," Tina announced and the table fell silent as they looked at Zan and Isabella.

Isabella looked around the table and lifted her head. "Hey. I, uh, I thought it was time for everyone to meet Zan. Zan, this is…"

She went around the table and introduced her different family members. He'd be lucky if he remembered one correctly.

They sat down in chairs that Tina found from somewhere and the family began to eat. There was chicken marsala and fettuccine Alfredo, three different types of salad and fresh bread. It was like eating at a restaurant, which didn't surprise Zan, considering what Isabella's family did for a living.

"So…" Isabella's father said as he glared at Zan. That was one person Zan didn't intend on forgetting. "Izzy tells me you asked her to marry her."

"Yes, I did," Zan replied. "Am I'm very lucky that she said yes."

"And you didn't ask me for her hand in marriage? Don't you have any respect for your elders?"

"Dad, come on," Isabella muttered.

"I apologize for not asking you first," Zan said firmly. "But I don't regret for a second asking your daughter to marry me. I feel beyond lucky that she'll be my wife."

"The ring is gorgeous," a woman in her mid-forties said, clearly trying to keep the meal peaceful. If Zan remembered right, he thought her name began with a *T*, and she was married to Isabella's oldest brother.

"Have you thought of any dates yet?" Tina asked. "We could plan a wedding for next fall. That would look beautiful with the leaves changing."

"We're actually getting married next weekend," Zan said absently as he grabbed another bread roll, completely missing Isabella giving him a short shake of her head.

It was as if he threw a grenade in the middle of the table. People started yelling over each other. Two of her brothers jumped up from their seats, one's chair crashing to the ground.

"You son of a— Did you get her pregnant?" her brother—Zan thought his name was Antonio—asked.

"What?" Zan was honestly shocked. "No, of course not."

"Oh, my god, we haven't even—" Isabella started to say before clamping her mouth shut, but her admission seemed to relax the atmosphere, but not by much.

"My former in-laws are in town visiting my children," Zan said. "They want to stay for the wedding, and there's really no point in waiting."

Her father's eyebrows shot up. "You have kids and in-laws. Seems like you come with the full package."

"Come on, Dad," her brother—Derrick…no, Dante—

replied. "This isn't the twentieth century. There are a lot of blended families these days."

The old man grunted a simple "humph."

"You won't be able to book the church in time," Tina said, an expression of concern on her face as she looked between her husband and daughter.

"We're getting married at Zan's house," Isabella told them, lifting her chin.

Her father's fist slammed onto the table. "I forbid it!"

Isabella glared at her dad. "As I said before, I don't need permission. I certainly don't need anyone telling me *where* I can get married." She stood up and grabbed Zan's hand so he had to get up as well. "Zan and I are getting married at his house next Saturday. I'd love for all of you to be there, but if you can't get over this, then I understand if you can't make it."

She turned to leave and Zan followed. There was nothing but silence as they walked back to Zan's car. Isabella didn't say anything once they were inside and he started the engine. He turned the car around and started driving to Meg and Tyler's house to pick up her car.

"I'm so sorry," he finally said. "I don't want to get between you and your family."

She wiped at her face and his heart clenched, knowing that she was crying because of something he'd caused.

"It's fine," she said. "This battle between me and my family has been a long time coming."

"We can get married in a church, if that's what you want." Zan wasn't particularly religious, so he had never even thought of a church service...let alone considered that it might be something Isabella would prefer.

Stubbornness settled on her face. "No. We're not changing our plans now. We're getting married in the garden next Saturday. Promise?"

She lifted her pinkie to him. He smiled and lifted his own, wrapping it around hers.

"I promise."

Chapter Seventeen

The makeup artist from Paul's show, *First Comes Marriage*, put the final touches on Izzy's face. Izzy continued to take deep breaths throughout the process, trying not to let her nerves take over. She couldn't believe she was doing this.

She was getting married to the man of her dreams. She knew by now that she had stupidly fallen in love with Zan Chen. Izzy suspected that she had fallen under his spell from the first day she'd interviewed with him. But when he offered to put their wedding on hold so that they could get married in a church, she knew beyond a shadow of a doubt that she was deeply, irreversibly in love with him. Zan was exactly the man she thought he was. He was good and gracious and kind.

And he was still in love with his dead wife.

They'd met in the library the previous day to go over the final details of the wedding. He'd just gotten off the phone with his lawyer, his features thoughtful, when she'd arrived in the room. She'd been shocked when Zan had asked her to meet him there instead of his office, but he insisted that once they were wed, the house would be as much hers as it was his. If she wanted to come into the library, she could. She'd nodded while trying to ignore the beautiful reminder of his first wife behind his head. When she'd asked him what the lawyer had said, he'd replied that the man had told him that things were looking up for him—not so much for the Westwoods.

"This marriage is going to be good for all of us—you, me, and the kids," Zan had said before launching into the updated details for the ceremony that Paul had given him.

She was thankful for her friends, who'd offered her a much-needed distraction. Later that night, Meg had picked her up and taken her to Julie's for a small bachelorette party. They hadn't had time to do anything elaborate, which Izzy was grateful for, knowing some of the things Meg had gotten up to when she was younger. It had just been just them and Kyleigh, and that was all Izzy needed. They drank good wine this time and talked. Not about anything serious. Silly things—such as preparing Izzy for life as a Holiday Boys' wife. By the time she was dropped off in the early morning hours, she'd felt like a load of stress had been taken off her chest.

"All finished," Heather said now, putting away her makeup brush. "You ready to see what you look like?"

Izzy nodded, though she was pretty sure she could show up in jogging pants and Zan wouldn't care, as long as they got married and he got his in-laws off his back. But she couldn't help but gasp a little when she saw her reflection. Her eye shadow was subtle, but it brought out the dark brown of her eyes. Blush on her cheekbones made them stand out prominently. Her hair had been pulled into a chignon with tiny white buds interlaced between the tresses. Izzy never thought of herself as beautiful, but she felt like she was in that moment.

"Let me grab your dress," Heather said, just as there was a knock on the door.

"Come in," Izzy called out, and Meg, Kyleigh, and Julie entered the room.

"Oh, wow, you look gorgeous," Meg said, coming over to hug her.

"Zan isn't going to know what hit him," Julie added.

"How are you feeling?" Kyleigh asked.

"Good. Nervous," Izzy admitted.

"That's perfectly normal," Kyleigh replied.

Heather came back into the room with her dress and helped her into it. When she was finally zipped in, she went back to the mirror. The dress was breathtaking. The bodice was tight, showcasing her breasts without making her feel like she was on display. It had an off-the-shoulder bodice with satin sleeves to keep her arms warm in the cool weather. The skirt of matching satin flowed down to her feet. The fabric was embedded with tiny white flower buds similar to the ones in her hair. It was gorgeous. She'd known it must have cost a fortune, but when she'd asked about the price, Jessica—the owner of the Bridal Barn, where the dress was purchased—told her it was a gift from Zan.

Kyleigh came over and hugged her. "I'm so glad it was you he fell for."

Izzy wanted to scream that he didn't love her. She was a means to an end. That he only had room in his heart for his dead wife. He'd even warned her about that when he'd proposed. But she didn't say anything. There was a softer knock on the door and Alice popped in, followed by two Asian women that Izzy didn't recognize.

"This is my grandma and Aunt Mei," Alice announced, so that Izzy understood she was meeting Zan's mother and sister for the first time.

"I..." She didn't know what to do here. She'd never had

in-laws before, and but she certainly hoped they weren't as awful as Mary's parents.

"It's so nice to meet you finally," Mei said. "I wish we could have met sooner, but this was the earliest I could get off from the hospital."

"Aunt Mei is a pediatric heart surgeon," Alice said proudly. "And Grandma was a principal at Clarington High School, but when she and Grandpa retired, they moved to California, where Aunt Mei lives."

Izzy looked at her future mother-in-law nervously. She could see where Zan got his looks from, because the woman in front of her was flawless.

She smiled at Izzy before giving her a hug. "It's nice to meet you. I'm Lin. I'm hoping you'll be able to convince my boy to come see his aging parents sometime. I keep telling him we're not going to be around forever."

Mei laughed. "Mom, you and Dad are healthier than Zan and I put together."

The older woman smiled before turning to Izzy. "My husband is very excited to meet you as well. He's catching up with Zan at the moment."

There was another knock on the door and Kyleigh went to answer it. Her husband, Paul, was on the other side. He gave his wife a tender smile before he looked at Izzy.

"We're ready when you are."

"She's ready," Heather said, giving her boss a thumbs-up.

The women left the room to take their seats, leaving her in the room with Alice. She took in the little girl's dress, which, like Izzy's, was satin and covered in tiny white flowers.

"You look very beautiful," she told Alice.

Alice hurried over and hugged her tight. "I'm so glad you're marrying my dad."

Warmth blossomed inside Izzy's chest before she lifted the girl's chin. "You ready?"

"Yes!" she shrieked.

They made their way downstairs and stepped into the backyard. To her left, behind the seating area, she could see Simon and Mrs. Hadley. The old housekeeper gave her a look that said she thought Izzy was clearly lacking. Izzy ignored her to look around the garden. It had been transformed into a fairyland, with sparkling lights covering all the trees and bushes. Flowers hung from branches, and a wooden arch—wrapped in white flowers—made up the altar. It was breathtaking against the orange and yellow setting of fall.

Zan's bandmates and their wives were sitting in chairs to the right of the altar, along with Zan's parents and sister. Astrid and Arthur were also present, but they had chosen to sit on Izzy's side of the aisle, probably to avoid Zan's family.

Izzy ached when she noticed how empty the seats were on the bride's side. There were only two people sitting there—her mother and Tonya. She blinked back tears at the realization that her brothers and dad hadn't come. Not even Dante. Izzy had no one to walk her down the aisle.

She heard a cough and looked to see Franki next to her, wearing a tuxedo.

"You didn't think I was going to let my favorite cousin get married without me, did you?" he asked.

She threw her arms around him. "Thank you," she whispered.

He pulled back and wiped a tear that escaped her eye. "Don't do that, you'll ruin your makeup." She laughed as he offered his arm to walk her down the aisle. "Dante wanted to come, but they had a big bar mitzvah at the restaurant. It was scheduled months in advance. You know how it goes—all hands on deck."

She did understand that. And she knew that her marriage was very last-minute. It didn't help take away the sting of them not being there. With her head high, Izzy started down the aisle to begin her life with Zan.

As she walked, she looked toward the altar and the figures standing there. Her gaze landed on Xander first. He looked handsome in his tux, his hair neatly styled. He didn't look as angry as he had been since she'd met him. He looked more resigned. Out of everyone present, he and Kyleigh were the only ones who knew the truth. It was sweet of him that he was willing to be his dad's best man, considering he knew the marriage was a fraud.

She moved her eyes to Zan and almost stumbled. He looked so ridiculously attractive. He wore a tux similar to his son's, but it molded to him perfectly, the layers of cloth doing little to hide his muscular frame. He gave her a crooked smile that made her heart dance. Was she seriously about to marry this man?

When they reached the end of the aisle, Zan stepped toward her and offered his arm. She let go of Franki to grab it with a trembling hand. His palm covered hers, locking her to him. She had a feeling that if she chickened out and tried to run, he wouldn't let her go.

Not that Izzy had any intention of running.

The man in front of them cleared his throat, breaking the spell that had wrapped around them.

"Dearly beloved..." the man began.

And in the blink of an eye, Izzy Rossi became Isabella Chen.

A couple hours later, Zan and Izzy danced around a makeshift dance floor, swaying to the sultry sounds of Norah Jones's "Come Away with Me."

"I like your family," Izzy said as they danced around the floor. She'd met his father after the wedding. The former pharmacist had greeted her with a twinkle in his eye, his warmth contagious. When she looked at him, she could almost picture what Zan would look like in thirty years, as long as he found the same joy in life that his father clearly had.

His lips turned down. "I'm sorry that most of your family missed today."

She looked over at where Tonya and her mom were sitting at a white-cloth-covered table, speaking to Lin and Mei. Izzy didn't say anything about her missing relatives as they continued to float around the floor. She wasn't going to let it ruin her day any more than she already had.

Zan hunched down so that he could whisper in her ear, the warmth of his breath making her shiver. "Have I told you how beautiful you look?"

"Oh, I'm not. I—"

"Don't think about finishing that sentence. You're absolutely stunning." His hands tightened on her waist, pulling her even closer to him.

She glanced up at him, her eyes lingering on his mouth. When the officiant had announced they were married, Zan had brushed his lips lightly over hers, barely making contact. That hadn't stopped her mouth from tingling whenever she thought of that moment. As she stared at the perfect bow of his lips, she wondered what it would be like to feel him even more. How would he react if she told him that she wanted their marriage to be real in every way?

Then she remembered that he'd once been married to a supermodel. He didn't seem to mind her body, and while she normally didn't care about her weight, she suddenly felt self-conscious of how she looked.

"Listen," Zan said, unaware of her inner turmoil. "I want to take you somewhere tomorrow. Do you have anything planned?"

She'd planned on sketching out the mural for Julie's store in between taking care of the kids. Just because she was now their stepmom didn't mean they weren't going to be her priority. They were the reason Zan asked her to marry him in the first place.

"Well, I don't think I'll be going to my parents' house tomorrow, so I thought I'd plan something for the kids or work on Julie's mural."

Zan frowned even as he pulled her in tighter. "You're not the kids' nanny anymore."

"I know," she said. "But you married me for the kids."

Zan opened his mouth to protest but closed it. What argument could he make? "My parents and sister want to spend time with them while they're here. That should free up your time."

"I'm sure your family would love to spend time with you, too," Izzy gently reminded him.

"But you forget, I'm on my honeymoon." He wiggled his eyebrows at her. Izzy blushed and he snickered in response.

When the song ended, Izzy stepped away to get some water, so Zan grabbed Alice and started twirling her around the floor.

"Izzy, we need to head out," her mom said as she came up to her with Tonya in tow. "But I couldn't leave without telling you that you were the most beautiful bride."

She hugged her mom. "Thank you for coming."

"I wouldn't have missed it. Not for anything."

Tonya hugged her next. "If it makes you feel any better, Tony is sleeping on the couch tonight."

"Perhaps I should make Gianni as well," her mom said with grim determination.

Izzy laughed. "I love you both."

They talked for a few more minutes before they left. Zan came over and claimed her for a toast. They continued to mingle and dance throughout the rest of the night, presenting a united front. When she started to yawn, Zan gently suggested, "I think it's time for us to say good-night."

She nodded, grateful for the thought of her bed. She wanted a moment to decompress, a place where she didn't have to hide how much it hurt that the men in her family weren't there for her today, other than Franki. Izzy knew they didn't approve of the marriage, especially considering it wasn't going to take place in the church. But it was hard not to see their absence as unforgivable, even if they had a conflicting event at the restaurant. Family should come first.

Zan nudged her toward the stairs. "Why don't you go ahead and get ready for bed while I check on the kids one more time?"

"Okay." She nodded again. As she headed up toward her room, she ran into the housekeeper on the stairs.

"Mrs. Hadley," she said.

The older woman shook her head. "What a disgrace," she muttered before heading to the main floor.

Trying not to let those hateful words affect her, Izzy dragged herself tiredly up the rest of the stairs. She opened the door to her room, but froze when she looked around. All of her things were missing. She walked over to her closest and found it empty of her clothes. Hurrying over the bathroom, she flipped on the light and saw that all of her makeup and moisturizers were missing off the counter.

"I had Mrs. Hadley move your things," Zan said from

the doorway. Izzy swung around to look at him with startled eyes.

She pressed a hand to her racing heart as she asked, "Why?"

"Well, " Zan said, "we're married now. It'd look weird if we didn't share a room, but if it makes you uncomfortable, you can move back into this room after Astrid and Arthur go home. They did indicate that they'd leave shortly after we married."

"Oh…" Izzy's stomach swirled in knots as she followed Zan to his room. Like the library, this was his sacred space, and one she dared not enter, other than that time she helped him when he was intoxicated. She entered the room now, pausing when she felt the thick carpet under her feet.

Zan went to one of the doors in the room and opened it. "Here's where you can find your clothes and shoes. All the drawers in the bathroom that are next to the right sink are also yours now, but feel free to reorganize the room however you want."

"Thanks," she murmured, knowing there was no point, because as soon as his former in-laws were gone, she'd be moving her stuff right back to her room.

"I'm going to take a quick shower while you get yourself situated, all right?" Zan asked.

"Sure," she replied, feeling suddenly nervous as he went into the bathroom.

On the other side of that door was a naked Zan Chen. She tore her eyes away from the wood barrier to take in the room again. Her gaze settled on the large picture of Mary and Zan above the bed. She stared at Mary's beautiful face, feeling like an intruder in another woman's bedroom.

Shaking off that feeling, Izzy walked into the ginormous closet. There were racks of clothes and floor-to-ceiling shelves for shoes. She walked over to a drawer in the wall and pulled it open, quickly shutting it when she saw a pair of Zan's black underwear. Going to the opposite side of the closest, she opened a matching drawer, and found her underwear and pajamas. She pulled out the most suitable thing she could, a red silk nightgown with thin straps. It was either that or one of her cami tops and boxers. She had a tendency to wear lingerie when she slept. It made her feel sexy. She never expected to have to wear it in front of Zan.

She grabbed the nightgown and some matching lacy underwear and went back into the bedroom. Her eyes automatically drifted to the picture above the bed. Izzy ached at the pure happiness on both Zan and Mary's faces.

The bathroom door opened and Zan came back into the room wearing nothing but a pair of navy blue boxers. His sculpted chest was on full display, his skin still gleaming from the shower.

"I'm, uh, I'm going to take a shower, too," she announced, hurrying by him to get into the bathroom. She shut the door before leaning against the bathroom counter. "Get a grip," she muttered.

Izzy tried to undo the zipper of her dress, but it was square in the middle of her shoulder blades, and no amount of squirming would help her get the zipper down. Briefly closing her eyes in defeat, she went back into the bedroom.

Zan was already in bed, scrolling on his tablet.

"Could you help me with this?" she said, waving at her dress.

"Sure," he said, putting the device to the side.

Izzy walked over to the side of the bed and turned away from him. She felt his fingers brush against her skin and tried not to moan. The feel of the zipper slowly coming down had her grasping for her bodice.

"There, it's down," Zan said. Before she could thank him, he pressed his lips against the newly revealed skin. Her breath caught and she turned her head so she could look at him with a raised eyebrow.

"You really did look beautiful today," Zan said before reaching for his tablet again.

"Um, thanks," Izzy replied as she tried to gather her wits.

With her heart pounding loudly in her ears, she walked into the bathroom, and shut the door quietly behind her.

Chapter Eighteen

For the first time in a long time, Zan felt inspired to write as he waited for Isabella to come out of the bathroom. He wasn't sure what finally managed to break him of his writer's block. Maybe it was because Astrid and Arthur had said they'd be leaving soon and they'd stopped bringing up taking the kids away—though he didn't trust Astrid to suddenly grow a conscience. Or maybe it was because for the first time in a long time, he felt a spark of life again.

Whatever the reason, he wasn't going to look a gift horse in the mouth. He felt energy flow through him as he tapped in some notes for an idea he wanted to explore later. He heard Isabella moving around in the bathroom, but Zan avoided looking in that direction.

He hadn't meant to kiss her earlier when he'd helped her undo her dress. But when he'd revealed that tempting skin of hers, he hadn't been able to stop himself. Zan had always thought Isabella was beautiful, even when he hadn't wanted to. But when he saw her walking down the aisle, she'd taken his breath away. She made him want things that he shouldn't. He'd told her that they could have any type of marriage she desired. He couldn't go back on his word now that he suddenly realized he wanted his wife.

His wife.

He waited for the guilt that always happened whenever he thought of any woman but Mary. Except it didn't come. The sadness was there. Of course, it was. He knew he'd always feel sadness over her death. But…*could* he move on?

He forced himself to focus on his work, latching on to the familiar adrenaline he always got when he wrote. He missed being able to create. His ability to tell a story was a part of his soul, and he'd thought the grief had destroyed something that was such an essential part of him. Having it return was like having a pet come back years after it had gone missing.

He heard the bathroom door creak open and he muttered, "Let me finish this thought I have for a story, and then I'll hit my light."

"Sure, don't worry about me."

Out of the corner of his eye, he saw a vision in red and glanced over in spite of himself. Zan stilled when he saw what Isabella was wearing—some sexy red number that fell down to her creamy thighs. He forced himself to remember that he'd left the ball in her court when it came to anything sexual, and he would respect that. Even if it killed him.

Isabella stood hesitantly beside the bed and he nodded at the spot next to him. She grabbed the covers and slid under them, her orange-blossom scent drifting over to him. He fought back the urge to throw his tablet across the room so he could grab her and bury his nose against the spot where that delicious smell was strongest. Her neck? Her hair? Maybe somewhere else?

He groaned at the thought, but quickly covered it with a fake cough.

Isabella glanced at him in concern. "Are you okay?"

While she was in the bathroom, she must have put on some type of lip balm, because her mouth *glistened.* Zan was horrified for three seconds that he might give in to temptation after all. Gripping the tablet harder, he jumped out of bed. "You know what? I really want to get this plot idea down before I forget. Don't wait up for me."

He ran out of the room like the bed had suddenly caught fire. As he went down the hall toward the library, he passed the kids' study. He paused when he saw sketches and paintings that were far too sophisticated for the children, though their own drawings were scattered around the room as well. His emotions warmed when he saw Alice's artwork. She'd painted their house in warm, bright colors—a reflection of her recent happiness, perhaps? There were even a couple that Xander must have done at some point.

The kids were doing so much better in the short time that Isabella had been with them. Alice was starting to smile more, reminding him of the bubbly girl she'd been before Mary died. And while Xander still had anger in him, he wasn't getting in trouble at school like he had been.

Things weren't perfect. Life never was. But they were improving. Thanks to Isabella.

He carefully picked up one of the larger paintings to take a closer look at it. Isabella had painted a single yellow rose from his garden, surrounded by a storm of green and blue swirls. The detail was incredible, but it was the emotion of the piece that struck him. Loneliness surrounded by chaos…yet there was a peace to it as well. The rose stood strong despite everything around it trying to tear it down. For some reason, the flower reminded him of his wife. Proud, living in pandemonium, but still going strong. He wondered if Isabella had painted it as a deliberate reflection on her life, or if her mind had created it subconsciously.

Regardless, it was incredible work.

He knew she was talented, but this was on another level.

Up close, it was just a bunch of thick lines of paint, confusing and nonsensical. It was when he took a step back that he could see the full picture.

Zan reluctantly put back the artwork and headed to his library. He already had one surprise in store for Isabella, but a new idea had formed in his head.

Going into his office, he called the one Holiday Boy who hadn't been able to make it to his wedding on such short notice.

Zan tapped his fingers impatiently on his desk as he waited for his friend to answer.

"Hello?" James said, sounding exhausted.

"Oh, hell," Zan said, rubbing at his face. "Did I wake you up?"

"It's all good, I was working pretty late. I just got home," James explained. "Can I say again how sorry I was to miss the wedding? I would have been there if I could."

James had built quite a reputation over the years for his renovations. While he normally liked to focus on homes in Detroit, he'd been offered an opportunity to restore a property that had once belonged to one of the country's first presidents. The museum who hired him was under a tight deadline and James hadn't been able to get away for the weekend.

"Don't worry about it, and I won't take too much of your time," Zan promised. "But there's something I wanted to talk to you about. I have an idea..."

Izzy felt completely humiliated the next morning. She hadn't seen Zan since he'd run out of his—their—bedroom the night before. Had he been so horrified at the idea of sharing a bed with her that he'd chosen to sleep somewhere else?

She had half a mind to remind him that it had been his idea in the first place for her to move into his room. She was perfectly happy to return to her original bedroom, thank you very much.

Izzy went into the bathroom to get ready for her day. She pulled on a sweatshirt and jeans after her shower, not bothering with makeup. What was the point? It wasn't like her husband was attracted to her. Going downstairs, she could hear Zan speaking with Mrs. Hadley.

"So what now?" the older woman said. "Am I to be housekeeper *and* nanny? This house is simply too big for one person to do both roles."

"I'm not asking you to," Zan said. "My parents will watch the children this morning. Isabella and I are going to enjoy a day to ourselves. It is our honeymoon, after all."

Izzy's cheeks heated. Was it really a honeymoon when the groom couldn't stand to sleep in the same room as his wife?

"And what about the day after?" the housekeeper complained.

"Mrs. Hadley," Zan said in a cold tone that made Izzy shiver. "If this job is becoming too much for you, let me know. I've certainly appreciated your years of service and dedication, but as we've previously discussed, if you're ready to move on to another opportunity, let me know."

She sputtered, "I never said that! I'm simply trying to figure out the logistics of your new circumstances."

Izzy stepped into the room. "Nothing is going to change here. I'll continue looking after the children." When Zan started to open his mouth, she rushed to continue. "I enjoy spending time with them. Besides, we can't expect Mrs. Hadley to do two jobs."

The woman gave her a look of pure scorn behind Zan's

back. Izzy controlled her own expression, so as not to convey how exhausted she suddenly was by everything. She went over to the counter where the coffee was and prepared a cup. She was going to need whatever caffeine she could get today.

She became aware that Zan was staring at her, but when she returned his gaze, his eyes quickly shifted away.

Great. Now, he couldn't even look at her.

"We'll head out as soon as you're done with breakfast," Zan announced.

She remembered that he'd wanted to do something this morning. She assumed it had something to do with their wedding, or maybe he wanted to readdress how things were going to be moving forward in their marriage. Her stomach was starting to feel queasy. She just wanted to get this day over with. She wasn't especially eager to spend time with him after last night.

Zan's father, Bo, walked in. He looked surprised when he saw Zan and Izzy.

"Hey! I wasn't expecting to see you two," he said. "Didn't you say you were going out this morning? I thought you'd be gone by now."

"We were just leaving," Zan explained.

Bo chuckled. "Your mom and sister have all kinds of plans for the kids. You might want to escape while you can, before you get suckered into wherever they're taking them."

"I'm sure Mr. and Mrs. Westwood will also be happy to lend a hand," Mrs. Hadley said, speaking up in favor of Astrid and Arthur.

"They're welcome to join us," Bo said, though his face went tight.

"They've had plenty of time to visit with the kids," Zan said. "If they want to join you, great. Otherwise, I'm sure they'll be busy packing their bags." He turned to Izzy. "And on that note, I think we should take my dad's advice and get out of here while we can."

"Sure," Izzy replied, then downed the rest of her coffee.

Once they were in the car and driving toward Holiday Bay, Zan asked, "Are you okay? You look a little pale. Did you sleep all right?"

"Yeah, I'm fine. It's just going to take me a minute to get used to the new environment." she replied. She wasn't about to confess that she'd slept like crap with his first wife's picture staring down at her all night while her mind raced, wondering where Zan had disappeared to. Curiosity getting the better of her, she asked, "What about you? Where'd you sleep?"

He gave her a somewhat sheepish grin. "I fell asleep at my desk. I started writing again last night."

He looked at her excitedly and she tried to ignore how the sight of his animated face made her mood lighten.

"That's great to hear," she murmured.

"It's not just great. It's a damn miracle. I haven't been able to write like that in years. I was so into my work, I didn't realize my eyes were starting to burn. I leaned back in my chair for just a moment. Next thing I knew, the sun was streaming through the window and I had a crick in my neck."

She smiled despite herself. "Next time you feel inspiration hit, let me know and I'll bring you a pillow for your desk."

"Deal," he said, his smile so wide that dimples popped on his cheeks.

He was so unfairly attractive.

Izzy tried to pull her mind away from that thought. "Where are we going this early, anyway?"

"I have a surprise for you," he said with that charm she loved. "You'll have to be patient."

"That's goes against my very nature. I don't know what the word *patient* means," she grumbled and he laughed.

But his ease seemed to lessen the closer they got to the heart of town. In fact, he seemed to be growing nervous about something. She was about to ask him what was going on when they finally parked. Izzy looked around in confusion.

"What are we doing here?" she asked as she looked at the old bank.

"You said you wanted to turn the building into an art gallery, so I bought it for you."

Izzy's head swiveled so fast her neck cracked. "You did *what*?"

"It's my wedding present to you."

"I—I don't know what to say," Izzy stammered.

Zan shrugged. "You can always say thanks, though you might want to hold off until you see the interior first."

He opened the car door and rushed over to her side so he could get hers as well. He leaned down and offered his hand, which she took, still too stunned by the morning's events to do anything but stumble after him.

He pulled out an old-fashioned key from his pocket and handed it to her. She stared at it like it had transformed into a bug.

"I can't accept this," Izzy said. "It's too much."

"Of course, you can," Zan insisted. "And like I told you before, if you don't want to accept me giving it to you as a gift…though you're my wife now. You're going to have to get used to—"

"Get used to you buying me buildings?"

Zan lifted his eyebrows. "That and whatever else you desire."

Izzy tried not to respond to that infectious look. "But—"

"Isabella." Zan cupped her cheek in his hand, instantly shutting her up. "I want to do this for you, whether you want to look at it as a gift or a loan. Please let me."

The seriousness in his eyes finally swayed her. She nodded and put the key in the keyhole, silently promising that she'd pay him back every penny someday.

They entered the large entry hall. Cobwebs hung from the ceiling, which was stained yellow with age. Dust and debris covered the dated decor. Somewhere in the distance it sounded like water was dripping, and the entire building smelled like a musty basement. But through the grime, Izzy could see the gorgeous woodwork she remembered from coming here as a kid, and the eighteenth-century floor tiles.

Zan gave her a strained smile. "I—I didn't realize the place was in such poor condition. Maybe we should look into different properties."

"Different?" she whispered. "This is perfect."

He relaxed slightly at her awe. "It's going to take a lot of work."

She nodded absently, already picturing how she wanted to do the lighting. "I'll pay you back, I swear."

He walked over to her and wrapped an arm around her waist. "I'm not concerned about that. Besides, I know a guy who can not only renovate this place to look exactly like your dream, but we can do it for little to no cost."

Izzy frowned. "What? This place is going to cost a fortune to fix."

"You know James Dallas?"

She nodded. "Of course. He's your bandmate."

"Do you know he also does renovations?"

She nodded. “I heard that.”

“I spoke with James last night and he said he could help with the project. And then I called Paul. A few years ago, Paul wanted to collaborate with James to do a renovation show in Detroit, but that fell through due to some personal issues on James’s end. Paul’s been trying to get him to commit to a new show ever since. So…that’s what they’re going to do. The renovation will be the premise for their new show. You’ll have three Holiday Boys involved in the project. Sponsors are already begging to be a part of it. It’ll also be a great way to boost the local economy.”

“Three Holiday Boys?” she asked.

Zan’s lips tugged into a small smile. “James, Paul, and myself. Though I’ll probably be there more as moral support.”

She stared at him in disbelief, then shook her head. “I can’t believe you arranged all this for me.”

“I wanted to,” he said softly.

“Thank you.” She looked around for the stairway, which had to be somewhere, considering the building was two floors, but there was a long wood divider running through the room that used to separate bank customers from employees. If the staircase was there, it was hidden. “Any idea where the stairs are?”

“No,” Zan replied as he started to walk toward the back of the building.

“I’ve always wanted to see what the second floor looked like. I hope it has the layout I have in mind for my apartment.”

Zan looked at her questioningly. “Your apartment?”

“Yeah,” she said before letting out a triumph sound when she opened a door hidden from the general public. Behind it was the set of stairs she was looking for. “I’m going to need somewhere to live after we eventually go our separate ways."

Izzy was so busy exploring her new space that she missed the way Zan's face suddenly darkened.

She swung around and hugged him. "Thank you. You've just made my dreams come true."

She let go and was halfway up the stairs when she thought she heard him, as he said, "Don't mention it."

Chapter Nineteen

Zan parked in front of the former dancehall that Paul had bought to use as a studio. After he'd purchased it, he'd told Zan that the place was convenient for filming *First Comes Marriage*, because it was in the center of town, but everyone knew he bought it because it was right down the road from Kyleigh's store. The sap.

Zan walked in and looked around, taking in the updated mocha-brown floors and baby-blue walls. Mounted on the pristine white ceiling was an industrial metal dome light that cast the room in a soft white glow. A large abstract painting of browns and blues was positioned on the wall behind the receptionist. Sitting behind the desk was a twentysomething blond man who looked like he thought he was too good to be there.

Zan walked up to him. "Hi, is Paul in?

The man, whose nameplate announced that his name was Chaz, looked up from his laptop in annoyance before his eyes widened.

"I… Mr. Chen, Mr. Rodriguez is in a meeting right now, but it should be wrapping up soon if you'd like to have a seat."

Zan nodded and sat on a brown leather couch that faced the wall opposite the main entrance. There were two doors on either side of another large painting. As he stared at the artwork, he couldn't help but feel it lacked something compared to Isabella's work. It didn't have that spark of life that made Zan want to take a closer look, so that he could try to get a glimpse into the artist's soul.

"Mr. Rodriguez can see you now," Chaz said a few minutes later.

"Thanks," Zan said, getting up and heading through the door on the left. He passed several rooms that he knew from a previous tour had been converted into studios. When he reached Paul's office, he could hear Paul and his business partner, Shawnee, speaking, so he knocked on the door.

"Come in," Paul called out.

Zan entered the office. This room was similar to the front lobby with its mocha-brown tiles, but the walls were sea-green instead of blue. Paul sat behind a massive dark-chocolate-colored desk that had a couple of pictures sitting on top of it. One was of Paul and Kyleigh's wedding day, and the other was a recent picture of Paul, Kyleigh, and Paul's stepdaughter, Holly.

"We were just talking about you," Paul said as soon as he saw Zan.

"Oh?" Zan said, sitting in the chair next to Shawnee.

"We're bringing *First Comes Marriage* back to Holiday Bay for our next season," Shawnee explained, "but we're trying to figure out the logistics. James has a small window where he can work on the art gallery, but that'll leave us filming two shows at the same time…"

"Which I told you we'll figure out," Paul said to his partner before explaining to Zan, "She doesn't think we have the capacity to film two shows."

Shawnee threw up her hands. "You know how many resources *First Comes Marriage* takes." Dragging her fingers through her short hair, she asked Zan, "Have you been inside the bank yet? How bad is it?"

Zan sighed wearily. "On a scale of one to ten? The building should be condemned."

"Awesome," Shawnee said, getting up from her chair. "I'll ask Chaz to update our calendars so we can get over there later and get an idea of what we're dealing with. We'll need James to join us virtually."

She walked out of the office muttering to herself.

Paul snorted as he watched her go. "Don't worry. Shawnee loves nothing more than to freak out over the littlest details. We'll get the building in tiptop shape for Izzy. Even if it's not part of the show. Consider it my wedding present to you."

"Thanks," Zan replied, not really hearing Paul as he thought about his exchange with his wife the day before.

"Something else on your mind?" Paul asked as he stared at his best friend. "You seem distracted."

"I..." Zan jumped up from the chair and started to pace around the office. "When I showed Isabella the building, she immediately started looking for the upstairs. She wants to convert it into an apartment for herself."

Paul's head tilted. "Is that a bad thing? You told me yourself that you only married her to get Astrid off your back. It sounds like Izzy's thinking about her future. It's smart."

"That's not the only reason," Zan said, feeling defensive for no reason. "I did it for the kids, too. They've been doing so much better since Isabella entered our lives. Alice is finally improving in school, and Xander is socializing more. I haven't received any concerned calls or emails from the principal in weeks."

But that wasn't the real reason he was upset. When Isabella mentioned moving away from him, something had settled inside him, making him feel restless. She hadn't just brought life back to his kids—he felt more alive when she was around. He loved the way they co-parented. He loved walking into the room she was in and smelling that addictive scent of hers. He loved how her features took on a dreamlike aura whenever she painted. He wondered if he looked the same way when he was writing, because ever since she'd become his wife, his creativity had burst wide open.

He loved…lots of things.

When he turned back to face Paul, his friend wore a smug smile on his face.

"What?" Zan snapped.

Paul's smile drifted away as his expression turned serious. "It's okay, you know."

"I don't know what you're talking about."

"You do, but I'll spell it out for you, anyway," he responded. "You're allowed to love again."

"I'm not in love with Isabella," Zan said shortly, though something inside him protested angrily at that declaration.

Paul leaned back in his chair. "You know I loved Mary. Spending time with you, her, and the kids were some of the best times of my life. So I feel like I can speak freely when I say, Mary wouldn't want you to grow old, alone and miserable. She'd want you to be happy. There's nothing wrong with you finding love again."

Zan stilled as he processed that statement. He finally stopped pacing only to collapse back in his chair. "I don't know what to do. I've treated Isabella like an employee ever since she started with us. I bribed her into marriage. She won't believe me if I suddenly tell her that I have feelings for her. Hell, I even assured her that I would never fall in love with her so she'd agree to marry me."

Paul slapped his palm on his forehead. "Have you always had so little game? Why in the world would you ever say that to someone, least of all someone as perfect for you as Izzy?"

"I thought it would reassure her. I wanted to marry her. I figured that if she didn't feel pressured, she'd say yes sooner." Zan ran a hand through his hair. "Stop judging and help me!"

Paul smiled again, and this time his expression was devilish, putting Zan instantly on alert.

"Don't worry," Paul said. "Here's what you're going to do. Trust me..."

Izzy had an idea for Julie's mural, but she wanted to find the reference she was looking for first. Hesitantly, she knocked on Zan's library door as a courtesy, but he wasn't there. He'd gone out to run errands before she even got up that morning, which left her feeling like an unwelcome bed partner again. Ever since they'd gotten married, he had either avoided sleeping in the same bed as her, or he was gone before she'd awakened, like he couldn't stand sleeping next to her for any longer than he needed to. It had been going on like this for a week now.

After a slight hesitation, she entered Zan's sacred space. She glanced at Mary's picture, taking in the perfection of the woman before turning to head over to one of the bookshelves. She thought she'd seen an old almanac there on one of the very few times she'd been in the room, and she wanted to get some inspiration from the cover. She'd just located the book when she heard the sound of someone clearing their throat. Swinging around, Izzy found Zan leaning in the doorframe.

"Oh!" Heat pooled her cheeks. "I'm so sorry, I know I shouldn't be in here—"

Zan's eyebrows snapped together. "You're my wife. Like I told you before, *mi casa es su casa.* You can come in here anytime you like."

"I was just looking for this almanac," she explained, pulling out the book. "I'll leave you alone."

"Isabella, wait," he said, grabbing her arm lightly as she started to brush by him. "Where are the kids?"

"Your parents and sister took them to the bay for the day. They wanted to spend a little more time with them since they're leaving tomorrow. I told your mom we could take them to the airport, but I should have run it by you first."

Zan frowned. "Why?"

"I shouldn't be making plans for us, and I should be watching the kids."

Zan still hadn't let go of her arm. His delightful cedarwood scent surrounded her.

"It's fine. You're their stepmom. You don't have to run those decisions by me. You're not their nanny anymore." He leaned closer to her and her heart started palpitating. "And again—" his breath whispered against her hair "—you are my wife now. We're a unit. You're more than welcome to make plans for us."

He gave her a half smile that did crazy things to her, then he let her go. And the way he said *us*. Was he…*flirting* with her?

Zan walked over to his desk and started rifling through some sticky notes he had placed there. "Speaking of plans, what are you doing tonight?"

"Other than the usual? Nothing." She'd planned on getting to know both sets of grandparents, since Astrid and Arthur still hadn't taken the hint and left. They were currently in town doing who knows what. But while they were still hanging around, she needed to convince them that they could trust the children with her so that they'd get off Zan's back. That was why he'd married her, and it was important that she didn't forget that.

"I want to take you on a date tonight," he said. Her eyes flew to his. She would have been less shocked if he'd announced he was becoming the pope.

"Why?" she asked.

He cocked his head as he looked at her. "Shouldn't I want to take my brand-new wife out on a date?"

Oh, right. It'd certainly help with their image as a couple in love.

"Okay, where are we going?"

He quirked his lips. "It's a surprise. But a dress would be appropriate."

She slowly nodded. "All right. It's a date."

And with her agreement, he sat down at his desk and opened his laptop without any further acknowledgement, causing Izzy to wonder what just happened.

Chapter Twenty

Izzy put the finishing touches on her makeup as Alice watched.

The little girl sighed dreamily. “You’re so pretty.”

Izzy dropped the small tube of lipstick in her bag and grinned at her stepdaughter. “You’re the one that’s pretty, but thank you.”

“Can I have some makeup?” Alice asked eagerly.

Izzy looked around her counter, then grabbed some blue eye shadow and putting the tiniest bit on her eyelids.

“Gorgeous!” she said as she leaned back.

Alice looked at herself in the mirror, blinking several times before she wrapped her arms around Izzy.

“I’m so glad Dad married you,” she said, causing a lump to form in Izzy’s throat. “I love you.”

“I love you, too,” she replied, squeezing the little girl to her. “Now, enough of this. I’ve got a date with your dad to get to.”

She tried not to show how excited she was as she ran a critical eye over her reflection. She’d worn a dark blue dress that had tiny cherries all over it. It had a scooped neckline that gave the smallest glimpse of her cleavage. She’d paired it with a white sweater and comfortable red flats. Her hair was piled into curls on top of her head.

"Well, I guess I'm ready," she announced, feeling suddenly nervous.

Alice took her hand and led her down to the kitchen, where Zan was waiting with his and Mary's families.

Astrid looked immediately disgruntled. "Alice, what is that on your eyes?"

"Blue eye shadow. Isn't it pretty?" she asked.

The older woman's mouth twisted downward as she looked at Izzy. "Don't you think she's a little young for makeup?"

"I think you look awesome, Alice," Mei said from where she sat at the kitchen table with her parents, Arthur, and Xander. It looked like they had an intense game of Uno going on.

Zan bent down and picked up his daughter, swinging her around until her smile came back, which had disappeared under her grandmother's criticism.

"You look amazing, sweetheart," he said, kissing her forehead. She threw her arms around his neck. Izzy wondered when they'd last had a relaxing moment together like this.

He put down Alice and she raced to join her family at the kitchen table. Zan turned to face Izzy, but halted as he looked at her, his gaze going over the curves of her body in a way that made her feel self-conscious.

"You said to dress up," she said, lifting her chin.

"You look beautiful," he rasped.

Izzy flushed as she returned his appraisal. Zan was wearing black pants with a matching dinner jacket. He had a white button-up underneath it that was open at the collar. He looked so ridiculously sexy. It was unbelievable that he was her husband.

"You ready?" he asked and she nodded.

"Don't stay out too late," Mei teased and he waved her off.

"We'll see everyone later," he told them as he walked over to Izzy. He put his hand on her lower back in a way that was becoming familiar as he guided her outside.

As he drove toward town, she asked, "Are you going to tell me where we're going?"

"Nope," he teased. "I've got a whole night planned for us. This night is about you and me."

She tried not to react at the implication that seemed to be in his words. She knew he didn't mean anything by it. Not when she slept under Mary's picture every night.

When they pulled into the parking lot of a familiar restaurant, her stomach turned with sudden dread.

"What are we doing here?" she asked, staring at Florentina's.

"It's the best fine dining in town," he said as he parked the car.

"It's the *only* fine dining in town," she muttered.

Zan laughed as he got out of the car. He walked over to her side and opened her door, but when he held out his hand to help her out, she didn't move.

"What is it?" he asked.

"I don't want to eat here," she said, not meeting his eyes. She was still too furious at her family for not coming to her wedding, and she had no desire to speak to them now.

He crouched down beside her. "Why not? Because of the wedding?"

"That...among other things. They don't approve of anything I'm doing right now. Not my marriage, not leaving the business, not my wish to start my gallery. Nothing."

"They're your *family*," Zan said with emphasis. "I don't want to be the reason that there's a divide between all of you."

"Trust me, there was a divide before you ever entered the picture." She sighed, though, knowing he was right. In a town as small as Holiday Bay, she was bound to run into her family at some point. She'd been isolating herself over the past few months, either staying at Zan's or hanging out at her friends' homes. She couldn't keep going like this, so she reluctantly got out of the car. Zan clasped her hand, giving it a reassuring squeeze.

"If things start to get ugly," Zan said as he leaned down so his lips brushed her hair, "I'll find the nearest plate of spaghetti and drop it in your nearest family member's lap."

She groaned as they entered the restaurant. "You're never going to let me live that down, are you?"

"Nope." He grinned. She tried not to stare at that mesmerizing smile of his as they approached her old familiar hostess stand.

"Izzy!" Luca said.

"Hi, Luca," she said, hugging him before turning back to her husband. "Zan, I think you met Luca at our last Sunday dinner, but this is my nephew."

Luca and Zan shook hands, Luca giving him a mock glare. "You better take care of my aunt or else."

Zan looked very serious as he said, "I plan on it."

"I wanted to come to the wedding," Luca explained, excitement all over the eighteen-year-old's face. "But I was touring St. Ignace College."

"And?" Izzy asked.

"It's definitely a contender," he replied and she beamed proudly.

"I'm so excited for you," she said.

"Thanks!" Luca said, then he shouted over his shoulder, "Ma!"

Izzy grimaced. As hostess, she was nothing but professional, but she was on Luca's turf now. He could present himself any way he wanted in front of customers.

As they waited, Izzy felt the niggling signs of one of her migraines. She moved her neck, trying to relieve some tension. She was about to ask why her sister-in-law was at Florentina's when the woman herself walked into the lobby.

Tonya smiled when she saw them. "Izzy!"

Izzy gave her a puzzled look. "What are you doing here?"

"Paige went into labor, so I told Antonio that I'd help out."

Izzy bit her lip. She and the restaurant's longtime waitress had worked together for years. "Is Paige okay? She wasn't due until next month."

"Yeah," Tonya assured her. "She had a healthy little boy. And speaking of little boys, have you spoken to my man-baby of a husband lately?"

"No." Izzy did her best of keep her expression impassive. "Not since we told everyone we were getting married."

Tonya's arms folded over her chest. "Luca, go see if our best table is ready for our honored guests. I have to go speak to my husband. I'll be right back," she said to Zan and Izzy.

A few seconds later, they heard from the back office, "Ow, Tonya, let go!"

Tonya returned to the lobby, firmly holding Antonio's ear in a tight grasp.

"Look who's joined us today," Tonya announced, finally letting her husband go.

Antonio rubbed at his ear before he said formally, "Welcome to Florentina's."

When Tonya reached for his ear again, Antonio held up his hands in defeat. "Fine!" Putting on his best face, he said to Izzy and Zan, "I'm sorry I didn't attend the wedding. Even though we had a bar mitzvah that day, and with your wedding being last-minute, we weren't able to cancel our event—" He rushed out the words, taking a wary step back from his ticked-off wife. "We should have still found a way to make it work so that we were all there for you."

"It's fine," Izzy said, feeling slightly better about the situation, thanks to Tonya's defense.

"It's not fine," Tonya said, before hugging Izzy and patting Zan on the arm. "I'm so sorry this bonehead put business before family. To make up for your brother's bull-headedness, dinner is on the house." When Antonio opened his mouth to protest, Tonya added, "In fact, you can have a lifetime of free meals."

"Oh, come on—" Antonio protested.

"For both of you," she added to include Zan in that offer.

Zan's lips quirked upward. "Thank you."

Antonio kept his mouth closed, so as to not get himself in more trouble.

"Luca," Tonya said as her son returned, "make sure our guests are comped for their meals."

Luca snorted at the outrage on his dad's face, knowing that Antonio wouldn't go against his wife. He grabbed two menus and said, "Follow me, please."

Zan grabbed her hand again as they went to their table. It had always been Izzy's favorite spot, since it overlooked Holiday Bay.

They soon ordered and began talking about the gallery's future. Izzy's tension loosened even further as Gio, Dante, and Enzo came out to awkwardly apologize for not coming to their wedding.

"You know how business gets," Enzo explained.

Zan had been quiet throughout most of the exchanges with her family, but he finally spoke up. "Is that any excuse to miss your only sister's wedding?"

And that was when Izzy realized that Zan was furious as he stared her brothers down.

"I apologize for not giving everyone enough notice, but that was on me, not Izzy," he said. "Had anyone in this family approached me about the situation, I could have compensated the restaurant for the previously scheduled event and found an alternative venue for the other family to have their bar mitzvah. I was too impatient to make Isabella my wife, and again, that's on me. But that doesn't give you all an excuse to miss your sister's wedding."

"You're right," Gio said. "But like you said, you gave us a week's notice and we didn't know there were alternative options."

"It's still no excuse," Dante said. "We should have been there for you, Iz, and we're sorry."

She couldn't say it was okay, but she did understand where Gio was coming from. Saturdays were their busiest nights, even without a scheduled event, and they hadn't given them much time. It still would have been nice to see at least one of them there.

She got up and hugged each of her brothers. When she reached Dante, he whispered in her ear, "I like him."

After they left, she sat back down. Zan's hand was resting on the table and she reached across the table to squeeze it. "Thank you."

He flipped his hand over so that their palms touched.

He smiled that special smile that drove her crazy and said, "You're welcome. Do you have any other family members working here that I need to guilt-trip?"

Izzy laughed, letting him go so she could lean back in her chair. "Not that I'm aware of, but I'll let you know."

There was only her father she had to deal with, but she'd save that battle for another day.

Chapter Twenty-One

After they finished their dinner, they headed outside, but were stopped by a couple of Holiday Boys fans who approached them excitedly when they saw Zan.

"She was always Team Jake," one said as she nodded to her curly-haired friend. "But you were always my favorite. I had *so* many T-shirts with your face plastered on them."

"Thank you, I appreciate it," Zan said, keeping Izzy within arm's reach.

"What are you doing in Michigan?" the fan asked curiously. "Visiting the other guys?"

"Among other things." He didn't mention that he lived in the area now.

"When are you going to release your next book?" the other fan asked. "You left the last one on a cliffhanger. It's been years."

Her friend elbowed her. "He lost his wife, show some respect."

"I've actually started working on the next book, but don't tell anyone," Zan said in a conspiratorial way that charmed both fans.

Izzy would have admired how they both stayed so composed, when she could tell they both wanted to freak out, but the ache in her head was turning into a persistent pain.

She cursed herself for not grabbing her migraine medication. She tried to discreetly move her head from side to side to relieve some tension, but it only made the nagging pain worse.

"If you'll excuse us, ladies," Zan finally said. He put his arm around Izzy's waist and pulled her toward the car. She was pretty sure the fans were taking pictures of them, but she didn't want to know if her backside would be plastered all over social media tomorrow. Not when her brain felt like it was about to pound its way out of her head.

"Where to next?" Izzy asked, hoping he would take them home.

"I wanted to show you around Clarington." Zan gave her a half smile and turned the car in that direction.

"What's in Clarington?"

"My roots," he replied. "I want to show you where I grew up."

They drove with only soft music on the radio playing as they headed toward the neighboring town. When they reached the center of the city, Zan whistled softly, which made Izzy wince, though thankfully, he wasn't looking at her. He was staring at the side of the high school, which had a huge mural of Zan and Paul on the side of it.

"Your work?" he asked.

"No." Izzy laughed despite her pain. "I guess you're hometown heroes."

"Yeah, I guess so," Zan replied, a trace of embarrassment in his voice. "Paul told me the mural was there, but I didn't realize it took almost the entire side of the building."

He turned right at the light. City buildings turned into family homes the farther they drove into the suburbs. Zan parked in front of a large, two-story Colonial. It was half-brick, half-beige siding with a large bay window in front.

"This was my childhood home," Zan explained.

"It's lovely," Izzy said. "Did you have a happy childhood?"

"For the most part. It was honestly pretty average. My mom was the high-school principal. My dad was a pharmacist. They both had big dreams of Mei and I going off to the University of Michigan to pursue medicine. Mei did what was expected, though she was happy to make the choices that she did. She loves being a doctor."

"And you?" Izzy said, rolling her head against the seat's headrest, the movement making her slightly dizzy.

"I always wanted to pursue something that would allow me to explore my creative side. My parents were angry when I joined Holiday Boys. I think they could have lived with my decision better if I'd gone off to Juilliard or done something respectable like that first, instead of joining a boy band right out of high school."

"Did they eventually accept it?" she asked. She hadn't noticed any tension between Zan and his family.

"Yeah," he said with a sexy smirk. "Once Holiday Boys topped the music charts and we became international stars."

"What made you decide to become an author?" she asked.

He copied her pose, leaning his head against the headrest so that he could look at her more comfortably. "I had a big publisher approach me on a talk show. By that time, James had left the band…though the general public didn't know it. He'd been struggling with severe stage fright and depression, thanks to the powers-that-be pressuring him to hide his sexuality. Jake—who's always been incredibly protective of his cousin—was the first to publicly leave Holiday Boys to pursue a solo career. He did it to protect James, but he took a lot of heat from the fans for that decision. Tyler, Paul, and I ended up doing a few talk shows to let the world know there were no hard feelings, and that we were ready to explore our own projects. The problem was, I had nothing to explore. That was when a publisher approached me and asked if I'd be interested in writing my autobiography. They thought being the first Chinese-American boy-band member to hit it big would make a good story. I told them no. I was only twenty-three at the time. I didn't think I had lived enough of my life yet to warrant a biography. But I did have a fictional story idea in my head that I'd been playing around with for years. I pitched it to them, and they said they wanted to see more. I locked myself away for six months and wrote my first book. The rest, you know."

"The rest being you became an equally famous author," she said, though she had to close her eyes. It was getting hard to focus, thanks to the pain in her head.

"Yeah, I..." Zan began, but stopped. She opened blurry eyes and saw that he was looking at her in concern. "Are you okay?"

"I..." She pressed a palm to her forehead. "I'm so sorry, but I think I need to go home. I'm getting one of my migraines."

"You should have told me," Zan gently scolded. He put the car in Drive and turned back toward Holiday Bay. "Do you get migraines often?"

"Not as much as I used to, thanks to a prescription I have, but I forgot to put extra pills in my purse tonight."

She sounded weak to her own ears. Thankfully, it wasn't too long before Zan pulled the car into the garage. She fumbled for the door handle, but he was already there, holding the door open for her. Izzy swayed when she stood up and he wrapped his arm around her so that he could direct her into the house. It was quiet when they entered, indicating that everyone was already in bed. He continued to lead her to their room. She flinched at the soft light of the bedroom lamp that had been left on. Zan steered her toward the bed and had her sit down.

"Where's your medication?" he asked.

"The top left drawer in the bathroom," she murmured, gesturing tiredly with her hand.

"Okay, I'll be right back."

Izzy kicked off her shoes and removed her sweater before fumbling with the buttons of her dress.

"Here," Zan said, moments later. He handed her the medicine and a glass of water. She gratefully swallowed it down, then tried to remove her dress again.

"Let me help you," he offered. She wanted to feel self-conscious about him seeing her in nothing but her bra and underwear, but in that moment, her head hurt too much to care. She didn't meet his eyes as he helped her remove the dress.

He threw it and the sweater on the chair nearby, before offering, "Let me grab your nightgown."

"Thanks."

He returned a short time later and drew the gown over her head. Before she could murmur a protest, he reached around her and unhooked her bra.

"Hey!" she said, quickly drawing her pj's over her chest.

"I figured you'd be more comfortable without it, but I can help you put it back on if you want." He sounded amused as he added, "I promise I'm not looking to cop a feel here, but you normally don't sleep with your bra on."

Izzy was starting to lose focus on the conversation. Maybe she should be offended about *something* in this situation, but she couldn't think of what. And how did he know she didn't sleep with a bra on? She didn't think he paid that close attention to her.

"No, it's fine," she muttered. She drew the nightgown down to her waist before sliding the straps of the bra down her arms, then pulled it the rest of the way off through the armhole of her gown.

He took it from her and threw it on the chair. "Can you stand up for a sec so I can pull the sheets down?"

Izzy did as instructed, which allowed the nightgown to fall down to her knees. Once she was lying on the bed, he pulled the sheets to her chin.

"Is there anything else I can do for you?" he asked.

"Something cold for my head would be great if you have it."

"Yeah, I think I can manage that."

Izzy thought she felt the soft touch of his lips on her forehead before he disappeared again. She stared at the ceiling before her eyes drifted to Mary's picture again. She was still looking at it when Zan came back into the room with an ice pack.

"I keep these on hand in case one of the kids gets injured," he explained, putting the gel pack against her forehead.

She sucked in a breath at the instant chill. It took her a few seconds to get used to the sudden coldness before she finally sank farther in the mattress in relief as the pain started to ease slightly.

"She was very beautiful," Izzy said.

"Who?" Zan asked absently as he sat beside her on the side of the bed. He got to work on loosening her hair and she groaned as his fingers threaded carefully through her locks.

"Mary," she murmured, looking at the picture once

more. "I've always wondered what it would be like to be that beautiful."

It was the last thing she said before sleep started to claim her. It was probably the pain that made her hallucinate Zan brushing a finger down her cheek.

But it was definitely her imagination that heard him as he whispered, "You *are* beautiful. And I'm going to make sure you know it."

Chapter Twenty-Two

Zan stepped out of the bathroom the next morning as quietly as he could. Isabella was still sleeping and he didn't want to disturb her. As he approached the bed, he noticed that the sheets had slipped down to her belly button. The gown she wore did little to hide the tantalizing curves of her breasts. Knowing that she wouldn't appreciate him ogling her in such a vulnerable state, Zan leaned down and pulled up the sheet so that it covered her. He paused as he looked at her sleeping face. A lock of thick hair had fallen across her face, partially covering it. He pushed it back, savoring the silky feel of her skin under his touch.

Isabella wasn't beautiful in the traditional sense. Her nose was slightly too big for her face, but it fit her features, and she had high, rounded cheekbones that stood out when she smiled. He thought back to their wedding day and that moment when he'd finally gotten to brush his mouth against those gorgeous full lips—like he'd been yearning to do for the weeks leading up to that day. He'd ached to feel them again ever since.

But the next time he kissed Isabella, he'd take his time learning that tempting mouth. Exploring it. To see if he could make her catch her breath as he tasted her tongue with his.

Zan jerked away from the bed. He was watching her sleep like some creepy stalker, not to mention, he was only up this early so that he could take his family to the airport. He didn't need to go downstairs with the very obvious desire he felt for his wife on full display. He exited the room, then headed down to the kitchen, where he heard his father say something and his sister tiredly respond.

As he entered the room, he saw the kids eating eggs and toast with his family, while Mrs. Hadley washed pans in the sink. Astrid and Arthur were nowhere to be seen, and Zan really hoped that meant they were getting ready to leave themselves.

"Where's Isabella?" his mom asked, looking behind him.

"She had a migraine last night so I thought she could use the extra rest."

Mei snickered. "Already getting headaches, and you haven't been married a week."

Zan gave his sister a dirty look. "Funny."

Alice looked between them, confusion clear on her face. "Why is that funny, Dad?"

"It's not," he replied, not about to have *that* conversation. Mei looked like she was going to go into convulsions as she tried not to laugh. It didn't matter that they were in their forties. Whenever they got together, it was like they reverted to being kids again.

His family went to their rooms to get their luggage, while the kids left to put on their shoes.

"Mrs. Hadley," Zan said as he pulled out his phone to check his email. "I'd like you to take the picture down that's behind my desk in the library. There's a beautiful painting in the kids' study of a yellow rose swirled in blue and green. I'd like that in its place. If you have any issues moving it, please see if Simon can help."

Mrs. Hadley looked like he asked her to shoot her best friend. "But…you want me to take Mrs. Chen's picture down?"

"That's the one," he said, thinking about the picture of Mary. His heart broke a little at losing it, but it was time to stop holding on so tightly to the past. Paul was right. Mary wouldn't want him to live the rest of his life in a state of mourning. "And the picture above my bed. You can move that one, too. Please use one of the other paintings available in the study. One that will fit the decor."

"And what am I supposed to do with Mrs. Chen's pictures?" she asked with a voice that sounded like she'd swallowed glass.

"You can put the one in my study in Alice's room," Zan said. "The other one can go in storage."

He rubbed at his chest as it twisted with long-remembered grief. The day he and Mary had taken the picture that currently resided in his bedroom had been one of the happiest of his life. The photo was one of sweet intimacy, showcasing the deep love they'd felt for each other. Afterward, they'd followed up their photo session with tender lovemaking. A few weeks later, Mary had been diagnosed with leukemia, and Zan's life became hell on earth as he'd watched his beloved wife wither away. He could still hear her sometimes, shut away in their bedroom, crying her pain into her pillow so that the kids wouldn't hear. He'd lost count of the number of times he'd stood outside their door, feeling helpless, knowing there was nothing he could do.

Zan shook his head to clear it of those morose thoughts. He'd moved to Michigan for a fresh start, to get his life back on track. That path now included Isabella, and it was thoughtless and cruel of him to expect her to see him as a real husband when he made her sleep under Mary's picture all the time.

"Please take care of the one in my study while I'm gone. Isabella's resting right now, so the other one can be removed once she gets up."

"Of course," the older woman said through locked teeth.

Zan murmured his thanks before running up to check on Isabella one more time, but she was still sleeping soundly. At least she didn't look as pale as she had the night before. He wrote her a quick note to explain that he'd taken his family to the airport, and then they piled into his Cadillac Escalade.

Once they arrived at their destination in Traverse City, Zan and the children walked with his family to Security and began saying their goodbyes.

"Come out and see us soon, okay?" Mei said as she hugged him.

"And bring your wife with you," his dad added as he gripped Zan's shoulder, pulling him to his side.

As the kids said goodbye to their grandpa and aunt, Zan turned to his mom.

"My boy," she said. As she embraced him, she murmured, "I haven't seen you smile this much in years. I'd lost hope of ever seeing you happy again. Isabella is good for you."

"Yeah, she is," Zan replied. His heart warmed, melting his earlier icy grief. Across the airport, he saw some fans taking their pictures, but his family was sadly used to the hoopla that came with being around him, and they ignored it.

As his mom pulled away, she patted his cheek. "Don't let her go."

"I don't plan on it," Zan assured her.

He watched them leave, feeling sad at their departure. He really had been living in a bubble the last few years, keeping himself distant, even from those who loved him most. He needed to make more of a concentrated effort not to push them away anymore.

"Hey," he said to Alice and Xander. "How about we get some brunch for Isabella and do something nice today?"

His children exchanged surprised glances.

"Together?" Xander asked.

"Yeah, of course," Zan replied.

"Yes!" Alice shouted, earning a frown from one of the security guards.

Zan grabbed her hand and the three of them left the terminal and piled back into the car. Once they reached Holiday Bay, they stopped by Franki's to get some breakfast pasties. Alice had to use the bathroom while they waited for their order, leaving Zan and Xander alone.

His son looked at him questioningly.

"What's on your mind?" Zan asked.

"Once Grandma Astrid and Grandpa Arthur leave, are you going to break up with Izzy?"

The idea of divorcing Isabella made Zan queasy.

"No," he answered. "At least… I don't want to."

Xander stiffened as he examined his father's features. He finally relaxed after a few seconds. "Good."

"You're okay with that?" Zan asked, somewhat surprised.

Xander scuffed his foot against the red tiled floor. "Even if I wasn't okay with it, you breaking up with Izzy won't bring Mom back. Besides, Izzy's really good at gaming."

A lump formed in Zan's throat. He reached out and ruffled Xander's hair.

"You're a good kid, you know that?"

Xander pushed his dad's hand away and muttered, "I'm not a kid."

But Zan could tell by the expression on his son's face that he was trying to fight back a smile.

Izzy woke up feeling better than she had in years. The crippling headache that she'd had the night before was gone. Her eyes fluttered to the alarm clock next to Zan's side of the bed and she staggered upright. It was almost noon.

It was then that she became aware of a couple of things. One, the dress she'd worn the day before was lying across the beige accent chair in the room, along with her bra. She didn't remember taking that off. She certainly never would have left her underwear out for Zan to see. And two…her mouth tasted like she'd been dining on garbage for the past week.

"Gross," Izzy mumbled. She took a quick glance down, relieved to see she was wearing a nightgown. After throwing the sheets back, she hurried into the closet to grab some pants and a blouse. She pulled some fresh undergarments out of the built-in dresser and then practically ran into the bathroom.

As she scrubbed her teeth, her brain tried to go back to what happened the night before. She remembered Zan taking her to Florentina's and her making peace with her brothers. She remembered the soft lull of the car as Zan drove them to Clarington, sharing little bits about himself that she'd never known before. And then she recalled how it felt like her head was going to explode and her world went blurry.

She was grateful that she felt so much better today. She hadn't had a migraine that bad in a long time. After taking a shower and getting dressed, she went back into the bedroom, noticing Zan's note for the first time. Guilt hit her as she realized she'd missed saying goodbye to her in-laws, but Zan mentioned in his note that he'd told them she'd been ill.

Glancing at the clock again, Izzy realized Zan had to be home from the airport by now. She wondered where he was. As she left their bedroom, she passed Mrs. Hadley on the stairs.

"Good morning," she said as politely as she could muster.

"It's not morning, it's afternoon, but I've seen to *your* stepchildren."

Izzy didn't miss the odd intonation in her voice. She didn't feel like dealing with Mrs. Hadley and her terrible attitude. She wondered what Zan would say if she brought up letting the older woman go. She knew that Mrs. Hadley had been with the family since before Mary was sick, but she was tired of her negativity all the time.

"Where are the kids?" Izzy asked.

"Xander is in his room playing on that awful device he loves. Alice is outside helping Simon in the garden. Mr. Chen is in his library."

He was most likely working, and as she didn't want to bother him if he was in the middle of writing, she decided to run an errand she needed to take care of.

"Will you tell Zan I've run out but I'll be back shortly?" she asked, already heading to where she'd left her sketchbook.

"Certainly," Mrs. Hadley said, before she muttered under her breath, "it's not like I have anything better to do."

Yeah, it was definitely time to speak with Zan about the woman.

A short time later, she pulled in front of Julie's store. As she entered, she found Meg holding a baby in one hand, while filming something in the other with a sly expression on her face. At her feet were two toddlers, a little girl with long red hair in pigtails and a handsome little boy with dark hair. They were playing with a large set of blocks and talking to each other in that baby language only little ones understood. Meg greeted her with a smile.

On the other side of the shop, Julie stood with her hands on her hips as she directed her and Meg's husbands to move a large, heavy-looking cabinet from one spot on the floor to the other.

"But do you think it takes up too much space in this spot?" Julie asked indecisively.

"For God's sake," Tyler groaned as he let go of the furniture to rub at his lower back.

Jake wiped at his sweaty forehead with the back of his hand. "Love, I think you'll make it look great wherever it goes."

"You're just saying that because you don't want to move it again," Julie said.

"You got that right," Tyler grumbled.

Jake waved off his best friend. "I'm saying it because it's true."

Julie walked over and kissed her husband's cheek before looking at the cabinet one more time. "Fine, it can stay here."

"Hallelujah," Tyler said, then turned to face his own wife. His eyes narrowed when he saw that she was filming them. "That better not get posted later."

Meg lifted an eyebrow as she shoved her phone in her pants pocket. "Or what?"

"Or..." Tyler walked over and whispered something in her ear. Izzy had no idea what it was, but Meg's face turned bright red.

She placed a hand on her husband's chest. "Don't flirt with me, Tyler Evans."

He winked back at her. "It's my favorite thing to do."

"Am I interrupting?" Izzy asked before she had to watch these happy couples get any mushier.

Julie swung around, a smile lighting her beautiful face. "Oh, perfect, we can get a second opinion. Do you think that cabinet—"

"Nope. No! No more. I'm done," Tyler announced. "And hello, Izzy. Nice to see you." He bent down to pick up his son. "Liam, my boy, how about you and I go feed the ducks at the park?"

His little miniature started instantly clapping. The little girl looked like her favorite toy was being carried away.

She turned big eyes at her father, her chin wobbling. "Ducks?"

Jake moaned before picking up his daughter. "Thanks, Tyler."

"It's what I do," Tyler said before asking his friend. "So you coming with us?"

Jake looked at Julie questioningly.

Julie nodded. "Have fun and thanks for your help. I love you."

"Love you, too," Jake replied before following Tyler out the door with his daughter.

Meg cuddled her baby daughter closer as she turned to Izzy. "Hey, Iz, what brings you in today?"

"I wanted to show Julie my sketches for the mural." She looked at Julie, who was now wiping at the cabinet with a rag. "If it's a good time."

"Yes, of course," Julie said. She grinned brightly at her. "Let's see what you've got."

Izzy held her breath as she showed the small sketch

she wanted to do. It was of Holiday Bay when it was still farmland. There were rolling hills and farmhouses that ran along the edge of the bay. It was the perfect blend of the rustic style and early Americana that was a huge influence for Julie's store.

"This is gorgeous," Julie said, awestruck. "When do you think you can start?"

"Let me talk to Zan and see. I need to make sure the kids are taken care of."

"Are you going to look into getting another nanny now that you're married?" Meg asked.

Izzy frowned. "I don't think it's necessary. I'm happy to help with the kids. Besides, I don't think Alice or Xander really needs a nanny at their age. They don't even need me as their stepmother."

"Don't say that," Julie said. "The kids have been doing great since you entered their lives. And Jake said that Zan is so much happier since you moved in. You're doing wonders for that whole family."

Meg rocked her sleeping baby in her arms. "So knowing that, why do you still look stressed?"

"I..."

Julie gave her a sympathetic smile. "Trust us, if anyone knows what it's like to be a Holiday Boys wife, it's us. You can talk to us."

Izzy slowly nodded. She soon began spilling all of her concerns to her friends. About why Zan had proposed and why she'd agreed in the first place.

"Wait! He bought the old bank?" Julie said. "That's awesome. I knew it sold, but I didn't hear to who. That'll be amazing. We can meet for lunch once you're up and running."

"It's pretty romantic that he bought it for you," Meg added, a dreamy expression on her face.

"It's business," Izzy said glumly. But she thought about last night and how caring Zan had been.

"Is it just business?" Julie asked as she watched Izzy's conflicting features.

"I—I had one of my migraines last night. Zan was so sweet and attentive. And sometimes I feel like he may be a little interested in me. But when I walk through the house, there are pictures of Mary in all the places that matter to him. In his library, where he spends the most time. Even in our bedroom above the bed. I feel like I'm living with a ghost."

Meg winced at that admission. "Look, I don't have any insight into Zan's mind. That might be more Kyleigh's expertise, since she and Paul spend the most time with him, but give him time."

"And for what it's worth," Julie added, "I saw how he looked at you at your wedding. He's crazy about you. He just doesn't know it yet."

"Typical male," Meg muttered.

Izzy smiled at that before her shoulders drooped. "I'm no Mary."

"That's a good thing," Meg encouraged. "He doesn't need a carbon copy of Mary. He *needs* you."

Izzy nodded but didn't say anything more. She couldn't—*wouldn't*—get her hopes up that someday Zan could love her. Not like she loved him.

When Izzy got home, she went to drop off her sketchpad in the study. As she walked by Zan's library, she noticed the door was open. She was about to walk by it when she heard her name called out.

"Hi," she said as she lingered in the doorway.

"Hi, yourself," he replied, his eyes warm as they traced over her face. "How are you feeling today?"

"Much better." She came into the room and sat opposite him. "Thank you for taking care of me. Last night was a bit of a blur, but I do remember you bringing me an ice pack."

She ignored the accompanying memory of him helping her out of her dress and bra.

"You're welcome," he replied. "I'm glad you're better."

"Did your family get off to the airport okay?" she asked.

"Yeah, they're airborne as we speak."

"I'm sorry I didn't get up in time to see them off. They must think I'm incredibly rude."

"Not at all. I explained you had a migraine and you needed the rest. They understood."

"I saw that in your note. I still feel bad. I'll call your mom later today once they land. I'd feel a lot better if I could at least thank them for all that they did while they were here."

Zan's lips popped upward. "Trust me, they didn't mind helping with the kids. I need to make more of an effort with everyone. I hate that Xander and Alice don't get to see their extended family like they should."

When quiet fell between them, she nodded at Zan's computer. "Are you working on your next book?"

"Yeah." A pleased smile formed on his lips. "It feels really good to get back on track."

"Well, I personally can't wait to read it," Izzy said.

He was about to pick up a pen to write down a note when he paused. "You read my books?"

"I *love* your books. You left Elliot and Elaine on such a cliffhanger. I need to know if they escape the Shadows or not. Did they get away with taking the Jewel of Pitcairn Island?"

He laughed. "I appreciate you being a fan. I'll let you read it before I send it to my agent, and you can let me know what you think."

"Really?" Izzy said eagerly. "That would be amazing!"

"I'm a little rusty," Zan admitted sheepishly. "It'd be great to get someone else's opinion first. I could end up writing a big pile of garbage."

"Nothing you write could be garbage," she said confidently.

He gave a tender smile that made her insides hum.

Looking down shyly at his desk, she said, "I should let you get to it."

She stood up, finally looking at the picture of Mary that she knew would be there. She froze when she saw her painting instead.

"What?" Zan asked when she didn't move.

"You—you hung up my painting. What happened to the one that was already there?"

She didn't say Mary's name, but she didn't have to. He knew exactly what she meant.

"It was time," he said simply. "And I really love your painting. You did an amazing job."

A thick knot of emotion formed in Izzy's throat and she swallowed hard.

"Thank you," she whispered, not just thanking him for his praise of her work.

She left him to his writing, but as soon as she was out of his sight, she covered her speeding heart with her hand. She knew hanging up her painting wasn't a declaration that Zan was in love with her.

But maybe it was a start.

Chapter Twenty-Three

A month later, Izzy woke to a warm arm splayed over her stomach, and a face smooshed against her shoulder. She smiled as contentment danced over her.

Even though Astrid and Arthur returned home shortly after Zan's parents left, Izzy never returned to her old room. She and Zan never talked about it, but there seemed to be an unspoken understanding between them that they wouldn't be going back to separate bedrooms.

They had a lot to talk about these days, and the only time they seemed to have alone anymore was while they were lying in bed about to fall asleep.

They'd talk for hours about the gallery, the kids, Zan's book. In addition to their various projects, news had broken about their marriage after fans had snapped pictures of her and Zan leaving Florentina's the night she had that crippling migraine. The world now knew that he had remarried and was living in Holiday Bay. While it had caused a bit of an uproar, people didn't seem to be too surprised that another Holiday Boy was off the market. Especially considering how Paul and Kyleigh got married on Paul's reality TV show. Compared to them, Zan and Izzy were almost boring...and they were both fine with that.

Izzy looked at the clock on the table beside the bed and

let out a breath. She needed to get up. She wanted to get the kids off to school and then she was meeting Lucas Beaumont from the mayor's office at the old bank. James was nowhere near getting any work started on it yet, but he had sent over an idea of what needed to be done. Because the structure was classified as a historical building, she needed to get her plans okayed by the town before they could get to work on the renovation.

She tried to move, but Zan's arms tightened on her in his sleep, as though he wasn't ready to let her go. She turned to look at him and her breath left her.

She loved him so much, but as much as she cherished these moments, she couldn't help but want more. They had gone on a few more dates since their first one, and a close friendship seemed to be developing between them, but that was as far as things had gone.

Zan hadn't tried to kiss her. He was tactile and always found excuses to touch her back or shoulder when they were around people, but that was it. No kissing. No rounding any bases. They weren't even up to bloody bat.

Maybe he wasn't attracted to her, though that thought felt like a stab to her insides.

She wanted everything from him. Love, sex, all aspects of marriage. But perhaps he was content with how things were. Cuddle buddies.

Biting back a sigh, she lifted his arm off her and slid out of bed. He groaned sleepily in protest, grabbing her pillow and burying his face in it. She smiled, love in her eyes as she brushed back his hair. Her eyes trailed up to the picture above the bed. Like in his library, he'd also replaced the picture of Mary in here with one of her paintings. It wasn't her best work, and she was currently working on another piece for the room, but it meant more to her than she could say that he'd made the gesture. Izzy knew she couldn't replace his first love, and she certainly didn't want to try, but she really hoped there could be some wiggle room in his heart for her. A small corner would do.

She crept into the closet to get some fresh clothes. She decided to wear a dress and business jacket so she looked somewhat professional for her meeting at town hall. After she showered and finished getting ready, she tiptoed back into the room, where Zan was still sleeping. One thing she'd learned about sleeping in the same bed as him was that the man could sleep through an earthquake and not wake up.

She left the room and went to make sure that the kids were also up. Alice was in her bathroom, brushing her teeth.

"Hurry up, sweet pea," Izzy said. "We need to leave soon and you need to eat breakfast first."

"Okay," she mumbled with her mouth full of toothpaste.

Izzy walked down to Xander's door. As was typical, she could hear his video game running.

"Xander, you ready?" she asked through the door.

He opened the door, wearing his headset. He was freshly showered and dressed, so she took that as a win. Sometimes he rolled out of bed and immediately started playing his games. She'd worry more about it, but during one of their matches, he'd confessed that he wanted to design games for a living. It wasn't just a hobby for him. It was his passion. She was all for encouraging it…as long as it didn't interfere with school.

"We need to leave soon. Did you eat breakfast yet?" she asked.

"Yes, ma'am," he said it sarcastically, but his eyes held humor so she let it slide.

"We on for tonight's rematch?" she asked.

A competitive edge gleamed in Xander's eyes. "Absolutely."

She smiled. "Be downstairs in ten minutes or I'm sending your dad after you."

He rolled his eyes. "He's probably still sleeping."

But there was no anger in his tone. They all knew that Zan's writer's block was officially gone. He'd let her read the first chapter of what he'd come up with so far, and she was already salivating for the rest of the book.

As she entered the kitchen, she froze when she saw the breakfast that Mrs. Hadley had laid out. The woman had gotten increasingly hostile, to the point where Izzy tried to avoid her at all costs. Izzy had spoken to Zan about it only once. He said that he understood the older woman wasn't for everyone, but she'd been with the family since before Alice was born, and while she sometimes irritated Zan himself, he'd promised Mary he'd look out for her. Not only that, but Mrs. Hadley had also cared for both kids after Mary had passed, and though she didn't seem to be the warmest person in the world, she did love the children and they loved her.

Izzy hadn't brought it up again.

But as she looked at the kitchen island already set up for breakfast, she took in the various carefully cut melons that the woman had laid out.

"Is there a problem?" Mrs. Hadley asked innocently.

"I can't eat any of this. I'm allergic, if you remember," Izzy said tightly.

"Perhaps it'll be good for you to skip a meal. You are heavily overweight, you know."

"What did you just say?" a voice said behind Izzy.

Izzy swung around to see Zan, his face contorted in

rage. She took a step away from him, but he wasn't looking at her. His furious eyes were locked on Mrs. Hadley.

Mrs. Hadley flushed. "Mr. Chen. I—I think you may have misunders—"

"Misunderstood? I heard quite clearly you telling my wife that she should skip a meal because you have issues with her body."

Izzy wanted to melt into the floor.

"I… I'm only looking out for your image," Mrs. Hadley sputtered. "You know what people said after those pictures of you two leaked."

Mortification imploded inside Izzy. While people hadn't been surprised to learn that Zan had remarried, they were surprised that he'd married *her.* Her plus-size figure had been a hot discussion across social media for a solid week until some political scandal broke.

"Mrs. Chen always carried herself with grace and looked the part of your wife," Mrs. Hadley went on.

"I'm not paying you to look out for my image," Zan said, biting out the words. "I'm paying you to cook and help with the kids, which you've also endlessly complained about, despite the fact that they adore you. I've put up with your negativity for their sake and because you were so good to Mary when she was ill, but I will not tolerate anyone disrespecting my wife in her own house."

"My apologies," Mrs. Hadley said stiffly. "I'll make something more suitable for breakfast."

"No," Zan said. "Mrs. Hadley, I greatly appreciate the years of service that you've given our family, but I don't think this situation is working out anymore. I think it's best if we part ways."

The older woman went rigid. "This is simply a misunderstanding that's gotten out of control."

"I don't think so," Zan said. "Mrs. Hadley, you're terminated, effective immediately. Pack your bags and leave the property. Anything you can't take with you will be shipped to you. Now, get out of my kitchen."

Mrs. Hadley looked at Izzy with pure hatred in her eyes. With her gray-haired head held high, the woman left the room without another word.

Zan grabbed on to the counter until his knuckles turned white. "Has she always been like that with you?"

"Yes," Izzy whispered.

He looked at her, regret all over his face. "I'm so sorry. I should have fired her when you asked."

"It's fine," she said, though she couldn't look at him anymore. She felt humiliated by the whole situation.

Zan pushed away from the counter and walked toward her so assertively, she took several steps backward until she felt the fridge at her back. His arms settled on either side of her, caging her in.

She opened her mouth to ask what he was doing, when he leaned down and kissed her so hungrily she saw stars. She froze for a second at the insistence of his mouth as it parted her lips, his tongue caressing hers.

He groaned as he pulled back slightly, and muttered, "I've wanted to taste you like this for so long."

"Zan," she said breathlessly as he bent down to kiss her again, gentler this time, but no less passionate. She slowly wrapped her arms around his neck, her fingers tugging at his hair. It was as if a switch had flipped inside him, and he pulled her more firmly against him as his lips worshipped hers.

He finally released Izzy, only to put his forehead against her own. "You're perfect the way you are. Your body is beautiful. If you only knew how many times I've imagined..."

Zan didn't continue, even though she desperately wanted him to.

Before she could ask what he was going to say, he took several quick steps away from her just as she heard two sets of footsteps approaching.

Taking a shuddering breath, she quickly turned and opened the refrigerator door to hide her face and cool off her heated flesh.

"Hey, Dad," Xander said. "I didn't know you were up."

"I wanted to have breakfast with my family," Zan replied, sounding cool and collected. Izzy didn't know if she should resent him for sounding so calm, or if she should do a happy dance at his mention of "family."

"Where's Mrs. Hadley?" Alice asked as she sat at the kitchen island and scooped some melon into her waiting bowl.

Zan went to the area where the coffeepot was and grabbed a mug. "Mrs. Hadley is no longer working for us."

"Why?" Xander asked with a frown.

"She was rude to Isabella and has been for a while. You know I don't tolerate bullying of any kind, so she was let go."

Alice's face saddened as she hopped off her chair. She ran to Izzy and hugged her hard.

"Are you okay?" the little girl asked.

Izzy smiled gently. "Yes, I'm fine, love. Thank you for asking."

She looked up to see Xander staring intently at her before his gaze shifted to his dad. His face relaxed at the protective expression on Zan's face, and a small smile appeared on his lips.

She didn't question the look as she grabbed a bowl of cereal. When she turned around, Zan had already placed a mug of coffee at the kitchen table for her. The kids moved their dishes there as well, and together, they sat down as a family and ate their breakfast.

Chapter Twenty-Four

As Izzy parked in front of the bank, her mind was still swirling with the events of the morning. She couldn't get that kiss out of her brain. Zan had shown a side to himself that she hadn't expected. It was like something had been building inside him, and it finally been unleashed the moment he heard Mrs. Hadley insult her.

She'd have to send the former housekeeper a thank-you note.

Her lips thrummed as she thought back to that kiss. She tried to shake off the memory as she grabbed the folder containing the plans for the bank and got out of her car. She needed to appear professional as she greeted the official who would either make or break her gallery before it even began.

Lucas Beaumont was already waiting for her, and nodded to her as she approached. He was the all-American boy—tall, blond, and handsome. The townsfolk had nicknamed him the Golden Boy, due to being the son of Holiday Bay's longtime mayor. He had also once been engaged to Meg. The couple had been together for years, and everyone had fully expected them to get married. But about six months before the wedding was supposed to take place, Lucas broke up with Meg. Her mental health had taken a toll, but she'd gotten back on track, and now she was happily married to Tyler. She'd also managed to forgive Lucas, and the two were now friends.

Izzy wanted to hate Lucas for hurting her friend, but there was something so sad in his eyes, she didn't have the heart to.

"Hello!" she said.

"Hi, Izzy, how are you today?" He was holding a binder in one hand but held out his other hand for her to shake.

"I'm really well, thanks," she replied. "You?"

"Can't complain." Though he had dark circles under his eyes that didn't quite match his carefree attitude. "I understand congratulations are in order." When she glanced at him in confusion, he added, "On your marriage. I know you've been married for a while now, but this is the first time you and I have had a chance to talk."

"Oh! Thank you," she said. "And I understand you're the reason that Mr. Farmington didn't tear down this building, so I should thank you for that as well. I've dreamed of owning this building for years. It's such a beautiful classic." She patted the pale brick exterior.

"I'm glad someone else appreciates it like I do," Lucas replied. "Are those the plans?" He nodded toward the folder she held.

"Yes," she answered, then handed them to him.

"Great, let's walk around and you can give me a visual of what you want to do."

They spent the next hour going over the details of the building. She showed him the upstairs, and explained that she'd planned on converting it to an apartment, though she secretly hoped she wouldn't need it now that things were shifting for the better with Zan.

"If it's converted into an apartment, will you be renting it out?" Lucas asked.

"I don't know. I guess I haven't really thought about it," she said, looking at the space with new eyes. If she did take on a tenant, the rent could go toward the gallery, or repaying Zan.

"If you decide to go in that direction, let me know," he told her. "I'm looking for a new place that's not as close to my parents'."

Izzy smiled at that. Lucas's mom was one of the most pretentious people she had ever met, and the mayor was a pompous jerk. It wasn't a bad idea to let Lucas move in. Lucas clearly loved the place as much as she did. It'd be nice to get someone in here who'd respect it.

"I'll definitely keep you in mind if I decide to rent it out." The two started heading down the stairs. "I'll need to talk it over with my husband first."

"Of course," Lucas said as their meeting came to an end. "Regardless of what you decide to do with the upstairs, I love what you have in store for the building. It'll be great to see this old gal rise from the dead. I don't think there should be any issues with your plans. But do me a favor and make sure that when you stop by city hall to get your permits that you ask for me." Lucas's mouth tightened. "My father's team had other plans for this space, and just between us, they aren't happy that the structure has been declared a historical building."

Izzy tried not to let her frustration show at that news. If Mayor Beaumont had his way, Farmington would have destroyed everything that made Holiday Bay great so he could build his monstrosity of a warehouse.

"Why wouldn't your father want to preserve this space?" She waved her hand around to indicate the gorgeous structure.

"Probably for the same reason that most lifelong politicians don't treasure things—money."

Izzy shook her breath and muttered lowly, "Someone should run against him."

Lucas stilled for a second, his face turning thoughtful. "Yeah, maybe someone should." Smiling grimly, he waved the paperwork she'd given him containing her plans. "I should go file this." He started walking toward the front door when he noticed a detail that was missing. "Hey, you forgot to write down the company who's doing the renovation."

"Oh, sorry! James Dallas," she said, looking at the chandelier above her. She really hoped they could save it.

A clattering noise drew her attention and she turned in time to see Lucas bending down to pick up his binder.

He brushed off the dirt that clung to the cover. "Sorry, did you say James Dallas?"

"Yeah, you know, from Holiday Boys? He does renovations now."

Lucas gave a stilted nod. "I know who he is. We went to high school together. We were…friends." Though there was a bitter twist to his mouth when he said it. "So James is returning to Holiday Bay?"

"Yes," Izzy said. "He and Paul Rodriguez are going to partner up and film a show featuring the renovation work on the bank. Paul's partner, Shawnee, should be filing the filming permits for that soon."

Lucas swayed on his feet. She took a step toward him in concern.

"Are you okay?" she asked.

He glanced at her and she sucked in a breath. He looked like he'd fought a demon and lost.

He gripped his binder tighter. "I'll get this filed for you. Take care, Izzy."

"Thanks, Lucas. You, too." She stared after him, confused by his reaction. But then another thought distracted her. She was going to be on the show with James.

Mrs. Hadley's hateful words sprung into her mind.

Glancing down at herself, Izzy bit her lip. What would Zan's fan base say when they saw her on TV? She didn't want to know, but she guessed it wouldn't be good.

Zan finished writing the chapter he'd wanted to get done before calling it a day. He was proud of the progress he'd made so far. Hopefully, in about another month he'd have the first draft written. It'd need extensive work after that, but as long as he got the bones down, he'd flesh everything else out later.

He stretched his arms over his head and his back gave a satisfying crack. Looking at his laptop, he saw that it was almost midnight. He regretted that he'd missed dinner, but Alice had brought him some pizza that they'd ordered, which he'd gratefully wolfed down. They were going to need to hire someone to replace Mrs. Hadley, but he'd talk that over with Isabella tomorrow.

He thought back to their kiss that morning and almost moaned. She'd felt incredible in his arms, womanly, her body pressed against his. She'd been so responsive, as though she'd been craving him as much as he had her.

He hadn't seen Isabella since, and he honestly missed her. He got up from his chair and left his office to find his wife. He didn't find her in the study, and she wasn't in their bedroom, either. It was too dark outside to draw, and she wasn't in the kitchen. Looking around with a frown, he made his way to the basement. He knew that she sometimes like to swim in the pool. But as he reached the final steps, he heard the familiar sound of the treadmill.

He leaned in the doorway and saw Isabella walking briskly on the machine. Sweat soaked the thin white T-shirt and dark leggings she wore. Her thick ponytail swayed damply against her shoulders. Exhaustion was clear on her face, but she didn't make any motion to stop.

"Isabella," he called out, but she didn't respond. He walked over to her and was almost to the machine when she finally noticed him and let out a scream.

She punched the button on the treadmill and slowed her pace. "You scared the crap out of me."

"Sorry," Zan said. His frown deepened on his face. "What are you doing down here this late?"

"Nothing," she said, not meeting his eyes as she continued to walk, breathing hard.

"Tell me what's going on in that gorgeous head of yours," he urged.

His eyebrows shot up when she scoffed in response. "Hardly gorgeous. Let's be honest. There's some truth to what Mrs. Hadley said. Mary was stunning, and we have Paul's show coming up, and your fans will see me on their TVs. People weren't exactly generous in their comments when they learned we were married. I just thought…maybe I should work on that before we start filming."

"Ahh…" Zan said. He reached over and shut off the machine, causing her to come to a slow halt.

He took her hand and pulled her off the machine before dragging her to the exit.

"Where are we going?" she asked.

"To the shower," Zan answered.

"What?" Izzy squawked as he led her to the bathroom that he normally used after his workouts. The shower was huge, big enough to easily fit eight people. Izzy stood stock-still as he flipped on the rain showerhead. It dampened his shirt and he stripped it off.

"What, uh, what are you doing?" she asked nervously.

"I want you to understand something. You and Mary are two very different people. Contrary to what people say, she wasn't this perfect paragon of a person. She was human, with flaws just like everyone else. I loved her, a part of me always will, but I wasn't blind to her imperfections, either. She used to count every calorie to the point of being fanatic about it. If she had a pimple on her face, she wouldn't go out in public because she was afraid cameras would capture her not looking her best." He stuck his hand under the water, making sure that it was the right temperature. He turned to face Isabella, ignoring the water running down his chest, soaking his pants. "It would drive me insane if you started worrying nonstop about how you look. Your body is perfect the way it is. All curves, and so damn feminine." He took a step toward her, not missing the way her eyes dilated at his approach.

"Do you have any idea how obsessed I am with your body?" he confessed. "It's a strain for me to keep my hands off you most days. The best part of my day is when I wake up in the morning with you cradled in my arms, my face buried in your neck so I can breathe you in. How have you not noticed how much I want you?"

He stepped closer to her, mere inches separating them. Zan reached for her hair and unbound it, raking his fingers through the soft strands. He then put his hands on the hem of her shirt.

"Can I take this off you?" His voice was heavy with need.

"Why are you doing this?" she whispered, not meeting his eyes.

He grabbed her chin and lifted it so she had no choice but to meet his eyes. "Because I want to show you how beautiful you are to me."

He wouldn't push her. If she didn't want this, he'd respect that. But when she gave a slight nod of her head, the relief that washed over him almost took his breath away.

He lifted her shirt, revealing the bright pink sports bra underneath with *Holiday Boys* written across the chest. When he lifted an eyebrow at her, she covered her face.

"Please excuse me as I disappear into the floor," she muttered against her hands.

His lips twisted with amusement, but he bit back the laugh that he desperately wanted to release. That was one of the things he loved about her. How she always made him want to smile or laugh. And he did love her. He was absolutely crazy about her. The idea that someone could hurt her because of him made him feel ill. He wanted to place her on the pedestal she deserved, far above the rest of the world, so that no one could ever make her feel like she was anything but perfect.

"I always thought Paul was the self-appointed narcissist in our band," he murmured, "but someday I'm going to make love to you and I want you to wear that bra. But for now..." He pulled it off her body, reveling in the rounded perfection of her breasts. He cupped them in his hands, worshipping one nipple with his mouth, and then the other. Her breath hitched with every teasing lick, a sound that he was already addicted to.

Zan pulled back so that he could reach for the waistband of her yoga pants, then pushed them slowly down to her feet. He then stepped back and removed his own pants and underwear. Her eyes locked on his body, her eyes widening when she saw how much he desired her.

"Never doubt that I want you," he said. He pulled her in the shower and maneuvered her so that her hair became wet. He grabbed some of his shampoo and cleansed her loose waves, before he reached for the bar of his cedar-scented soap. He ran it up and down her arms, around her back, before trailing it across her collarbone.

"I'm sorry to have to use this on you," he said as he put the soap back on its shelf after lathering some in his hands. "I go crazy whenever I catch your scent. I never knew the smell of orange blossoms could be so intoxicating."

Zan moved his fingers over her breasts again, circling the tips in a soapy foam before exploring farther down her belly.

"I—I feel the same way about you," she said. "I..."

Her fingers tightened on his shoulders as he let one hand drift down further, dipping between her thighs to tease her. Isabella's head flew back and she let out a delicious moan. Zan bent down and licked the rapidly beating pulse at her neck.

"You have no idea how gloriously woman you are," he murmured wetly against her skin. "But I'm about to show you."

And then...he did.

Chapter Twenty-Five

Izzy's body buzzed as she lay on her side, facing Zan on their bed. After they'd learned each other's bodies in the basement shower, they'd moved things upstairs to their room. They made love a second time, unable to keep their hands off one another.

As they caught their breaths, peace poured over Izzy. She was overwhelmed with the love she felt for this man as her hand traced the hard lines of his abs. "Tell me something."

"Hmm? What?" Zan asked, his fingers capturing hers when they started drifting lower. "Woman, I'm in my forties. Give me a little recovery time."

She giggled before returning to her question. "I don't know. Tell me anything. Something that no one else knows."

His eyes crinkled at the corners. "Something that no one else knows, huh? Okay, I think your body was made solely for my pleasure, and I'm excited to test my theory shortly."

She lightly slapped him on the chest. He laced their fingers together, bringing the back of her hand to his mouth so he could kiss it.

"I'm serious," she said.

Lines formed on his forehead as his face turned thoughtful. "Okay, I wouldn't say this is top-secret news, but only a few people know."

She propped up on her elbow. The sheet fell from the top half of her body, exposing her breasts. "Oh?"

He looked at her and groaned at the sight she presented. Leaning over, he gave her nipple a quick kiss before he leaned back against the mattress again.

Izzy barely heard him over the blood racing in her ears, so that when he finally gave his answer, she had to ask him to repeat it.

"What was that?" she asked.

"My first name isn't Zan."

"Get out of town," Izzy said. She moved so she could lie half over him, her thigh going between his legs, her chin resting on his chest.

"What's your first name then?" she asked.

"Ping."

"Ping? Ping Chen?"

He smirked at her. "Not very rock and roll, right?"

"Where did Zan come from?"

"It's my mother's maiden name. Technically, my full legal name is Ping Zan Chen. When I met Paul in elementary school, we decided we'd work better as friends than as rival singers, and we formed a two-man band. The movie *Wayne's World* was big at the time, and there's this scene where they rock out to Queen. I became obsessed with the band, and since I knew music was going to be my life, I changed my name to something more rock and roll, like Freddie Mercury did. And… Zan Chen was born."

"Oh, my god," Izzy laughed, burying her face against his bare chest.

He pulled her more fully on top of her, a smirk on his face that made her want to kiss him.

"What?" he asked with a mock glare. "Am I not as sexy now that you know my name is Ping?"

"Definitely not," she joked before he flipped her on her back.

"I'll have to see what I can do about that," he promised. Zan returned his attention to her breasts, teasing and taunting them until she arched against him.

"Isabella," he murmured against her skin. "I know last night got away from us, but should I use protection?"

It took Izzy's brain a second to break through the sensual haze he'd doused it in. "I'm—" she breathed. "I'm on the pill."

"Good." He moved his mouth to her belly button before moving even lower. And then, Izzy forgot what they were talking about in the first place.

"Well, I'll say this," James said as he settled in the chair opposite Zan. "We've got our work cut out for us. It's going to take a lot to get that building up to code."

"But now that you've seen it in person, you think it can get done?" Paul asked from the computer monitor. He hadn't been able to join Zan and James in person due to starting the new season of *First Comes Marriage*, but he didn't want to miss their meeting.

"It can be done," James promised.

"Thank God," Paul muttered. Someone yelled at him off camera, and he snapped back, "I'm conducting business right now." Turning back to them, he said, "Listen, I'll catch up with you both later, okay?"

He didn't wait for their reply as he exited the meeting.

Zan leaned back in his office chair. "I'm glad you could make it, man."

"Thanks—me, too." James angled his head as he looked

at Zan. "You look better than the last time I saw you. Happier."

Zan couldn't stop the grin from popping onto his face. "Things are going really well with Isabella. I didn't think I'd ever feel this way again, but I'm crazy about her."

"That's great. I'm really happy for you," his friend said, and Zan knew James meant it. He'd attended Mary's funeral. He knew what a mess Zan had been.

Zan observed James. "What about you? You ever think about entering the dating pool again?"

James cupped the back of his neck. "Nah. After what happened with Mason, I'm good with staying single."

Zan grimaced. He wanted James to find the kind of love that the rest of the Holiday Boys had found. The record company had really done a number on him by forcing him to stay in the closet. He hadn't told any of them about the pressure the executives had placed on him. They didn't find out about that until much later. It had taken James years to get his life back on track, only to meet and marry a man that was more interested in his fame than him. As soon as James's husband found someone more powerful in Hollywood, he'd left him, and James had been alone ever since.

"So..." James said. "Why did you want to meet at the house instead of Paul's studio?"

"I have another project I wanted to get your thoughts on," Zan said, getting up from his chair. He took James up to the attic.

James shoved his hands in his pockets. "It has potential. Lots of natural light. What do you have in mind?"

"I want to build a studio for Isabella. Somewhere she can paint when she's not at the gallery. But I want to keep this between you and me. This isn't for the show, and I don't want Isabella to know about it. I know you're going to be stretched pretty thin with the gallery renovation, though."

Zan wanted to give her something that was just for her, something that would make her not want to use the apartment she'd planned above her gallery. They needed to talk about that soon, because there was no way Zan could let Isabella leave him.

James gave him a half smile before joking, "You're so whipped." He pulled out his phone, and opened up his measuring-tape app. "I can put my secondary crew on this project."

"Awesome, thank you." Zan looked around uncertainly. "Do you think she'll like it?"

James chuckled before he threw his arm around his friend. "Yeah, man. I think she'll love it."

Chapter Twenty-Six

Izzy busied herself with plans for the gallery. She'd become an expert at video calls thanks to constantly meeting with Paul, James, and James's interior design partner, Kitty. She'd also started traveling throughout the region to speak with local artists and make connections to get the gallery fully stocked by the time she was ready to open. It was a long shot, but she hoped that the building would be ready in time for the holidays the following year. There was nothing more magical than Holiday Bay at Christmas, not to mention that the more established shops in town could bring foot traffic to the gallery, since it was in the center of town.

When she wasn't going around looking for potential artists, she was working on the mural at Julie's shop. And when work wasn't taking up her time…there was Zan.

Zan and the children had become her entire world. Even though they'd found a new housekeeper to help around the house, Izzy still made sure to take the kids to school in the morning and pick them up in the afternoon. No matter how busy Zan was with his book, he always made sure he was available at dinner so they could eat together.

He had also decided now was a good time to start working on a secret project for the third floor. He wouldn't tell her what it was—just that it was a "work in progress." The only other thing he said on the matter was that there was a lot of construction going on, so for safety reasons, she and the children needed to stay away from that floor.

As for their nights…those were just for her and Zan. They spent most of their time making love like the honeymooners they were, but there were also the long conversations she looked forward to having with him. The more Izzy got to know him, the deeper she fell in love.

Everything in her life seemed to be clicking into place, with the exception of one area.

She was still at odds with her father. While she'd talked with her mom over the past four months that she and Zan had been married, she hadn't gone to their house since the fight with her father. Izzy didn't know how they would get past it. She was her father's daughter, after all, and as Dante had once pointed out, they were both stubborn to no end.

So, of course, fate intervened.

Izzy had an in-person meeting at the gallery with James and Kitty to discuss bathroom placement and design. She wanted to get there a little early. Sometimes Izzy liked to stand inside the building and just enjoy the silence of it all, knowing that it was hers.

As she hurried up to the old door to get out of the cold, she heard someone call her name. She looked over her shoulder and saw her brother Dante walking toward her, wearing a thick winter jacket and hat to protect him from the falling snow.

"Hey, sis," he said, giving her a clasp on the shoulder. "What are you doing in this neck of the woods? I thought Zan had you locked away in his castle."

"Funny," Izzy replied before biting her lip nervously. She wanted to show Dante what all of the fighting and leaving the restaurant had boiled down to. This. This building meant everything to her, and she suddenly *needed* to share it with her brother. "Do you, uh, do you want to see what I've been up to recently?"

His dark brown eyes—so similar to hers—sharpened with interest. "Yeah, I'd love to get caught up."

Izzy swallowed over the lump of emotion in her throat before she finished unlocking the door to the bank. "Come on in."

Her brother followed her inside. They hadn't made much progress yet, but James's crew had already started some light demolition and major cleanup work. The interior already looked ten times better than it had the first day she'd toured it.

Izzy showed Dante around and walked him through the different plans that she and James's crew had come up with so far.

"So..." she finally said nervously. "What do you think?"

Dante looked at everything with amazed eyes. "What do I think? I think this is incredible."

"Yeah?" She had to confirm.

"Yeah, absolutely." Dante reached out and wrapped an arm around her shoulders, giving her a quick side hug. "You're doing it. You're actually living your dream. I'm so damn proud of you, Iz."

"Thanks," she replied, a weight lifting off her shoulders at his words. "None of this would have been possible without Zan. He really believes in me."

Dante stared at her profile for a moment, then smiled. "You really love him, don't you?"

"Yeah," she admitted. "I really do."

"Come over for Sunday dinner," Dante encouraged. "We miss you, sis. You know how stubborn Dad can be, but he misses you, too. Please come. You can bring your family.

We should get to know Zan better now that you're married to the man, and he means so much to you. You could bring the kids, too. You know how much Dad loves his grandkids. They might help make the situation less tense."

He said it like a joke, but they both knew he had a point, and the truth was, Izzy did miss hanging out with her wonderful, chaotic family.

"What do you think?" she asked Zan later that night as they were lying in bed.

They were facing each other as usual, their lower limbs entwined together. Above them was the new painting she'd completed the other week. It was of their back garden, the day they were married in the golden leaves of fall. It was home and warmth, and she loved how it turned out. So did Zan, when she'd presented it to him as a belated wedding present. He'd shown his appreciation in a way that still sent euphoric pleasure all over her body whenever she thought back on it.

Zan traced her cheek with his thumb. "I think if dinner with your family is something you want to do, I'm all for it."

She melted. Sometimes she thought that Zan might love her—times like now—but he'd never said the words, and she wasn't going to push him. She knew who'd owned his heart. She should be happy with what she had from him—his kindness and affection. She just couldn't help but want a little more.

Like his love.

No big deal.

She felt his eyes glance her way a few days later as their family drove toward the Rossi household. Alice was practically bouncing in her seat, eager to meet her new cousins. Xander had his head buried in his tablet.

"Are you nervous?" Zan asked when he noticed how her leg kept jumping up and down.

"A little," she confessed.

He picked up her hand and held it, his thumb playing with the black diamond of her engagement ring.

"We're here for you," he murmured, even though Alice and Xander had started arguing about something in the back seat. Zan finally said to them, "Enough!"

Both children quieted, though they didn't stop glaring at each other.

"See what I mean?" he murmured for Izzy's ears only, and she bit back a smile as he continued speaking to the children, "Today is an important day for Isabella, so you two need to be on your best behavior. Got it?"

They both murmured their agreement. As Zan pulled up to her parents' house, she could see that everyone was already there. They got out of their car and walked to the front door. After a hesitant breath, Isabella knocked. It took a few moments before her mother opened the door, looking confused.

When she recognized who it was, she held her arms wide open. "Baby!"

"Mom!" Isabella replied, almost collapsing into her mother's embrace. The sweet scent of her mom's favorite perfume tickled her nose. The scent was home.

They broke apart and Tina turned to look at Zan. "Hello! It's so good to see you again."

"Thank you," he replied, looking relaxed compared to the first disastrous time he'd come here. "I don't know how much of an opportunity you had to speak to the kids at the wedding, but these are my children, Xander and Alice."

"It's lovely to see you both again!" she said to them. "You're both so beautiful."

Xander looked like he wanted to be anywhere else, but Alice preened at the attention.

They entered the house just as a group of five teenagers went hurrying by, heading for the nearby staircase.

"Luca!" Izzy called out.

The eldest broke away from the group and came over to them. If anyone could help Xander fit in, it was him.

"What's everyone up to?" Izzy asked. "Gaming?"

"Hey, Aunt Izzy. Yeah."

She nodded. "Which game?"

"*Elden Ring*," Dante's daughter, Calista, said.

Xander perked up at that. Izzy noticed and made the introductions.

"I know you," Calista remarked. "We have third-period English together."

"Yeah," Xander replied, not looking at any of them.

Izzy could tell he was nervous. He didn't need to speak for her to know that he really wanted to make a good impression with this group, who loved to game as much as he did. So she added, "*Elden Ring* is one of Xander's favorite games."

"What level are you?" Calista asked, her eyes fiery. She was almost as competitive as Izzy was.

"One hundred and fifty," Xander responded.

Luca looked around the group before offering, "You want to come with us?"

Xander looked hesitantly at Izzy and Zan, who gave an approving nod. Xander tried to act casual as he said, "That'd be cool."

But he practically ran up the stairs with the others.

Alice tugged on her hand. She was starting to get upset, tears forming in her eyes.

"What's up, sweet pea?" Izzy asked.

"I don't like video games," she responded.

"That's okay," Izzy replied. "I want to introduce you to someone else."

They went into the living room where Gio's daughter, Sophia, was watching a movie.

"Hi, Soph!" Izzy said as they entered the room. "Can I introduce you to my stepdaughter, Alice?"

"Hi," the little girl said, pulling her gaze away from the screen for a half a second. She was a year younger than Alice. She had the same coloring that Izzy and the rest of them had. She wore her black hair in two braids that were offset by the thick-framed glasses she wore on her adorable face.

"Hurry, sit down," Sophia ordered Alice. "Laurie is about to propose to Jo."

Alice's face lit up. "You like *Little Women*?" she asked, forgetting her nerves as she sat next to the other girl.

"Yes, Laurie is so handsome," Sophia said, her voice going dreamy. "He's the most perfect guy to ever exist."

"I *so* agree!" Alice responded, perhaps a little to enthusiastically, because Izzy turned to see Zan looking at the TV with a disgruntled expression.

"What?" she asked.

"Aren't they a little too young to be getting boy-crazy?"

"Oh, darling," she said jokingly. "One is never too young to be crazy over Theodore Laurence."

"Is that right?" he responded with a quirked eyebrow.

"There's something about a man who's tall, dark, and handsome," she said, batting her eyes at him.

He snorted and brought her to him so he could kiss her.

"Besides," Izzy said, "I was about Sophia's age when I had *your* pictures all over my walls."

"That's different," Zan replied.

Izzy quirked an eyebrow at him. "How so?"

"Because," he joked, "I'm clearly cuter."

She laughed just as his lips brushed hers again.

"Oh, come on," a voice grumbled from the hallway.

Izzy turned to see all four of her brothers standing there, looking at Zan like they were going to throw hands or something.

"What's going on?" Izzy asked.

"Nothing," Enzo said innocently. "We just wanted a chat with our new brother."

Izzy instantly went on alert. "What?"

"Don't worry, baby sis. We won't hurt him," Gio added angelically. "Much."

Dante came up to Zan and wrapped an arm around the other man's shoulder before looking over at Izzy. "We're going to show Zan here how we make *braciola alla griglia.* I promise we won't actually hurt your beloved hubby."

Antonio grumbled, "I don't remember making that promise," and then they all walked away.

She started to trail after them, but her mom called her into the kitchen. "Just because you're a married woman, doesn't mean you can't help with the meals," she told her daughter lightly.

"Hey, Izzy," Tonya said. She was standing next to her brothers' wives.

"Hey, everyone," she replied.

She started making a salad. Through her vantage point in the large kitchen, she could see through the windows that her brothers and Zan were talking as they stood around the grill. Antonio had a very serious look on his face as he spoke to Zan about something, his expression intense, his hands waving around.

To Zan's credit, his body language was relaxed and he

didn't respond to any of the animosity that Antonio was dishing out. Zan responded to whatever her oldest brother said, and Antonio's lips quirked upward. Izzy's tension lessened at the sight of that small smile. Zan was truly a miracle worker.

Everyone was present and accounted for. With the exception of one.

"Mom," Izzy said after she finished chopping the lettuce. "Where's Dad?"

Tina stopped exchanging gossip with her daughters-in-law and said, "He's in his office."

She gave Izzy a nod.

Taking a deep breath, Izzy headed to the front of the house and to the room left of the front porch. She knocked on the door but didn't receive a response. That had never stopped Izzy before, though, and she entered the room.

The room hadn't changed much since her parents had bought the house in the late eighties. Her dad's office had the ugly wood paneling that people considered high-fashion back in the day. Shaggy, lime-green carpet covered the floors. Her father was sitting in his black leather chair behind his desk. He had the restaurant's ledgers in front of him. He liked to do things by paper instead of electronically, and Antonio still respected him enough to take the time to print them out for him.

Swallowing nervously, Izzy said, "Hello, Dad."

Her father's head shot up. His eyes narrowed when he saw her standing there. "Isabella."

She almost winced. Her family only called her *Isabella* when she was in trouble. There was only one person who used her full name consistently these days, and that was Zan. But the way he said it was more pleasure than punishment.

Izzy lifted her chin. “I thought it was time for you and me to talk,” she told her dad.

He turned his head away from her. “Got nothing to say at this point.”

“So that’s it?” she said angrily. “You’re never going to speak with me again?”

Her dad leaned back in his chair. “What would you like me to say?”

Izzy sat in the chair in front of the desk. “I want to know why you’re so mad at me.”

“I told you why,” her dad snapped.

“This isn’t about me not getting married in a church. It’s not like you even regularly attend. So tell me what this is really about.”

Her dad’s nostrils flared. “I came to this country with only the hope of marrying your mother and building a life so that you and your brothers would lack for nothing. I grew up poor, but I built our dream from the ground up with my own two hands. For you! It’s our legacy.”

He waved his hand at the ledger.

This was, of course, about the restaurant. It always was. Her teeth were practically clenched as she said, “But it’s *your* dream. It was never mine!”

“And you never told me that!” he said, getting visibly upset. “You lied to me all this time.”

Izzy stiffened. She had no idea what her dad was talking about, unless he was referring to her marriage bargain with Zan, but that had been just between them, Zan had promised.

“I don’t know what—” she began but her father interrupted her.

“You were unhappy all these years and you never said anything!” her father clarified. “You think I wanted that for you? You should have told me, instead of running off with the first man who gave you a different option."

"I didn't run off with Zan," she said. "Our relationship started off merely as employer and employee. But I don't regret my decision—"

"Clearly," he replied shortly, waving a hand at the large ring on her finger."

"Okay…" she said, trying to rein in her temper. "I should have told you that I wanted to do art instead of working at the restaurant. I'm building a business for myself—I've already been booked to do a mural for Julie Reynolds's store. And my gallery is going to be featured on James Dallas's new show. I'm—"

"See, this is what I'm talking about," her father said impatiently. "You should see the happiness and pride on your face. How am I supposed to look you in the eye knowing that I pressured you into such misery?" Her father's face crumpled and he put his face in his hands.

"Dad." Izzy got up from her chair and hurried around the desk to grab his wrists. "Working at the restaurant gave me a solid understanding of what it means to run a business. I'm going to use that knowledge to have the best gallery in Michigan. It's because of you that I'm going to get my dream."

"I ruined your life," he said.

"No, you didn't, Dad, it wasn't that. You and Mom gave me the foundation I needed to succeed. And now, I have everything that I've ever wanted. My art, an incredible husband, two amazing stepkids…"

Her dad's eyes softened as he looked at her. "Do you love him?"

Izzy nodded. "I do. Very much."

He threw his arms around her and hugged her tight.

"I'm sorry I've been such a *stronzo*," her father whispered against her hair.

"I'm sorry, too. I should have been more up front with you," she said before she stepped away from him. "Now that we've gotten that out of the way, would you like to meet your new grandchildren?"

Her dad smiled, the first real smile she'd seen from him in a long time.

"I'd love to."

Chapter Twenty-Seven

A few weeks later, Izzy stood in the kitchen discussing the week's menu with their new housekeeper, Simon's niece, Roberta. Zan and the other Holiday Boys had been on tour for the last three weeks in Europe. It was the nature of his job, and Izzy knew that she needed to get used to it. But that didn't mean she didn't miss him like crazy.

They made sure to have virtual dates every day so they didn't go too long without seeing each other, but it wasn't the same as having Zan in the flesh right in front of her. She missed kissing him good-night and waking up in his arms. But thankfully, he was scheduled to come home that evening. Which was perfect timing, since it was also Alice's eleventh birthday that Saturday.

After Izzy finalized the birthday party plans with Roberta, she headed for the library. She stopped in to check that the kids were in their rooms first. Xander, per his usual, was playing some new online game that Luca and Calista had gotten him into. Alice was sitting on her bed, working on a school project. Izzy's heart soared at the eagerness she saw on Alice's face to complete whatever task she was doing. Six months ago, she would have been crying about homework.

Izzy walked into the library, where she'd left her sketchbook. She was working on a mural for the Bridal Barn. After she'd finished the one for Julie's store, her mural business had exploded overnight. She was in high demand, not just in Holiday Bay, but all over Northern Michigan, as word got out about her work.

As Izzy began working on different projects, she'd taken to visiting their library to look up ideas in Zan's large assortment of books. He didn't seem to mind. In fact, he put a chaise longue in the room, and they'd work in there together for hours. Sometimes she'd get tired and would fall asleep to the sound of his fingers tapping the keys of his laptop. Other times, she'd ask his opinion on an idea she had, or he'd ask her what she thought about a certain plotline he needed to flesh out.

Hanging around Zan in the library was one of her favorite parts of the day. Lying on her chaise longue now, she looked over at Zan's empty desk, and she almost crumbled.

He'll be home soon. Just a few more hours.

Izzy yawned. She was so tired lately, but she had a feeling she knew why—at least, if the pregnancy test she'd taken earlier was accurate. She wanted to wait until Zan got home before visiting a doctor for an official diagnosis. If she was indeed pregnant, she wanted Zan to be by her side every step of the way. He deserved to see his child on an ultrasound at the same time she did.

Izzy chewed on her lip. She wondered what his reaction would be. He was such an amazing father, but in a few years, Xander would be off to college, and Alice would officially be a teen. Zan would be in his mid-forties by the time the baby was born. Would he want a little one at this stage in his life? When she'd told him she was on the pill, he'd said, *Good.* She'd been so careful not to miss any doses. The only thing she could think of was that maybe her migraine medication might have somehow messed with the birth control and made it less effective, but if that was the case, she certainly didn't remember her doctor warning her about that.

Her hand nestled over her lower body. She hoped he'd want their baby. Izzy didn't even have the official confirmation yet, but she already loved this hypothetical child fiercely.

Trying to focus on her drawing, she found her head drooping despite her best intentions and she nodded off. Her phone rang who knew how many minutes later, and excitement leaped inside when she saw Zan's name.

"Hello?" she rushed out.

"Hey," he replied.

"Where are you?" she asked, hoping against hope that he was already stateside.

Her heart sank when he said, "Canada. There was some trouble with our plane—"

Izzy shot into a sitting position. "Are you okay?"

"Yeah, we had to refuel in Quebec, and when the pilot was ready to start the engine again, he heard a noise he didn't like. Thankfully it happened before we were in the air."

Izzy's hand went over the pounding in her chest. Just the thought of them having engine trouble while they were in the air made her want to roll up in a ball and cry.

"What are you going to do?" she asked.

"We're looking into taking a commercial flight home. Paul won't stop complaining about it—"

"I'm not complaining," Paul yelled from somewhere in the background.

"Sure, cupcake," someone else said—it sounded like Tyler.

Izzy smirked. "Tell him that there's sure to be a fan on

the commercial flight who will *absolutely* make a big deal about being in his presence."

Zan snorted. "You've been hanging around me too long."

"Speaking of," she said. "Do you think you'll still get home tonight?"

"Yeah, I'll be there before you know it. I can't wait to be with you again."

"Me, too," she said softly, her hand drifting to her stomach.

She heard some further conversation in the background, and Zan said, "Listen, I have to go. See you soon."

"See you soon," she repeated. She wanted to tell him that she loved him, but she didn't dare. Emotion wasn't supposed to be a factor in their relationship. It didn't matter that she loved him.

Izzy got up from the chaise longue with her sketchpad in hand and walked over to Zan's desk. If she continued to lie on the longue, she most likely would fall asleep again and she'd never get any work done. So despite her exhaustion, she forced herself to work on her project sitting in his luxurious office chair.

She lost herself to the artwork for the next few hours, before she heard someone in the doorframe. Roberta asked hesitantly, "Izzy?"

She glanced over at her housekeeper. "Hey? What's up?"

"There's someone here to see you. She's being really persistent."

"No need to keep me waiting by the front door like some kind of intruder," Astrid said from the hallway, and Izzy went rigid. She gave Roberta a short nod and the housekeeper let the older woman into the room.

Astrid looked around, her mouth twisting when she saw

the painting behind the desk. "What is that hideous thing? Where's Mary's picture?"

Izzy frowned. "That picture is in Alice's room. How did you know it was in here before?"

"Because I saw it the last time I was here." The woman walked farther into the room without a welcome and sat opposite Izzy, her body held regally.

Considering how private Zan had been about this room prior to his marriage to Izzy, she very much doubted he let his in-laws explore what he considered to be his personal space.

"What are you doing here?" Izzy asked as politely as she could.

"What do you think? It's my granddaughter's birthday this weekend. Surely you didn't think we would miss it?" Izzy glanced at the door, half expecting Arthur to follow his wife in, but Astrid continued, "Arthur's back at the hotel. We didn't want to intrude."

That was a first.

"Zan isn't here," Izzy explained, "but he should be back later this evening."

Astrid looked at her fingernails as though she was bored with the conversation. "I understand that he went to Europe without his children."

"The kids have school," Izzy said, defending him. "And I'm here for them."

Astrid scoffed. "And who are you in the grand scheme of things?"

"Their stepmother," she said coldly. Izzy might have let Astrid get away with whatever she wanted last time she'd visited them, but she wasn't about to let the older woman push anyone around in this house again. Not in *her* home.

Lifting her head, Izzy added, "Perhaps it would be better if you returned when Zan is here."

Astrid's lip curled. "Look at you, acting as though you're the queen bee."

"That's exactly what marrying Zan made me," Izzy said, getting to her feet. "I think it's time you leave."

"But you're not really married to Zan. Not in the way it matters, are you, pet?"

Izzy stiffened. "I don't know what you mean."

"He married you to get me off his back, didn't he?"

"You're delusional," Izzy whispered. She thought she heard a noise in the hallway and looked over, half hoping that Zan would be standing there, even though she knew he wouldn't be home for a while. Unfortunately, no one was there to help get her out of this situation.

Astrid leaned back in her chair, "Do you know who absolutely adored my daughter, Mary? Mrs. Hadley. A fantastic woman, if I've ever met one."

"Well, she's not here, so perhaps you should—"

"Oh, I know that. She works for me now." Astrid's face turned smug at the dismay Izzy couldn't quite hide on her face. "And she told me quite a few interesting things about your relationship with my son-in-law."

The way she said *son-in-law* made Izzy stiffen. How dare this wretched woman come in uninvited to Zan's sanctuary and then have the nerve to speak about him with such disdain?

Izzy crossed her arms over her chest. "What are you actually doing here?"

"I'm here to take my grandchildren back to Maine."

Izzy's world dropped away. She put both hands on the desk and glared at Astrid. "That's not happening. You have no reason whatsoever to take the kids away from their father."

"How about the fact that he let a woman he barely knew into his home…and forced her presence into the lives of two impressionable children. Not to mention that the whole marriage is a fraud."

"It's not a fraud," Izzy replied weakly.

"Mrs. Hadley says otherwise. In fact, she's willing to swear in court that your marriage was never consummated."

"How on earth—" Izzy's cheeks burned with humiliation. Mrs. Hadley was responsible for changing their bedsheets. She probably knew more intimate details about Izzy and Zan's marriage than either of them were aware.

She raised her chin. "The marriage has been consummated and is very real. I'll swear it in court. You have absolutely zero rights here. I love Zan and we are extremely happy together. It's clear that you love your grandchildren, so let me give you some advice. Stop this. If you keep threatening Zan every time you come to visit, all you'll be doing is driving a further wedge between you two. He's the parent here, and he can deny you access to the kids if you keep pushing him."

Astrid gave her a frosty look. "Are you threatening me?"

"No, I wouldn't do that," Izzy said, barely holding on to her temper. "I'm promising you."

Astrid stood up finally, towering over her. "Then apparently we'll see you in court."

Izzy responded coolly, "I want you to leave my house. And next time, call before you come over. You're not welcome here otherwise."

Astrid's nostrils flared, indicating her fury. "We'll be returning on Saturday for Alice's birthday. She'd be hurt if we aren't there."

Izzy could barely spit out her response. "Fine. But after that, if you show up here uninvited one more time, I'll call the sheriff and have him physically remove you."

The older woman looked like she was about to have an aneurism. She left the room without another word.

Izzy collapsed in Zan's chair, shaking all over. What had she done? Had her temper made things worse for Zan? She was sure that Zan had an NDA on file for Mrs. Hadley. Izzy had to sign one when she'd started working here. He had to have some legal recourse against the woman for running to Mary's parents with such damaging information about their marriage. Maybe he could even sue her. Something needed to be done about the woman, because what was stopping her from spreading more lies…this time to the press?

Izzy didn't know how long she stayed in the library before she finally pulled herself together. It had to be dinnertime, if not later, given how it was starting to get dark outside. She wondered why Roberta hadn't told her, but then she remembered that the new housekeeper had gone to her friend's wedding that evening. She'd planned on making the kids lasagna, but it was too late for that. It looked like they were about to have a pizza night. Or maybe they would drive over to Clarington and get some Chinese food. She was craving it, despite how awful her evening had been going.

She got up from the desk and went to Xander's room. He was no longer playing his game. Surprisingly, he was doing homework on his computer, his fingers flying over the keyboard.

"Hey," she said from his open doorway.

"Hi," he replied, looking at her questioningly. "Is it time for dinner?"

"So about that," Izzy replied. "I lost track of time. What do you say we order a pizza from Florentina's, or maybe we can take a drive and get some Chinese food. Do you have a preference?"

"Nah, both sound good to me. Let Alice choose."

She gave her stepson a proud smile. "That's nice of you. You're a good brother."

He grinned at her. "It's her birthday week. This is the one and only time I'm letting her choose dinner."

Isabella snickered before heading to Alice's room. The door was shut so Izzy gave it a respectful knock.

"Alice?" she called out. When the young girl didn't respond, Izzy tried again. "Alice?"

There was still no answer after a few moments, so she slowly opened the door. There was a chance that her stepdaughter had her headphones on. But to her surprise, the room was empty. Maybe she was in the home theater.

Izzy made her way down to the basement and popped her head in that room. A trickle of concern shimmered down her spine when she didn't find Alice there, either. She began searching room to room without any sign of the little girl.

Izzy finally went back to Xander's. "Have you seen your sister?"

Xander made a face. "She went storming by a while ago, crying about something."

Izzy grew more alarmed. "Do you know what she was upset about?"

"Nope," he replied, turning his attention back to his keyboard.

"I can't find her," Izzy stressed.

"She's probably out in the gardens or something."

"It's too dark and cold to go walking around in the gardens." Izzy pointed at the window, finally getting Xander's attention. "Help me search the house again."

He sighed deeply. "Fine."

But the indifference melted away to worry as they searched the house without any luck.

When Xander and Izzy met in the kitchen a half hour later, their faces wore matching grim expressions.

Because Alice was gone.

Chapter Twenty-Eight

Despite the lateness of the evening, Zan was in a great mood. Touring was always exhausting, especially when they had to cram in as many dates as the Holiday Boys had during the past three weeks. They'd been overdue to tour Europe, so it was nice to see their fans there. But Zan was more than ready to get home. Aside from missing the kids like crazy, he wanted to see Isabella so much it hurt. The amount of times he'd fantasized about their reunion, and the many things he planned on doing to his wife once they were alone, would have made a grown man blush.

"He's got that look on his face again," Paul grumbled as the group walked into the first class lounge, waiting for airport security to bring them their luggage. Zan ignored his best friend.

He was almost desperate enough to get home to wait at the baggage carousel, but he knew he'd be recognized. He didn't want any delays—and if fans spotted them there were always delays—so he had to wait in the lounge with the rest of the guys.

"Leave him alone," Jake told Paul. "He's still in his honeymoon phase."

"I don't remember ever wearing that sappy look when Meg and I got together," Tyler said.

“Yeah, that’s because you were worse,” James grumbled from where he was sitting in a cushy armchair, thumbing through his phone.

The sight of the device reminded Zan that he’d left his phone on airplane mode. He grabbed it from his jacket, then pulled up his settings and reconnected it. Seconds later, it exploded with notifications of missed calls and texts. Frowning, he looked to see that he had a dozen calls from Isabella and a few from Xander. His stomach turned over as he read his wife’s last text: Please call me as soon as you see this.

He moved to the other side of the lounge and dialed her number. As soon as he heard Isabella’s voice, he relaxed slightly. “Hey, sorry. I just landed and got your—”

“I’m sorry,” she cried. “I’m so sorry.”

Zan went back on alert. “What’s wrong?”

He could see his friends turn their attention toward him.

“It’s Alice. I can’t find her anywhere.”

“She’s probably in the basement. Did you check the—”

“Zan, Xander and I both checked every inch of this house. I even have my brothers here searching the grounds. We can’t find her.”

“I’m on my way,” Zan told her and hung up. To hell with his bags. He’d get them later.

He turned to see his friends standing beside him.

“What’s wrong?” Paul asked, concern lining his face.

“Alice is missing,” Zan said, feeling dazed. “I need to get home as soon as possible.”

“The driver should be waiting for us,” Jake said.

“I’ll get our bags and meet you back in Holiday Bay,” James offered.

“How will you get there?” Tyler asked.

"I'll take an Uber," James said. "Don't worry about me. Keep me updated, okay?"

Zan gave his friend a grateful nod before he, Paul, Jake, and Tyler rushed out of the building and into the waiting limo. It had just started to snow, making the roads slippery. Zan thought he'd go out of his mind during the forty-five-minute drive back home.

When they hit the city limits, Zan told the chauffeur, "I need you to drop me off first. Get me there as soon as you can, and I'll pay you double what the record company did."

"Yes, sir," the driver said enthusiastically.

Once they drove down his long driveway and pulled up to the house, Zan jumped out of the limo. There were a line of cars he didn't recognize parked in the drive despite it being almost midnight. Every light in the house seemed to be on. There was a chaotic feeling in the air that made Zan sick. The rest of his friends followed him out of the car. He looked over his shoulder at them questioningly.

"You don't think we're seriously going to leave you to this alone, do you?" Paul asked.

Love for his friends conflicted with the terror in his heart as he hurried into his house. As soon as the door opened, he shouted, "Isabella! Xander?"

"We're in the kitchen," she called out.

Zan hurried into the room with his friends following. Both of Isabella's parents were there along with her four brothers, a couple of her nephews, Xander, and Simon. Zan didn't notice any of them. He only saw Isabella, her eyes swollen from crying.

He hurried over to her. "Any updates?"

"No," she said, her voice hoarse. "Zan, I'm so sorry."

"What's been done so far?" Paul asked behind him.

Antonio spoke up, telling them everywhere they had searched so far.

"I called Sheriff Richards," Isabella said. "He and his team are searching around town."

Zan grabbed her hand as the others started going over other areas they should consider.

"Come with me," he said, his voice low and urgent. When they were in the entry hall, he continued, "Tell me everything that happened today. Was Alice upset?"

"No," Isabella said, not meeting his eyes. "Everything was fine. We had a normal breakfast and lunch. She seemed to be her normal self. I checked on her before I went to the library and she was working on a project for school. She was in good spirits. I went to work on my sketches, but lost track of time after Astrid showed up—"

"Wait, what?" Zan interrupted. "Astrid was here. Why? What did she have to say?"

Isabella continued to avoid looking directly at him as she told him about their ugly exchange.

"Isabella." He put his hands on her shoulders until she finally met his eyes. "Is there any way Alice left with her?"

She frowned. "No. When Astrid left she went in the opposite direction of the bedrooms."

Zan let go of her shoulders to run a hand through his hair. "We need to go speak with her."

"She's at the hotel."

"Come on," Zan said.

They hurried into the kitchen, where the rest of the group still was. They explained where they were headed while the others agreed to start a wider search around town.

Zan and Isabella rushed to the garage and jumped into his all-wheel drive Land Rover. The speed that he drove would have made him lose his license if a cop pulled him over, but he didn't care. The only concern he had at the moment was finding his little girl. She was out there in the cold. As they drove, Isabella made a call to the police station. Arrangements were made to have the sheriff meet them at the hotel.

Once they arrived at Hal's Hideaway, they met the sheriff in the office area. Hal, the hotel's owner, sat behind the check-in counter, looking tired.

"Sheriff Richards, Izzy..." He nodded at Zan. "Mr. Chen. I received a call from Dorothy over at the police station. She said you needed to speak with me, Sheriff?"

"Yes, we need to get the room for a Westwood, Astrid and Arthur."

"Oh yeah, that snooty woman," Hal replied. "They're in room one-oh-three."

Zan and Izzy were out the door again before Hal even finished speaking. The sheriff followed shortly behind.

"Now, look," the sheriff said, "I know emotions are running high, but we have procedures we need to—"

Zan arrived at the door and banged on it so hard his hand hurt.

Arthur opened the door, looking disgruntled. "What is the meaning of...?"

"Alice!" Zan called out, pushing past him. His frantic eyes darted around the room, taking in Astrid, who was lying in the bed, the sheets up to her chin, her knees tenting them. Was Alice under there?

Zan went over to his mother-in-law and ripped the sheets away. "Alice!"

She wasn't there.

"How dare you?" Astrid said. "Sheriff, I want him arrested immediately."

"Where's Alice?" Zan demanded. He turned to search

the bathroom, but Isabella was already there. The sheriff had taken to looking under the bed.

Zan looked at him hopefully, but the man shook his head regretfully.

"What…you're looking for Alice?" Arthur asked, looking horrorstruck.

"What did you do with her?" Zan snapped at Astrid.

"We—we haven't seen her," she said, starting to look as upset as he felt. "How could you lose her?"

"Don't you dare!" Zan shouted. "You came into my house, threatened my wife, and now you're accusing me of losing my daughter? Go to hell, Astrid."

The sheriff's cell rang and he answered it. The expression on his face switched from professionalism to relief.

He put his hand over the phone and said, "They found her." He turned his attention back to whomever he was speaking to. "Bring her to Hal's Hideaway. That's where her parents are."

Isabella let out a heavy breath of air. "Is she okay?"

"Yeah," Sheriff Richards said. "One of my deputies found her at the bus stop. Apparently, she didn't know it only ran once a week. It sounds like she was running away. They should be here in a few minutes."

"Oh, thank God," Isabella murmured. She swayed on her feet and Zan grabbed her waist, instantly steadying her.

He felt like crying himself. He started shaking as his adrenaline dissipated. He pulled Isabella against him, buried his face in her neck, and released a shuddering breath. She wrapped her arms around him, and they held each other tight.

"If this doesn't prove you're unfit to raise my grandchildren, I don't know what does," Astrid said, seething.

He turned around to find the older woman pulling on her robe while glaring at him.

"Astrid, now is not the time," Arthur said, sounding bone-weary.

"I disagree. In fact—"

She didn't finish whatever she was going to say because a car pulled up to the hotel room. Isabella and Zan rushed outside to find a young deputy opening the back door of his car, revealing Alice. She had her winter jacket on and a hat that the cop most have given her to keep her warm.

"Alice," Zan said. She looked at her dad and immediately started to cry.

"I'm sorry," she sobbed. She ran at him and he picked her up, holding her securely against his chest. He didn't know if he would ever be able to let her go again.

"What were you thinking?" Zan asked, even while he held her tighter. He felt Isabella standing closer to him and he reached out and wrapped an arm around her so that she could be a part of their embrace. "Why did you run away?" he asked his daughter.

"I—I overheard Grandma talking to Izzy earlier. Sh-she said that you and Izzy aren't really married."

"She's wrong," Zan told her. "We are very much married and that's not ever going to change."

Alice turned eyes to him that were so broken it felt like someone suddenly punched a hole in his chest. No child should ever experience that much trauma and pain before they're even eleven.

"You're really married?" Alice asked. "You love Izzy?"

"Yes, we're really married. And, yes, I love Isabella. Very much."

He felt Isabella stiffen next to him, but he couldn't look at her to see how she was reacting to his confession.

Alice looked so heartbreakingly lost as she repeated with empty, defeated eyes, “I heard Grandma, though, Dad. She’s going to take us away from you and Izzy. I don’t want to leave you. I love you, Dad. And I love Izzy, too! That’s why I was running away. If I can’t stay with you, then I’ll live on my own.”

She started to sob. Before Zan could even respond to that statement, Astrid spoke up.

“But, darling,” she said, coming up beside them, instantly putting Zan on edge. “Don’t you want to go back home to Maine? You can have any room in our house that you want, and you can see all your old friends.”

“No!” Alice sobbed harder. “I want t-to stay with my dad and Izzy.”

Zan could see Astrid’s shoulders droop as the fight in her body deserted her.

“Okay,” she finally said after a few moments of listening to Alice cry. She looked at Zan, looking pallid. “I only ever wanted what was best for them. If they want to stay here with you, I won’t interfere with that.”

“Are you saying…”

“I’m saying I was wrong,” Astrid admitted, looking every bit her age. “I’m not going to fight you on this anymore. The children should stay with you.”

Chapter Twenty-Nine

Zan felt weary to his soul as he put Alice to bed. He'd had to carry her since she fell asleep on the way home. He'd talk to her tomorrow about running away. He was too grateful at the moment to do anything but hold his baby close. Zan didn't know what he would have done if he'd lost either of his children.

And then, after he put Alice to bed, he wanted his wife.

Isabella had been quiet on the way home, her face turned away from him to look out the window. He'd asked her if she was okay a couple of times, but he only received one-word answers. He guessed that she was as exhausted as he felt. Between the delays with his flight, learning Alice had disappeared, and his confrontation with Astrid, he was ready to drop where he stood. But he pushed through, helping Alice change into her pj's before he tucked her in for the night.

As he stared down at his daughter, he ran a hand over her light hair, so much like Mary's. Another wave of tiredness hit him and he left her room, shutting the door softly behind him. He was only a few feet down the hall when he heard crying. Frowning, he realized it was coming from Xander's room.

He lightly tapped on his son's door. "Xander?"

"Come in," he called out.

Zan walked in to find his son lying on his stomach, his head buried against his pillow.

"It's late. Are you okay?"

"Yeah, just tired. I want to go to sleep now."

Zan reached over and put a hand on his shoulder. Xander stiffened but didn't turn to look at his dad.

Giving him a light squeeze, Zan said, "Have a good night."

He was almost to the door when Xander called out, "Dad?"

"Yeah?"

"It's my fault that Alice ran away."

Zan frown at him. "What do you mean?"

Xander turned on his side and Zan could see his son's face was tearstained, his eyes red and swollen. "If I had paid more attention to her, if I hadn't been so busy playing my stupid game, none of this would have happened."

"No!" Zan's heart broke for the second time that night. "This wasn't your fault."

"But I—"

"Xander, stop." Zan came back and sat at the edge of the bed. "I know things have been crappy since your mom died. If it's anyone's fault, it's mine. I uprooted both of you without even discussing it with you first, and I've been so lost in my grief, that I wasn't there for either of you when you needed me the most. That's something I'll have to live with for the rest of my life. And if I made you feel like you had to be responsible for Alice, then I'm sorry for that, too." He reached out and wiped at a tear running down Xander's cheek. "Things are going to get better. I promise. We're going to start acting like a family again."

"You, me, Alice, and Izzy?"

"Yeah," Zan said, warming at the idea. "Are you good with that?"

Xander's face scrunched as he looked down at his bedsheets. "Do you love Izzy?"

Zan nodded, not willing to hide it anymore. "I do. Very much."

His son's face softened. "Okay."

Zan inspected Xander closer. "Are you good with that?"

He nodded. "I like Izzy. She makes you happy. She makes all of us happy."

"Yes, she does," Zan said. He leaned down and kissed Xander's forehead. "Get some sleep, okay? We'll talk more in the morning. I love you."

"Love you, too, Dad,"

Zan left his room and headed to the one he shared with Isabella. Part of him hoped that she would already be sleeping. The other part wanted her to be awake, so that they could talk and get caught up. More than anything, he just wanted to hold her.

She was doing neither of those things. When he walked into the room, she was carrying clothes from the closet to the open suitcase on the bed. There was another bag already packed on the ground next to the bed frame.

His earlier exhaustion disappeared in an instant as he realized that Isabella was packing to leave him. It certainly wasn't how he expected to find her.

And it sure as hell wasn't going to happen.

"Do you mind telling me what's going on?" he asked, barely able to rein in his fear and anger.

Izzy paused when she saw Zan in the doorway, looking as mad as a storm coming across the bay.

"What does it look like?" she said as she continued to

pack her socks in her suitcase, her heart shattering into a million pieces with every move.

"It looks like you're leaving me," Zan said, his tone like ice.

"Then why ask?" Izzy replied. She couldn't deal with this right now. She needed to get away from him before she completely broke down. It wasn't every day that she found out she was pregnant and that her marriage was over.

Zan folded his arms over his chest. "Care to explain why?"

"It should be obvious," she said, trying not to let her hurt show.

"Look." Zan stepped closer to her but stopped moving when she stiffened. "If this is about Alice, that wasn't your fault."

"I should have been watching her—"

"What is with everyone blaming themselves?" Zan muttered, running an impatient hand through his hair. When she looked at him questioningly, he said, "I just left Xander, who was also blaming himself."

Izzy's eyebrows drew together. "That's preposterous, it wasn't his fault."

"That's what I said, and that's what I'm also telling you. We can all blame ourselves. Hell, I wasn't here. I was off touring the world. But if I'm going to blame anyone about this situation, it certainly isn't going to be anyone currently under this roof." She could feel Zan's eyes boring into her. "So now that we've settled that, why are you continuing to pack?"

She was in the middle of refolding a shirt. Tears blurred her eyes, making it hard for her to see.

"Izzy," Zan said and she looked at him in surprise.

"You don't usually call me that." The last time he had, he was drunk, and it'd been the anniversary of Mary's passing.

"Because *Isabella* is beautiful, just like you."

She wiped impatiently at a cursed tear that escaped. "Please stop."

Zan walked over and grabbed her shoulders, turning her so that she faced him directly.

"Talk to me, Iz. Tell me what's going on in that gorgeous brain of yours."

She shook her head, trying not to let his sweet words affect her. "You told Alice that you love me. I never thought you would lie to your own child."

She tried to pull away from him, but he wouldn't let her go.

"I didn't lie."

"Sure." Izzy couldn't meet his eyes. "I'm going to spend the night in my old room. We can talk more in the morning."

"No."

Izzy's eyes snapped to his. "What do you mean *no*?"

"I mean exactly what I said. No. You're not leaving. You're sure as hell not sleeping away from me. We're going to talk this out."

He finally let go of her, only to turn and grab her bags, taking them to the closet and chucking them inside.

"Hey!" she said.

Zan came back and grabbed her hand before drawing her to the bed. He gently pushed her until she sat on the edge.

"Give me ten minutes," he ordered. He eyed her, waiting for her to respond. When she finally nodded, he left the room.

He came back nine minutes later, out of breath.

"Come with me." He grabbed her hand and led her into

the hallway. When he started taking her to the third floor, she looked at him in confusion.

"Are you taking me up here for nefarious reasons?" she asked.

"Don't tempt me," he muttered. "Given the unhinged thoughts going through your head right now."

When they reached the third floor, she looked around, her eyebrows drawing together. Zan and James had been busy. He'd asked her to keep everyone out of the attic due to the construction, even going so far as to lock the door leading to the floor. They had taken down some of the walls, making it a lot more open. There were several skylights newly installed on one side of the room, and there was a large outline drawn into the wall on the other side.

Zan caught her looking at it and said, "We're going to remove part of that wall, so we can build a walkout patio that overlooks the garden."

Something inside her clenched at that. The gardens were just one more thing she loved that she'd have to let go.

Her eyes finally settled on the large blanket in the middle of the floor, candles lit next to it.

"It looks nice," she said, ignoring the blanket. "I'm sure it'll be great for whatever you have in mind for it. Now, if you'll excuse me—"

"I wasn't being truthful before," Zan admitted.

She flinched. She already knew he'd lied to Alice. "Right. Can I go now?"

He cupped her cheek. "I know exactly what this space is going to be. It isn't some random project. I asked James to turn it into an art studio for you."

Izzy's eyes flew to his. "What?"

Zan looked sheepish. "You can't paint outside in the

winter—it's too cold—and I want you to have a place to work when you're at home."

She was shell-shocked. "You did this for me?"

He shrugged. "There's not a lot that I *wouldn't* do for you."

Izzy shook her head, hope and disbelief competing inside her. "Zan, I—"

"I'm not looking to give you up, Izzy," Zan whispered, his face more serious than she'd ever seen it. He pulled her to the blanket and he sat on the floor, bringing her with him.

"But..." Izzy shook her head. "You only married me for the kids. Now that Astrid said she won't fight for custody—"

"I married you because I *wanted* to marry you," Zan replied. When she scoffed, he said, "You don't believe me? Ask my attorney. He called me the night before our wedding and confirmed that there was no way Astrid would get custody of the children, despite the Westwoods's connections. The kids are healthy and happy, not to mention I have well beyond my means to take care of them. And...well, let's just say that Arthur has made some bad investments over the years. A lengthy custody battle wasn't something they could really afford."

"Then why..." Izzy began.

"I told you why. I love you." Zan lay down, pulling her beside him so that his lips could capture hers. He released her, then muttered, "I finally found someone that makes me feel alive again—who treats my children like they're her own—and you want to...what? Leave me? Divorce me? Forget it."

He turned her so that she was lying on her back. He settled between her thighs, caging her in with his arms.

"But you love Mary," she whispered.

Zan stilled, his thumb moving to trace over her bottom lip. "There's a part of me that will always love Mary. She's the mother of my children and we had a happy marriage," He rested his forehead against hers.

"I understand that, I do," Izzy insisted. "It's just that… everyone knows how *much* you loved her. How can anyone else compare to a love like that?"

Zan unbuttoned the top two buttons of her blouse, kissing the crest of her breast. "You shouldn't feel like you *have* to be compared to her. I never thought I could love again, but then you came into my life, and from the day we had your interview, I knew I needed you. I just didn't understand the drive behind my need at first. But I do now. I can't let you go. Please don't make me." He unbuttoned the rest of her shirt, kissing his way down to her belly as he went. "I love you. On a level I never knew was possible, just as deeply as I loved Mary. I love you so much, Izzy."

"Isabella," she murmured, her fingers threading through his hair, pulling on the strands lightly.

He let out a guttural sound before returning to her mouth, kissing her, his desperate need making her own rise up to match his. She hesitantly put her arms around his neck, pulling him closer until he settled more firmly against him. Izzy could feel his desire for her against her body and she arched into it in invitation. It didn't take them long to shed their clothes, their hands touching. Seeking. And finding.

When he finally moved inside her, Izzy couldn't stop the words from spilling from her lips. "I love you. I love you."

Zan stilled briefly before he began a pace that soon had her body clenching in ecstasy. Her release triggered his own and he shuddered inside her.

Zan found her neck and he nibbled there lightly. His

chest heaved as he said breathlessly against her skin, "Do you mean it?"

"Yes," she replied, her eyes swelling with ecstatic tears, grateful to finally be able to say the words. "I love you."

She'd tell him about the baby tomorrow. They had a whole future of tomorrows ahead of them. Izzy couldn't wait.

"I love you," he repeated back, kissing her cheek, her chin. "I love you so damn much."

"Do you promise?" she said, holding up her pinkie.

He pulled back to watch the smile on her lips and he groaned, capturing her mouth once more with his own. Zan released her to wrap his pinkie around hers, a grin tugging at his own lips.

"I promise."

* * * * *